THE BELOVED

R. L. MARCELAIN

ARCHWAY
PUBLISHING

Archway Publishing books may be ordered through booksellers or by contacting:

Archway Publishing
1663 Liberty Drive
Bloomington, IN 47403
www.archwaypublishing.com
844-669-3957

Because of the dynamic nature of the Internet, any web addresses or
links contained in this book may have changed since publication and
may no longer be valid. The views expressed in this work are solely those
of the author and do not necessarily reflect the views of the publisher,
and the publisher hereby disclaims any responsibility for them.

ISBN: 978-1-6657-3530-8 (sc)
ISBN: 978-1-6657-3529-2 (e)

Library of Congress Control Number: 2022923156

Print information available on the last page.

Archway Publishing rev. date: 12/13/2022

True love is a rare gem, real blessed are those find it.
Not many are in pleasure of it.

Udaya N.

PROLOGUE

Life can be so unpredictable. Humanity, I have realized, can be so blinding. A person never considers when something might happen, how one event can change their eternity or destiny. Never in my existence did I believe that life could end as it did. Shocking was the truth. The horror of that night and by whose hand death came. Though I have not seen that blood-sucking parasite in many decades, I still remember the pain and tragedy she caused. Losing my first love and my soul the same night felt like my heart was being crushed under a thousand pounds.

Everything we ever had died that night. My rebirth through fire and blood did nothing to quench the pain of losing not only my soul but also my love, my life, my entire world at that same moment. It became a never-ending agony for years. There was once a time where I thought that I had found it. I realize now that it was not meant to be. As lovely as she was, and as happy as I thought I felt now, it was not true everlasting love. So many secrets she kept to herself, so many hidden truths that she took to her grave. It took my stepdaughter coming of age and into her power for the truth to be revealed of who she truly was. Many decades have passed since that moment in my life, and here I am, alone again. I decided to concentrate on my birthright, and my company endeavors, with the hope of finding peace in my heart again.

It is the year 2008. It's been well over a century since the fates changed my life in ways I never thought possible. There are moments like today when I look back on my human life. The world continues to evolve and advance in frightening ways. I miss the simpler times during my human life. It was so pleasant and full of love. Now everything felt complicated. Sometimes I just want to have a break from it all. I want to find a way to go back into the past. So many what-ifs. What if my wife and I had never stayed in England? What if we'd never settled down in London? Would she be alive? Would my life not have changed? She desperately wanted to travel, and I never gave her the opportunity. I was so preoccupied with my own success as a business owner that I never made time for her dreams. Some days it still eats at me. I can never correct my mistakes. I live every day with that shame and guilt. The only solace I could give her spirit was taking her with me when I relocated to America.

When I relocated to Ithaca, New York, I bought a country estate and buried her under an oak tree, fulfilling her dreams in one manner. I no longer live there. However, I still visit the property occasion. It is days like this when I feel a sense of peace. I feel Eliza's spirit with me, I feel a gentle hand caresses my cheek, and a light breeze moves through my hair. I wish I could dream so I could see her once again.

The years evolve, and society changes. With this so does my stature in the public eye. My name, Hunter Eldridge, in the last several decades has grown to celebrity status, and I was surprised to be named most eligible billionaire bachelor by *People* magazine." I'm deeply moved that the magazine even took notice of me. Being in the spotlight does have its strain, the damned paparazzi are very annoying, but I am happy about my accomplishments. The small store that my father left me has exploded into a corporate chain. The bonus was a partnership with Starbucks in most of my stores. Ten years ago, I was blessed to open a publishing house as well. E. H. Publishing has had success with multiple top-selling books and won numerous awards.

I'm grateful for my success and the benefits packages that accompany it, but were I being honest with myself, I'd admit that I feel empty. It has been several decades since I felt a woman's embrace. I pray that I will one day feel that heavenly touch, if God wills it. I stare out the balcony of my penthouse, gazing at the view of the Chicago skyline. As I'm nearly finished with my mug of coffee, the alarm on my iPhone 8 beeps, letting me know the time currently is nine in the morning.

"Time to head to the office," I said to myself. I stand from my reclining sofa and make my way back inside. "Good morning, Mrs. Fuentes," I greet my housekeeper.

"Good morning, Mr. Eldridge, how are you this morning?"

"I am doing well. How is the family? I hope your daughter is feeling better."

She smiles and updates me about her daughter's surgery as I sit at the counter waiting for her to finish making the coffee. Once finished, she sets the mug down in front of me. Dark roast coffee with caramel creamer and six spoonfuls of sugar, just how I like it. I thank her for the beverage, and she informs me that she is going to start the laundry as she walks out of the room. Once I am finished, I enter my en suite bathroom. The room, I reconstructed as a wet room. There is a glass wall that separates the shower from the bathtub. The bathtub is rectangular, resembling a miniature pool, with steps on either side for easy access. There are heating jets that can be remotely turned on.

Someday I hope to share that tub with a special woman. I shake those thoughts out of my head as I strip down and step into my shower. The back wall is paved in stones, with a waterfall-style shower head pouring from it. I stand under the water, trying to push the depressing thoughts from my mind. I do everything I know of to relax myself under the stream of water. This may be my birthday, in more ways than one, but I will not let my mind become crowded with grief and loss. I need to keep looking forward.

Once I'm finished with my ablutions, I dress in my favorite cream-colored shirt, paired with charcoal pants and suit coat, finished with a power tie. I gather my business bags and documents together, and I quickly stop by my private office connected to my bedroom. I open my private fridge and grab a bottle of O negative. After I securely stash it in my office bag, I say a farewell to my staff and head to the lower parking garage. I quickly locate my Audio R8 Spyder. I love this car. Silly, I know, but I feel like Tony Stark driving it. I pull out of the underground parking spot, using the remote control to lower the roof of the car.

Something happens that I don't expect. As I pull up to the stoplight, the most addictive scent instantly steals my senses. I grip the steering wheel a bit tighter and try to ignore it. However, the moment I start to drive again, it grows stronger. This succulent perfume shakes me and makes my mouth water, pushing my physical urges into overdrive.

"What is that amazing smell?" I snarl. The beast inside of me wants to capture the owner of the heavenly scent. I take another deep breath to inhale cinnamon and vanilla. I lower the top to my car and adjust the tinted windows so no human can see me punch my steering column. I do my best to mentally fight off the urges I feel. This scent is sweetness, so sweet and pure it stirs my senses to a frenzy. I have not smelled anything so appealing.

As the aroma dominates my senses, the smell brings recognition, like a fragrance I know so well from a time long ago. Reminiscent of an era long gone. During a time of love and eternal bliss with my precious gem. Memories come to my mind. Eliza! Good God, this is Eliza's scent. It can't be. Could she be alive? Could she have been transformed as I? No. It can't be. I cannot lose myself to hope. I feel her spiritual presence with me, yet the mind is powerful and can play tricks. This person! This cannot be just a coincidence. I must find this person. I need to know for sure. I drive a little further until I am able to find a parking spot. Once, I park my Audi R8, I run from the car, making sure no one is around to notice. I decide to follow the trail. I run throughout the entire city of Chicago. I'm thankful in the moment to be a vampire. We have the ability to run incredibly fast. Humans wouldn't notice. They'd think that a strong gust of wind blew past them. It's funny how humanity portrays us in movies and shows. Honestly, the Flash would be a perfect vampire. Yeah, we can run that fast. Humans can't track our speed.

The overwhelming need to find her and claim her is so strong. I have no idea who this person is. I try to dismiss the idea that it is my wife, yet who else could it be? Who else could possibly have her heavenly scent? Could this mysterious woman be her doppelganger? I have heard in my life that such rare phenomena exist. I had never met one myself. However, after spending the last one hundred years as a vampire, I now believe that anything is possible.

The more I run, the more I breathe in its intoxicating aroma. This scent, it captivates me. It pulls me in and makes my body yearn for times long gone, for love, for life, and everything I thought I would never have again. I start to race toward nothing yet somehow everything I could ever hope to have again, while thinking about Eliza and every turn my life has taken since. Has it really been so long since I have been with my love? The moments I held her, touched her, and worshiped her body? Time for an immortal seems to bleed together. Everything moves by so fast you don't even realize that a century passed by in the blink of an eye.

Time slips away, and no matter how much we want to, we cannot turn back the clock. What is done is done. I cannot bring her back; all I can do is reflect on the loving memories I had with her. I make my way back to my car after searching for her. I need to leave here. I need to move forward and arrive at the office soon. I know that I should not engage with this situation. My logical side tells me Eliza has passed on long ago and gone to heaven. My heart yearns for her. I want my wife. After all this time, I still crave her. As I drive away, the memories begin to flow, and my mind is overwhelmed with what my heart longs for.

My name is Hunter Eldridge, and this is my story.

CHAPTER 1

I recall the final day of my human life. It is a beautiful autumn day in the month of October. The year is 1860, and I live in London, England, a beautiful and majestic city. I love everything about living there during that time. The shops, the meat markets, the seafood markets, the opera house, the baker's house where my wife and I enjoy visiting on Sunday mornings after morning mass. We love to buy the bread, which is freshly made daily. Each shop is owned by hardworking families. The stores have been in service since the year AD 1250. The baker adds in fresh berries and spices like cinnamon as a sweet bread. It tastes heavenly. Eliza always loves to buy raspberry tarts.

The palace is a beautiful sight to behold. I remember in the early years of my marriage. I visit the royal court with my love and her family. So many servants hustling around, as the king would issue orders to be obeyed. Sometimes, I miss the way life in London used to be. It has been so long, so many years since I could recount my life during that time. It was a life that shined with true love, peace, and happiness. I look at this world that exists today, and it seems that continues to fall away. In Victorian England, there is no social media, no digital or media distractions. Everything is centered around a family environment. I was raised to become a successful, hardworking man from childhood. When I become of age to be a man, I leave it behind and enter the service of the king's military, enlisted for five years until I am released. I will never forget the day I step into my father's shop and see the most beautiful woman I have ever beheld.

I have just returned home from the military. I serve in the king's army. I was a soldier for the king for more than ten years. My current battle is the Anglo War, in the year 1845. I am so happy to finally return home and bid my soldier days goodbye. I have seen more blood and death than I have ever wanted to see in my life. I excelled in the ranks and earned the rank of lieutenant. As I bid adieu to that life, I look forward to quiet mornings and seeing my family.

I arrive in London on the ship *Erebus* from the military base in India. Aunt Loretta, my father's sister, meets me at the docks as I depart from the ship. She embraces me in a tight hug and makes me promise to never leave again. After our reunion, we make our way toward the carriages that line the street near the harbor. As we walk, we talk, and she brings me current on everything that has transpired at home. After walking a few blocks, we arrive at the family carriage and drive that she used to collect me. I hold her hand and assist her as she steps inside.

As we travel, we talk, and she catches me up on everything that has been happening in my absence. I learn grave news, which my mother's brother had passed away while I was in service. I hang my head in prayer and sorrow. I hold her hand as she continues to talk and regale me with everything she knows. I love my aunt; she is a wonderful soul. My mother's family all reside in various parts of Ireland. My sweet mother, Nora Rose Reilly, had been arranged to marry my father by her family. They were farmers and shepherds, and her childhood life had been poor and a bit of a struggle that could not be completely said when concerning my father's family.

The Eldridge family has always been a bit more well off, not individuals of extreme wealth, but our finances are very much manageable. So when my father took a fancy to her during a visit to

Ireland, he asked for her hand and offered to provide financially for her family so their farm and livestock would be well taken care of. During my youth, I rarely saw my maternal grandparents. Looking back now, my uncle and grandparents have gone to heaven. I feel foolish for wasting so much time, and I wish I would have made it more of a priority to visit.

I stay in the carriage with my aunt until the family home comes into view. It is a beautiful home. Outwardly, the house is made of cream-colored brick. There is a large wraparound porch with a brick stairway. I enter the house and take in its grandeur. A grand staircase sits dominant in the main entryway. To the right is the parlor where my mother used to enjoy embroidery, knitting, and painting as she had tea with her lady friends. To the left of the staircase is the smoking room and library, where my father entertained his colleagues and conduct business.

I set my bags down on the window seat in the parlor. I proceed to walk down the hallway next to the stairs and make my way toward the kitchen. I am welcomed by the smell of duck roasting in the oven and something else that makes my stomach rumble. I smile as I see the family cook, Ms. Grasty, busying herself in the kitchen.

"Hello, Martha," I say to her. She whirls around. Her hand flies toward her chest in fright. "Master Eldridge!" she says as she smiles and curtsies. "I had heard word that you would be arriving home. I will say this house will be much more pleasant now that you are here."

I nod in agreement. Living with my father, I can only imagine what she has been through. Thinking about the old geezer makes my blood boil. I know I will have to visit him at some point. Perish the thought of him returning home later this evening to find his son eldest son, myself, returned home for war. The son that I was who wanted nothing to do with his business. The night I told him that was a great uproar in this house. I had to leave before he tried to beat me to death. I had been just barely age sixteen years old at the time.

I had just become a man, and I'd thought that what my path was in life. I was young and adventurous. The idea of being a soldier had been some glorious path to me, but I know better now. I know that I will swallow my pride in time and do his bidding. I learned from my aunt during the ride that all of my other siblings have departed. None wants to live near him.

I steal a piece of bread from the cooling stone near the oven. I retrieve my bags from the parlor and ascend the stairs to my room. I lay my bags in the cupboard. I decide to lie on the bed and rest myself. After such a long journey, I feel exhausted.

After a few hours of relaxing, I seek out a maid and request to use the bathhouse. Once I am finished with my daily ablution, I dress and leave the house. I walk to the livery stables.

It is a happy relief to find that my horse is still well cared for. I have a beautiful black stallion named Magnus. I stroke his mane. He lays his head on my shoulder, showing me that he missed me. I strap on his saddle and mount him. It feels good to be with him again.

As I ride Magnus into town, I dread facing my father. My siblings and I have never been on the best of terms with him. However, he is my father. I try my best to give him respect by associating with him regardless of how emotionally draining it is on me.

I ride Magnus into town and up to the storefront. I step off and walk into my father's bookstore. The store is a bit empty except for a few customers who are loitering around. I walk around trying to find someone who can assist the various people who need help. I can hear my father in the back room. It sounds like he is in his office.

My father has a young apprentice named Gregory Tierney, a young chap who is finishing up his schooling and is working toward attending Oxford in the fall. There is also a Matilda Smithers who works in the store for my father.

I find the young man in the storage room going over items.

"Mr. Tierney, where is my father or Ms. Smithers?"

A look of confusion forms upon his face. His brows draw together. After a few moments of silence, where I presume he is thinking of my question, he speaks and informs me he is not sure of their whereabouts. I decide to check my father's office. Upon approaching the door, I immediately hear muffled cries of ecstasy. I don't have to walk in to understand what is happening. I walk away from the room, disgusted by what I heard. My father is getting his sexual fill from his own clerk in his office. I turn toward the entrance, determined to leave. The need to mount Magnus and ride away from this place is strong. I need to get far away from the sick, perverted man. Nothing has changed about him. He used to have flings with various young women while my mother was alive.

It is at that moment, just as I am heading toward the door, that I see her. She is the loveliest woman I have ever seen. She is wearing a blue, high-collared dress with a lace front. There is a gold necklace adorning her, with a locket that is encrusted with diamonds. It is almost as lovely as her. Her hair is curled in the dressy fashion of the maidens of the day. She is sitting in a corner area where a little tea table is positioned. I observe her as she sits, eating cookies and enjoying her tea while weaving a knitted pattern. Her eyes watch the craft she is creating, while also observing a book of poetry. I know from that day that I want to share my life with her.

I decide to be brave, and I walk over to her and introduce myself. She drops her book, and in a gentlemanly fashion, I retrieve it for her. Her eyes catch mine, and it is like I can't look away. She looks so much like a dark-haired angel. We spend some time sitting together, enjoying each other's company and becoming acquainted. Sometime later, she excuses herself to leave. I suddenly panic. I have not been given her name, and I feel I can't part.

"Please, Miss, I have to have your name," I tell her.

"Elizabeth Carlisle. However, you may refer to me as Eliza," she says with a smile. Then she leaves, and I feel my heart nearly lose its beat. I ride Magnus home, with Eliza's face in my every thought.

During the next several weeks, I can't remove her from my mind. Her voice, her smile, and her eyes sparkled and caught my heart for eternity. I fell deeply in love with her. I decide that I need to see her. I inquire around and find we both attend the same cathedral, and we know mutual people. My friend Fredrick Dunn is kind enough to inform me where her family resides. That night, I go to speak with her father. I need his permission to court her. I can feel my stomach twist in knots as I ready myself to look presentable as a reputable man in society. Insecurities and doubts plague my mind, a little negative voice continually telling me, *She's superior to your family. This will never last.*

I grit my teeth, attempting to squelch the malicious words. Oddly, it doesn't sound like my voice. I resist these dark thoughts, praying for God's strength and blessing. I feel in my soul that she is meant for me.

I ride my steed Magnus to their home. It is a ways outside of London, a magnificent country estate, much more lavish than my father's. I walk into the parlor, the stained glass windows, the marble flooring, and wood-carved moldings on the walls showing its splendor. The finest wallpaper, silk curtains, and luxurious tapestries hang on some walls.

I continue to walk around the house, not straying too far from the entryway. I marvel at the artwork that is mounted on the walls. In the foyer near the grand staircase, there are two large beautiful paintings. One is of a man who appears proud and dominant. This, I surmise to be Eliza's father. The other is a family painting. It shows my beautiful Eliza, her lovely mother, her father, her sister, and her two brothers. The entire scenario appears as royalty. I know just by seeing her parent's home that she was born into a greater wealth than my family. The only person in my family who would match this level of prestige is my uncle in France.

I am lost in these thoughts while I await the meeting with her father. I have been told stories about him. He is a man of honor, not only that, but of great stature, and haughty. I pray that my meager life as the son of a store owner will be acceptable.

He walks toward me, we shake hands, and I follow him to his office to discuss. I remember feeling as if this were the longest night of my life. He has such a superior aura. I come to know that he was previously a military general who now is one of the king's councilmen in the military. Eliza's mother is the daughter of an earl. It is clear in his manners that his family holds high standards of association and marriage. We continue talking for the next hour, becoming further acquainted with each other. I can see he had already formed an opinion of me.

I share with him my family. He inquires about our social status, our income, our occupation, our potential for higher living. I inform him that, to my knowledge, my family originated years ago from royalty in Europe. Currently, I recently returned home from war. My father owns a well-established business that I will acquire upon his death. My sister and brothers have moved on—they live elsewhere. I inform him that I have an uncle in France who is much higher in society. However, he is not a respectable fellow and treats his family poorly. He makes a scowl at the thought. I am starting to feel as if I should not have come. I love Eliza. However, I know it is hopeless. I can see this from his body language and how he observes me. I feel my fears confirmed when he informs me that, though he respects me for serving the king, he doesn't find me a qualified suitor for his daughter. I deeply inhale, and I start to leave with a heavy heart. How can I feel my heart hurt when she is not mine yet?

I walk to the door, feeling my heart breaking. I can hear Eliza calling my name. I try to continue away from their home. Yet, the minute I heard her screaming for me, my heart will not let me leave as I wish. Her father tries to stop her. He is ordering her to return to her room. I become infuriated, as he is telling her to mind her place, the situation is not her concern. However, to my delight, she will not go quietly and is demanding to see me. I turn to see her lovely face. She tells her father how we met, and that her heart can't suffer to be without me.

Tears stream down her cheeks. Her eyes hold sorrow and longing for me. It feels as if our souls are trying to become one with each other, but there is a barrier being drawn. I feel my soul cry as she cries. Her father, I can clearly see, is becoming enraged. Honestly, at this point, I no longer care what he thinks. Seeing her longing for me makes my heart soar. It shows me that true love is like a rare gem—it can only be captured once, and if you love strong enough, it will always stay with you.

That night, I know I have found the love of my life. It is as if everything that felt broken in my universe is finally made whole. Once her father sees her pain, and her strong desire to be with me, he can't reject her. We court for three years. It feels as if heaven has decided to come to earth and grant me happiness. We enjoy leisurely strolls along the London harbor. I greet her with flowers and a new book every week. I learn that she is very educated. She enjoys reading as much as I do. We feel as if we have been made for each other.

During our courtship, I also begin working under my father. This is not something I originally wanted. There is more I want to do with my life than work for that man as his protégé. My father's partner, Garrett Wilkins, seems a more likely candidate than me to fill the role of becoming the store owner. I learn from my father that he wants to keep the business in the family, so I begrudgingly accept.

I am his protégé for three years. During that time, I learn the importance of record keeping, the importance of consumer relations, customer satisfaction. It is part of my duty to keep account of the company finances, taking record of literary inventory. He grooms me on the duties of scheduling clerks' hours of work. I learn many things that will help me for decades to come. Garrett is also a great help when my father is not around. We grow close. I look at him like an uncle. He says one day that it is his charge to groom me in every way that will help me succeed.

As time moves on, Father can no longer function. Father has developed a cancer and becomes very ill. The doctor does his best and delivers a remedy called laudanum that nullifies the pain in the beginning. However, as his condition worsens, there are some days where his pain is so tremendous that he does not wish to move from bed. Any movement is met with screams of pain. It is so nerve-racking on Eliza, the servants who attempt to care for him, and me. I take the liberty to inform my siblings of his health state. However, none of them return a letter. It is the following year in 1848 when we finally say farewell to him, and he is laid to rest next to my mother in St. Patrick's cemetery.

It is the year of 1849 when I feel it is time for our courtship to progress to the next level. My business is starting to boom stronger than ever. My father had never had such a thriving store. Perhaps it shows how much the citizens of London didn't care for him.

After I assume command, I decide to remodel the store and add my own tastes to it. I also speak with Eliza for her womanly advice. I learn from her that she enjoys interior decorating, so she helps me mold the business into my own brand. It is the month of March, and business has shown to be strong. I muster my courage and arrange a meeting with her father, Mr. Carlisle, to arrange for Eliza's hand in marriage. I can tell that her father still disapproves, yet he will not utter a word against it.

I decide to wait a few more months before making my proposal. It is the month of June. The night of my proposal is perfect. We attend the opera with her family, a performance of *Romeo and Juliet*. It lasts several hours, and soon we leave the theater. We walk along the cobblestone streets of London, enjoying the night air. The moonlight shines in the night sky, and with the streetlamps lit, it is a romantic moment. We find a bench near the waterfront to sit and rest as we gaze at the stars. I hand her a bouquet of roses I have been keeping with me. I have placed a wrapped candy in the center that will catch her eye. The wrapping is covered by a beautiful diamond ring. She plucks on the candy, and her eyes light up.

She then gasps as I bend a knee. Smiling, she begins to lightly cry. "Elizabeth Pearl Carlisle, every day with you is like heaven on earth. My love, keeper of my soul. Please fulfill the longing in my soul. Dearest, sweet Eliza, please say that you will do me the honors of becoming my wife?" She is smiling, her eyes filling with tears. She kneels down next to me, takes my hand in hers, and whispers her desire for me to become her husband and keeper of her soul.

I take her into my arms and hold her tight. She made me the happiest man in the world, and I promise her that I will never let her go. In my heart, I whisper, *Even if death may come, I shall keep you in my heart for eternity, my beloved.* I hold her face as I whisper my love for her. Her eyes shine with love and contentment. I hold her close and bury my face in neck. I inhale her sweet scent. She is my love, my life, my everything that I want for the rest of my days.

Our wedding day is elegant, like a scene from a fairy tale. It is the happiest day of my life. We are married in St. Peter's Cathedral. Father Drury officiates our union. I remember that day. I have such chills through my body, and I am intensely happy. So many of my friends and family have gathered to celebrate with me. Both of my brothers arrive to be my groomsmen, and my sister graces us with her presence. Despite her bastard of a husband's objections, we are happy to see her safe and home.

Watching Eliza walk down the aisle is like stepping into a dream. Her gown is white as pearl and complements her beauty. Her raven-colored hair is fashionably braided in a way that resembles a crown. She wears lace gloves and a silk veil. I praise God for giving me such a divine angel as Eliza. We exchange our vows and become one. I wish I could give her a honeymoon. The best that I am able to give her is a weekend trip to Wales, where we stay at luxurious rooming house where we become one as husband and wife. That night, I think we will last forever. I never knew how wrong I could be.

CHAPTER 2

The years move onward. Fifteen years of marriage filled with undying love flash by faster than expected. The last day of my life starts with a beautiful morning. I sit in my lounge chair, enjoying the cool air of London on my balcony, looking at my beautiful wife with a warm feeling of contentment filling me. I still remember our words that morning. They will forever be in my soul. It is a wonderful autumn day in October. I can see the children next door playing on the lawn as, just like us, their parents sip their tea. I have never cared for tea; I know that's odd, being from England. My wife drinks her tea while finishing her needlepoint. With a smile, I turn toward her with love in my heart.

"Eliza, you are my rare gem of love. Stay with me forever," I say to her lovingly.

She giggles and smiles. "Hunter, you are my prince, whom I wish to love forever."

I nuzzle my head in her neck. She giggles in delight. I whisper in her ear. "My darling, I'm never going to let you go," I tell her as we embrace.

I am taken away every day at the sight of her. She is everything I could ever have wished for. She is so beautiful, eyes as blue as the sea, long, wavy, black hair currently tied up in a respectable bun, pink full lips I could spend hours kissing. Eliza has luscious curves and a perfect bust. Her dress respectfully shows her curvy form. There are many days I would love to stay home and explore those curves.

"Sunday mornings are the best day of the week. Do you not agree, Eliza?" I look into the beautiful blue eyes I feel as if I could dive into and never swim out of. So perfect, so lovely.

"Yes, dear Hunter, I dare say they are."

We talk about how we would like to spend our day. We talk about mass and what to do later in the day.

I am not a strong believer. My experience with war has left me to question God's purpose. However, I have always attended to pray for atonement and to see my wife happy. I know that Eliza prays for my soul to return to faith. Secretly, I hope for redemption for my wartime sins.

"We could always go to the bakery store after service. Perhaps that delicious bread you favor is ready for sale. Afterward, if you want, we can take a walk along the lake to watch the ships and tide roll in."

I nod. "That sounds like a very good idea, my lady."

She giggles again.

"Then, this evening, since it is my birthday," I whisper sweetly in her ear, "I will make you mine again, just as I did so many years ago." Eliza turns deep crimson as she blushes and hurries out of the room to get our coats to attend morning mass.

As we travel in the carriage, she reminds me of something. "Oh, Hunter, don't forget: my parents invited both of us to their manor for dinner this week."

Ah, how could I forget the in-laws. My only peace with my wife is when we don't associate with her family. However, they are her parents, and I don't wish to hide her.

"Sure, we can attend on Tuesday if you wish."

She beams at me. "Splendid! I will send a message so they are aware." She kisses me on the cheek while I frown. "Hunter, don't be cross. They love you."

I scoff. "They wanted you to marry the Duke of Wilmington."

She looks at me. "Yes, but they know I love you, and it is only because my grandfather was one of the king's financial advisers, so they wanted us children to marry into the court or royalty."

I turn my head away. I know her family. I would never tell her that they are uptight pains in the arse.

"They love me because I'm Catholic," I retort.

She rolls her eyes and playfully smacks me on the chest.

I cannot help but pull her into my arms. "I will do my best to be pleasant on Tuesday and not kill your father."

She gives me another playful smack, and I chuckle while escorting her inside the cathedral.

We arrive at mass and make our way inside. We are greeted by some of our friends. We embrace our loved ones and pass the parishioners who are stationed in the entryway to welcome guests.

"Good day, Mr. Eldridge, Mrs. Eldridge. How lovely to see you both this morning," says Deacon Phillips. I shake his hand as we enter. Eliza gives my hand a squeeze, says her hellos, and walks away, seeking the other ladies.

"Good morning, Deacon Phillips, God has blessed this day, indeed. The sunny weather is very pleasing, is it not?" I say to him. We stand for a while exchanging pleasantries. I turn to watch Eliza as she greets her friends. I love her smile as she chats excitedly, no doubt becoming filled in on the latest gossip. Her smile is like a beautiful beacon of light in a dark room. Her face glows with love, adoration, and happiness. I am truly blessed; God has given me the perfect woman as a wife.

I walk over to her ladies' group. "Darling, I believe the service is about to begin. If we may take our seats?"

She quickly takes my arm. "Oh yes, of course, dear," she says while waving to her friends. We sit in the cathedral for the next hour as we learn and listen to how to grow closer to God and accept his love wholeheartedly. Once service concludes, we say our goodbyes to the other parishioners and proceed onward to the next place on our agenda.

We take the short walk to the market, enjoying the beautiful day. As we stroll, I spot someone riding a black stallion like mine. I do often miss my stallion, Magnus. It had been many years, and he had been such a fine horse. He'd slipped in the stable during winter and sustained a fatal injury. Sending him away had been the most painful day. Today, I would have loved to ride him. The horse moves on, pulling me away from my memories. Suddenly, I feel very off about something. I look around, trying to find my uneasiness. Seeing nothing amiss, I decide to ignore the feeling.

Eliza and I are walking when we look up to see that we are stopped in front of the apothecary store. As we stare in the window, I notice our neighbor Bathilda working behind the counter. The woman is tall and willowy, with red hair currently fashioned in a bun style. She wears a burgundy dress with a high lace collar, and is wrapped in a shawl. I notice her assisting customers with tinctures and bottles that look as if they hold medicine with odd shades of red, green, and blue. Most medicine I have seen is clear liquid. Somehow she managed to find a way to add color. As I stare at her, I have a feeling of dread come upon me. I, at times, am amazed she is a friend of Eliza's. I do not dare say a word. However, the woman makes me uncomfortable. Every time she is over, I have this feeling of danger, and I swear I catch her watching me from the corner of her eye. This happens when Eliza is not paying attention or not in the room.

Just as I am lost in thought, she turned toward the window and smiles at me. It scares me to my core. I wave at her and look away.

As Eliza and I continue to walk, we see a commotion across the street.

"Hunter, what do you think is happening?"

I look at her. "I don't know." At that moment, we hear the pop of what sounds like a pistol being fired. Everyone screams and scatters as we witness the market attendant being shot and a masked man rob his cart. We stand by, watching the authorities arrive on the scene.

Just as we are observing the incident, Eliza screams and falls. "Ah. My purse! Oh my. Hunter! That man stole my purse and shoved me over, ow. I think I hurt my ankle!"

I see red. How dare he hurt my love? "Where did that piece of filth go?" I snarl in fury. A bystander assists me to help Eliza find somewhere to rest. I check her to ensure that she is indeed all right. My assistant, who was kind enough to come to Eliza's aid as she fell, helps me pull her to her feet gently. He is an older man, dressed in a suit coat, dress pants, and a top hat. He turns toward me and says, "The man ran around the corner."

"Thank you, good sir. Eliza, I shall go and fetch your purse from that filth," I whisper to her.

"Hunter, I'm afraid."

I hold her close to ease her worries. I kiss her and whisper, "Fear not, my love. I will attempt aggressive persuasion only if the situation warrants it."

She nods and lets me go.

I take off around the corner, running as fast as I can. Stopping abruptly, I come upon a curious situation. Eliza's purse sits on some steps. However, I don't find the man. He has simply vanished. Could he possibly have noticed me coming for him and abandoned it? I entertain these thoughts until I get a disturbing feeling that I am being watched. I turn to leave the alley and notice something frightening, a red puddle on the ground, a good amount of it. I don't need to examine it to know what it is, blood. The chilling feeling grows. I look around, only to see a figure hidden in shadow further down the alleyway.

I run from the place, every nerve in my body screaming in terror. Once I am around the corner, I am happy to return Eliza's purse so that we might continue our day. I realize that with her injured ankle we will have to go home. I arrange for a carriage to carry us there; she is sad that we will have to postpone the rest of our plans. We arrive at home; I carry her upstairs to lie down so she will not aggravate her foot. I am still filled with boiling rage at the bastard who'd hurt my wife. I believe that any respectable man who was in love would have felt the same way.

After I sit her on the bed, I call for one of our maids to attend to her needs. I walk away from the room to give her some privacy. I head down the stairs, only to find Garrett Wilkins waiting for me in my study. Perplexed by his sudden visit, I walk into the room to see what he has to say.

"Hello, Garrett, to what do I owe this surprise visit?" I ask him.

He stands to shake my hand. "Good afternoon, Hunter. I apologize for this abrupt meeting. I wanted to bring over the weekend reports on progress."

I nod. I really wish we had a faster way of communicating than these spontaneous gatherings. He hands me the reports and takes a seat at my desk as I study them. He discusses with me progress, areas of recession, and overall expected future growth in our store.

We have talked about expanding to other areas outside England. I would love to expand to different areas in Europe and America.

"How is Eliza?" Garrett asks.

I am unsure why, but for a brief moment, I catch a quick scowl on his face. I feel as if something is trying to warn me about Garrett. I ignore my negative thoughts, and I detail to him our day, all of the excitement we had witnessed. His eyes fill with fury, but something unreadable as well. It is as if he is privy to a secret that he will not share.

I feel compelled to question his behavior. "Garrett, may I inquire something?"

He nods while observing me.

"Is there anything the matter?"

He looks at me curiously. "Not that I'm aware of? Is everything all right?"

In this moment, I feel as if I should have my guard up. "Can you tell me? Every time you come to visit my house, you ask of my wife. However, your countenance says you are hiding something. You have a cold glare that touches your eyes. Is there are reason why I should think you hate my wife?"

He stares at me for a moment. I gaze at him, daring him to lie to me. He assures me he asks for polite reasons. For some reason, though, I feel as if he was not being honest. We end our conversation and continue to focus on our records. A few hours later, I walk Garrett out and bid him good day. I find Eliza awake and returned to her needlepoint.

"What are you making, my dear?" I ask her.

"Oh, I'm making a doily for my sister's new furnishings. She and her husband have recently moved into new dwellings closer to the palace."

Ah yes, Minerva Carlisle is betrothed to the son of a lord to our beloved Queen Victoria.

Eliza has shared stories with me about her every time we go to port. Recently, her sister had returned from a voyage to Spain. I see the sadness as Eliza looks away to the horizon. I know what is in her heart. She longs to leave England forever. She dreams of traveling abroad to America or France. She craves the ability to find new adventures, to see what lies beyond the horizon. I love my wife, but she is so sheltered.

I know we are very happy together, yet I can see her sadness now as she gazes out the window of our lovely home.

"I wish I could understand why we cannot travel as well."

This is just something that can't happen right now. I don't want to lean on her family's money either.

"Sweetheart, I know you dream of traveling. I dream of seeing the world with you. Right now, as you know, I don't have the time." I want to build my financial success.

"Very well."

I continue. "Eliza, the business is booming very well. There have been talks that Lord Byron is going to visit my shop."

Eliza has a beaming smile. "Oh, Hunter. That's fantastic."

"Yes. It is. Therefore, no matter how much I would love to take you to see the world, I cannot."

Eliza looks down at her feet. "Hunter, perhaps I can arrange for myself and maybe Bathilda since you're so busy?"

I become enraged. "No! Absolutely not!" I can't understand what it is, but that woman makes my skin crawl. Something about her screams trouble. "I will not have you go anywhere alone with her. End of discussion."

Eliza smiles shyly. "Yes, Hunter."

I realize that I've upset her. "I'm sorry, my dear. However, I don't want you going on any trip by yourself, not without me and not with her. I can't explain it, but something about her screams danger." I am afraid that something will happen. I don't want to lose her.

Eliza rolls her eyes. "Oh Hunter! Seriously! You read John William Polidori too much," she says as she scoffs at me.

I see red. "Eliza! Enough! Do *not* give me an attitude!"

She looks down. "Yes, dear."

I feel bad and try to rein in my temper. Why can she not see my fear, how dangerous that woman appears? I know I have been harsh, but I am trying to protect her.

I walk with Eliza and ponder many things about our oddly disturbing neighbor, Mrs. Morris, or Bathilda, as Eliza calls her, and if I dare say, I think about my business partner Garrett Wilkins as well. There is something so different from everyone about the two of them. Garrett and Bathilda both have facial features that seemed paler than the average person. Their eyes are very weird. Bathilda, with her red hair, has deep green eyes, yet there are times when she becomes angry that her eyes change a shade to black. I don't understand how that is possible. Garrett is nearly as tall as I am, with black hair and gray eyes.

Most women I have heard describe his eyes say they are captivating. I see women try to fawn over him because of his good looks, yet I will be honest that he terrified me when he becomes angry. His eyes turn black as sin. There is a fire in their depths that looks to be straight from hell. I have thought at times about dismissing him out of fear. I am too terrified that he will attack me. I am a retired soldier. However, the power that radiates from him is otherworldly. I feel cold chills when associating with either Bathilda or Garrett.

I know that if I were to be honest with anyone, many would remark that I was starting to lose my senses. I know that it is illogical. However, it feels entirely unnatural. Something about Garrett and Bathilda is dark, ancient, and powerful. I dare not speak my fears.

There have been times at work when Garrett doesn't notice I have heard him talking to himself, and his eyes go completely black or turn blood red. Some days, I hide myself in a separate meeting room. Peering discreetly through the cracked office door, I make sure to observe my business partner from a distance where he will not suspect. I keep myself calm, so he will not sense anything. I watch as he makes haste to the back door of our store. There, another person meets him and passes him a bottle of red liquid. To my horror, he snaps the man's neck. I stay hidden until Garrett leaves. Fear takes root in my bones. I can't unsee what I have seen, yet I can't do anything concerning it.

I have had similar situations at my house as well. I am sitting one day on my promenade deck. I see Garrett at Bathinda's house. That is how I know that they are acquainted. What I see, though, seems rather odd. As seen through a window, they both seem to be kissing a maid on her neck. I quietly make my way back inside my house and decide to close the window shade just in case they might have seen me lounging. The scene looks very weird, but it is not a scene that anyone could ever forget. After returning to my bedroom, I realize I have neglected my paper on my chaise lounge. I decide to

quickly retrieve it. Then I shut the door once I am inside, and I feel
the strong urge to lock my doors. I hear Eliza calling my name from
the parlor room downstairs. So I descend the staircase in search of
my ailing wife. I keep these dark thoughts in my mind because no
one will believe me. If what I have seen is the truth, and their secret
becomes uncovered, they will no doubt kill me.

CHAPTER 3

As I walk into the lounge, I find Eliza relaxing on a sofa, I call our maid Betsy and request her to fetch the physician so he can attend to my wife. Dr. Blythe arrives within the hour to examine her. He has been my family doctor for decades. Dr. Blythe was friends with my father. From my understanding, they knew each other from age eleven and attended secondary school together. I pray that Eliza is well, that nothing serious is the matter. I cannot wait for tonight. It is my birthday, and I intend to celebrate with her.

I want to try one more time toward conception. I don't know why, every time we try, something constantly happens, and the baby doesn't survive. I'm beginning to wonder if God is punishing me for my time in battle or if dark forces are at work here. There must be an explanation. Is this an attack from evil powers that lurk in the darkness? Those who follow Satan? Are my ancestors angry with me? The doctor said we were both physically healthy. I pray to God every night for answers and to protect my children's souls. One reason I doubt my faith is this: it feels as if he doesn't hear me when my children continue to die, and Eliza mourns every one of them. She fears she's infertile and her family will see her as a disgrace. I don't care what they think. I still will love her.

I'm so engrossed in my thoughts I don't hear Dr. Blythe walking toward me.

"Mr. Eldridge?"

I snap out of my thoughts. The doctor is standing near the doorway to the dining hall where I'm currently seated on the window seat. I raise my head, noticing him. I invite him to sit down with me and discuss his examination. I'm relieved to learn that her ankle is only sore, and nothing dangerous has happened to her.

We stand up. I signal one of our maids, Demaria, to come prepare lunch as I go to check on my wife. I hear Eliza calling my name.

"Hunter? Hunter?"

I immediately approach her and inquire if she's well. She informs me that she feels much better and asks if we can continue with our day. I'm a bit hesitant. However, she tells me that she would like to take the buggy, and I instantly feel better. Demaria enters the room, and we request

As our coachman is driving the buggy, I decide that I want to stop by the store. I inform Eliza that I intend to stop in for a minute.

She gives me a scowl. "Really, Hunter? On your day off, you are going to work. What about our day we have planned?" I immediately silence her disapproval with a passionate kiss. Then I assure her that I'm not working. I'm just going in to tell Garrett an idea I have about expanding my company.

I walk into the store and greet everyone. I see in the corner of the store my apprentice Thomas Dersley.

"Hello, Thomas, how are you doing?"

The boy turns to the sound of my voice. "Hello, Mr. Eldridge, I'm doing well, sir." The boy smiles at me.

"Splendid, how is your father? I heard that he was not feeling well."

He frowns at the mention of his father. "Yes, sir, he has been diagnosed with the sickness. The doctors have said that it's very progressive, moving forward very fast. They fear that nothing can be done to help him."

My heart was breaking for him. "My wife and I will pray for you next week in mass." I offer him a paid holiday so he can be with his family.

The boy looks at me with happiness in his eyes. "I would be so honored, sir. I know it has been hard on my mother."

I shake his hand. "Think nothing of it. I will mention it to Garrett." I give him a nod as he walks to the door. I walk into my office; I don't find Garrett anywhere in sight. However, clerk Fredrick is at the corner desk, tending to the books. I ask Fred if Garrett has not arrived, yet and he tells me that he has stepped out for lunch.

As I depart, I make Fred aware that I'm leaving, giving him a note for Garrett mentioning my decision regarding Thomas's family. Fredrick nods and goes back to his task. I walk out of the store, and Eliza is waiting for me across the street at the flower boutique. I watch her as she enjoys her time there. We have been married for fifteen years, and I have loved her every moment since I first met her. Married life is not easy, yet through patience, love, and working together, we make it work.

I cross the street to join her.

"Hunter, I grew bored, and I saw these flowers that are just so lovely." My wife has always loved roses, red. I buy them for her every anniversary. Red roses and pearls are her favorites. She has always been a classy lady.

"You don't have to explain. I know your love of botany."

She smiles at me and blushes. "What took you so long?" she asks me as we make our way back to the storefront where our coachman, Reginald, is still waiting with the buggy.

"I do apologize. It is Thomas Dersley's family. His father was just diagnosed with cancer. They fear that it is progressive, and nothing can be done."

"Oh my, that is terrible. I pray God to be with them." My lovely wife, she has always been a devout believer and a kind soul.

"I pray the same. I gave him liberty to return to his father's side and have left instructions for Garrett Wilkins to give him a lump sum to compensate his family." I pray that it will be sufficient for them.

She nods and gives me a disapproving frown at the mention of Garrett. "Hunter, I know it is not my place. However, I don't feel comfortable with him working for the company."

I look at her more sternly than I mean to. "Eliza, no, it is not your place."

She looks at me in shock, and I soften a bit. "He has been with the company since I was a boy. He is a top-notch partner in the company. I have no cause to dismiss him." I shake my head, I can understand her fears. He's so mysterious and sometimes frightening. Nevertheless, I was always taught as a child to accept him like family. "Everyone is different, but we must still love the person, and family is important." my father always said.

I know secretly she's terrified of him but remains friendly and polite so she doesn't offend him. "Hunter, I understand what you say. There is something about him, how has he managed to remain the same for thirty-five years without seeming to age?" She looks at me with morbid curiosity.

I have questioned the same. "I don't wish to know. He is a stellar partner, and I respect that he's a private person, as I am. It has no effect on his work abilities, so I will not snoop or pry, nor should you."

"Yes, Hunter, I regret speaking my mind on the matter," she says in a subdued voice.

I want to erase this conversation. It is my birthday. I don't want to fight with her when we rarely argue. "Let us continue our day. If I recall correctly, today is my birthday. I would like to end our day by taking you out to the opera and dinner. How does that sound?"

Eliza's eyes lit up when she heard this. "Oh, Hunter. I adore the opera! That is a splendid idea. Thank you, my love."

We continue with our day. We do everything that we intended to do. When we arrive back at our house, I cannot stand another minute being away from her. I pull her into my arms and she kisses me with passion.

"Thank you for today, Hunter. It was indeed a perfect day." Her eyes sparkle like the stars.

"You're welcome. I love you more than my own life. Each day with you is perfect. My wife, my love, my life, my everything, my Eliza, I never want to let you go," I whisper to her as I take her hand and pull her toward the stairs.

In a shocking move, I lift her into my arms like a new bride.

"Oh." she says.

I nuzzle her neck. "Before we go to dinner, I'm going to make you scream my name," I tell her as I carry her up the stairs to our room. I lay her down on the bed, and I crawl over her. I roll her on her stomach and undo her dress, pulling it off. I undo her corset while planting sweet kisses on her neck. She moans my name. Just as I have her corset off, I slip my hands underneath her and begin to fondle her. She pants and squirm. I roll her onto her back and remove my trousers.

I have not had the pleasure of being with my wife like this in a while, so I decide that I'm going to enjoy this, enjoy her. I roll her on to her backside and decide to make this moment special. I undo my bow tie, wrap it around her wrists, and secure her to the metal frame.

I whisper in her ear, "I love you so much."

She moans, "Oh God, Hunter, I love you too."

I chuckle as I nibble on her earlobe. "I'm going to make you scream my name," I whisper to her again as I reach over into her nightstand, finding her eye mask. I slide it on to her face, hiding her beautiful eyes.

I start to pepper kisses down her neck. I pull her down farther on the bed, stretching her a bit, but not too much. I crawl back over her. I give her a swift kiss on her lips, biting softly on her lower lip.

She gasps and pants. I seal her lips with a passionate kiss as she opens to me. My tongue entwines with hers. I start to caress her lovely skin. I guide my hand very gently across her skin. Moving from her collarbone to her perky mounds, I start to kiss down her throat, taking one of them in my mouth. She arches her back. I smile as I continue to give it attention.

My hand still gently moves, light as a feather down her stomach, until I reach her heated core. I start to move my hand around her heated button. She lets out a wail as her back bows off the bed. She's my everything, and I love how I can make her feel like this, how she makes me feel in every way. She starts to scream and moan my name. I smile wide as she wraps her legs around me. I reach over to loosen the restraining bow tie, and I slide myself into her wetness. I begin to slow movements. Then as she starts to come undone again, I start to move faster and harder. I lose myself in the passionate embrace of my wife as I make love to her for the rest of the afternoon.

I cannot think of a nicer way to celebrate my birthday than buried in my love. I hope a conception sticks this time. We have dreamed of having children. After several miscarriages, I don't understand what the issue is. *Please, God in heaven, grant us a child! Grant me a son.*

CHAPTER 4

I remember those moments of carnal love and bliss with her as if it were yesterday. I could not wait until the evening when I would take her out for our date to celebrate my birthday. I had everything planned. Nothing in our lives was supposed to go so wrong as it did. I had even decided to share our night with her family.

It had been many months since I took my lady to the opera. Once upon a time, it had been one of our favorite pastimes with times. Sadly, though, I consumed myself in work matters. My business was growing at an incredible rate, and without realizing it, I start to leave Eliza behind. Not this night, though! I instruct my servant Benjamin to go to the carriage house and make sure that the horses are ready for departure. He bows and heads out the door to do my bidding.

My maid Edna approaches me. "Master Eldridge?"

"Yes, please make sure that Mrs. Eldridge is making herself ready to depart."

She bows her head. "As you wish, sir," she says as she leaves the room.

I don my coat and my hat and then step outside into the evening air. I decide to take a walk to the carriage house and wait inside the buggy for Eliza. As I wait, I hear a female voice calling to me. I turn my head and notice my neighbor, Mrs. Morris. She watches me. It gives me the feeling of a cat watching a mouse, waiting for the right time to strike. She smiles at me and waves, but it is bothersome.

I still remember the moment she moved into the house next to ours nearly a decade ago. Her husband was the first to greet us. He was a wonderful fellow. Honestly, I don't recall what happened to him. He has not been present for several years. Eliza and I have discussed the odd situation, which perhaps they divorced quietly. My wife was the first one to build a friendship with her. Eliza has always been a kind person unless she has a bad feeling about someone. It baffles me. I don't understand how Eliza doesn't feel the same feeling I have. Bathilda disturbs me, but Eliza has had her over for tea on numerous occasions.

While Eliza is present, she's a wonderful guest, and they've grown close as friends, that is, while my wife is in attention to her behavior. Last week, Eliza invited her to join her book club. I remember that day well. I was sitting on my promenade deck while the ladies were reading and having tea on the veranda.

The other ladies ended the session, and Eliza was showing them out of the house. Bathilda stayed behind. I became bothered as Bathilda looked up and watched me with a mischievous look, a salacious glint in her eye.

As I try to ignore her even now, I have the same feeling. Before I can leave the area and head back into the house, she speaks.

"Good evening, Hunter," she purrs.

I responded kindly, "Good evening, how are you tonight?"

"Oh, I'm doing wonderfully," she purrs again. She keeps giving me a look like she's waiting for me. I don't understand it.

"How is your shop coming? Are you getting any business?" I ask her to try and make pleasantries

"Oh, marvelous. Yes, I was quite busy today. Luckily, I still get customers interested in alchemy. My grandmother used to get many requests. We thought over the years it had become unheard of. I'm happy to be wrong."

We both laugh. I don't understand why I laugh. Perhaps I'm just being polite.

"You have plans for this evening?" she asks me, and I nod.

"I'm taking Eliza to the opera. Her favorite play is showing tonight, *Hamlet*. It is my birthday, but I love doting on my missus." I smile, thinking of the surprise waiting for her.

"Oh, how wonderful. I love the opera, such beautiful music, and some have bittersweet songs of woe," she says to me, her eyes looking a bit vacant as if she were remembering something.

"Yes, I suppose some of them do indeed," I agree with her.

Eliza finally steps out of the house, and I'm very thankful for her company. It is already evening. I order my driver to pull the buggy around to the front of the house. It is October; however, it is not too late yet to be very cold. I ask Edna to please grab Eliza a shawl or small duvet for the ride. The maid brings everything I ask for, and we begin to travel. It is a far walk to the opera house, and my lady is adorned lavishly with clothes fitting to attend the opera.

I notice Mrs. Morris is still watching. Tonight, she has a serpentine smile that is most unnerving. It sends chills down my spine. I'm grateful that Eliza is conversing with the driver and doesn't notice the neighbor's frightening yet baffling behavior. Not wanting to be rude, I still wish her a good evening.

As we pass Bathilda's house, Eliza notices her, and we both wish her a good night as the horse and buggy travels down the street. Right before we are completely out of sight, I distinctly hear her say directly to me, "I'll see you soon, my love." I'm deeply troubled, but I let an impassive mask settle on my face. I don't want to worry Eliza.

It is a scenic ride to the opera house. We talk about numerous details. I talk to her about the business, its progress, and I share with her how someone from parliament visited my store recently to purchase a book. It was the best day in the store. We had never received a visit from the Duke of Prescott's wife, and she was a lovely woman.

"Oh, I remember her. She's wonderful. It has been so long since I have associated myself with anyone from parliament. I probably wouldn't recognize anyone," Eliza says with a sad tone.

"I have never been fortunate enough. However, if you ever wish to go, just to see your old friends, I would love to meet them."

She looks at me with happy surprise. "You would!"

I shake my head, smiling at her. "Of course, you are my love, my everything. Your world is mine as well."

Eliza leans over and gives me a passionate kiss, then blushes as she looks around.

"Do not fret. I don't believe that our driver Reginald would never be offended since we are happily married," I tell her as I trail kisses down her neck. I lower the front of her dress trying to reach her cleavage.

Eliza moans softly. "Hunter don't make me a mess before the show."

I continue to nip and suck on her neck and whisper, "Why? It's so much fun!"

She tries to push me away, and at that moment, Reginald informs us we have arrived.

Once we are safely inside, I cover Eliza's eyes and tell her that I have a surprise for her. She giggles like a schoolgirl, playing along. The attendant takes some time checking in our coats, and our usher shows us to our seats. I take my hands off her eyes, letting her take in the box view.

"Hunter. Oh, my heavens! How did you secure this?" she asks me.

I point over to where her parents are sitting, also watching the show. Her eyes tear up. She waves to them and then turns to give me a swift kiss. "Thank you, darling," she says, and we spent the evening watching *Hamlet*.

The hours grow long. I can see that Eliza is starting to become very tired. We gather ourselves and walk to retrieve our coats from the attendant. We bid them goodnight; we exit the opera, and I remind Eliza that we still must go to dinner.

She took such a lengthy time getting ready that I had to push dinner plans to after the show. I have not told her, but we are having dinner with her parents. I will endure this. I'm informed that her sister's family will be joining us at a supper room. I ask the attendant to please have our coachman Reginald bring the buggy around. We both step in and head toward the dining place. She sees where we are and squeals in delight.

We embrace and head inside where her family is waiting for us. From the look in her eyes, she already has guessed at the surprise that I have in store. Once inside, we spend the evening socializing with her family. For me, it is enough to bore me to tears, and I want to leave. I'm grateful when she's finished so we can make our way back home.

By this time, the hour is very late, and the sky is black. I stand from my place at the table and suggest that, since she's so worn, we may depart to go home. Eliza says that she would like to walk and enjoy the cool night air. She confides in me that, though she's tired, she would like to gaze at the stars by our old spot where I proposed and enjoy its nightly beauty. I know I should instead just bring her home. However, I cannot deny her request. It has been many years so we have enjoyed a night like this.

We start down a path near the harbor. At this moment, a very eerie feeling starts to grow in me that we are not alone. Among the darkness and streetlamps lit with candles, I see dark shadows quickly moving around us. Oh, how I wish that there were someone else on this path tonight. I immediately regret my decision to take a moonlight stroll with her when we are both already weary.

I try to walk Eliza faster, and as I do, the feeling continues to grow into a sickening part of my stomach. I will do anything to protect my wife. I urge her to run.

"Hunter, what is the matter?"

I cannot shake the feeling that we are being followed. I'm so terrified. "I don't know. I love you. I don't want harm to come to you."

Her eyes are wide with terror, and she attempts to move faster. "Oh, God in heaven, help us." She prays as she shakes in fear. We start to run; Eliza quickly slips off her high-heeled shoes to run faster. I know the truth. Deep down, I know it is too late. Whatever this is, we cannot outrun it. We still try. We must fight for our lives against this hour of darkness. At that moment, I realize that running will do nothing. I wish I brought my saber with me. I stand and decide to fight. I push her behind me.

"Show yourself." I shout into the darkness, and before I can understand what is happening, I start to hear a sadistic laugh from somewhere in the darkness. I do not know what is happening. It feels like gusts of wind keep engulfing us. I hear the laugh come from a different directions, as if we are surrounded. However, I do not see anyone else present. Whoever this is moving very fast, like the wind. The anxiety we feel keeps building, and the feeling of being trapped is continuing to grow.

Whatever, this is, it is running in circles around us. Suddenly, it stops. I reach behind me to fasten my hand to my wife. Something suddenly hits me like a cement wall. I feel myself thrown away from her as the side of my body hits something that feels like I tree. I groan in pain, sure that I just heard something break. I stand up and begin to walk forward, ignoring the pain. Before I can find her, I hear Eliza scream in the darkness of night.

"Eliza!" I scream, to no avail. She's gone, and I fear for her soul. If there is a God above, please let not my fears be true!

I fall to my knees. All I hear is Eliza gasping in the darkness. There is a sucking sound, and I hear a thud. I cannot stop the sobs that fall, as I assume God has forsaken me and Eliza is dead. As I lift my head, I'm terrified beyond belief. *This is it. Now it is my turn.* I have had so many times during battle to die. How ironic that it should happen on the night of my birth. I see a figure in the shadows of the walk. It appears female. Everything is so confusing tonight.

All I can think at that moment is, *How could this have happened to us?* I stagger back to my feet to either fight or await my imminent death. My soul fills with dread, and a voice brings about a shocking revelation as to who is responsible for this night of slaughter.

"That takes care of that wench. Do you know how long I have wanted you, watched you, and couldn't do anything because she was always around!"

I feel myself shaking and sobbing at the bitter truth of my wife's death. Her voice pulls me into focus. It is a voice that, even through my utmost confusion, I begin to recognize.

"Yes, Hunter, she's lost to you. She was never meant for you. You have always been mine!" she laughs sadistically.

My melancholy turns to rage as she continues to laugh at me. As I'm pondering these horrific events, she steps into the light. My heart hammers in my chest. I stare at her with recognition. I knew she was dangerous. Somehow, I always knew. I never should have let Eliza near her. I stare at the woman who has been my neighbor for nearly a decade.

"Mrs. Morris!" Eliza's so-called best friend.

"Hello, Hunter, my love."

I stare at her in disgust. I notice the red liquid on her lips. The foul stench of blood is in the air. My stomach rolls at the odor while my head is screaming. My heart breaks with grief once again. I know what she is. I feel as if I have known this whole time but refused to see the truth. She's a creature of the night, a vampire.

She smiles. "Oooh, I love it when they realize what's about to happen. The screaming. The fear in the eyes. Not you, Hunter, my pet, not you. You are special, and you're mine!"

I tremble in fear. As futile as it may be, I try to run and scream. She just stands there in the night, watching me like a fierce predator waiting for the kill.

My eyes strain and catch sight of a still shadow laying on the ground in the distance. I know it is my love lying lifeless. Her soul has already gone on to God and left me behind. Just as I believe I'm escaping; she's in front of me grabbing me.

"Oh. My love, never run from a vampire!" She laughs as she throws me to the ground hard enough that I feel the impact sear through my body. I still try to crawl away from her. I'm a short distance when she picks me up and begins to lick my neck. She starts kissing and sucking on my neck hard while stroking my length. I feel so ashamed and wish for death.

"Come for me, Hunter," she purrs.

Frozen in fear, I wait for her to kill me. I have a desire inside me to fight her off, but I know it is useless. I scream in pain as I feel her bite deep into my neck. A second later, she's ripped off me. I hear a loud thud, and glass shatters.

She groans as I imagine she's thrown into something, possibly a streetlamp. I immediately recognize Garrett's voice. "Hunter, oh my God."

I hear a sudden sharp gasp. It sounds as if he mumbles something in a language I'm not familiar with. My body lies weak before him.

"Bathilda, what have you done!" Garrett screams.

I try my best to crawl away when I suddenly feel pinned down. I can only imagine that he somehow has noticed my wife's body. I hear him growl. Then I don't feel him. I hear what sounds like a brawl. I suddenly notice her body skid right by mine.

"Hello, love," she says as she licks my neck, sealing my wound. At this moment, after she does this, it is as though my body lights on fire. My neck feels as if molten lava has been poured into it.

I cry in agony. Death would be a better gift than this fire I feel is starting to consume me. I writhe and beg the heavens for death. Eliza! My wife, my love, I cannot go on without her. I grit my teeth enduring the excruciating pain. My head feels as if there are fifty war drums beating. I try to focus on my surroundings and the terrifying battle that is occurring between a man who has been my business partner and something of an uncle to me during my life and a woman who was a neighbor.

Garrett may have been my father's best friend, but he has always been terrifying, yet I was taught to love him like family. I realize now as an adult I was refusing to see what they truly were, what Garrett Wilkins truly was, and what I was now becoming. Eliza saw it all along. Had my years of association with him blinded me to the truth? I used to snark at my wife for speaking ill of Garrett. Would things have been different if I listened to her? A part of me is relieved he's here. However, I cannot understand how he knew where to find us. Something about this entire scenario, the more it fills my mind, is not making sense. I start to question other things my mind never allowed me to entertain previously. How long have they been watching us? Did they plan this moment?

Garrett answers my thoughts as though he heard them, informing me that Bathilda loves hunting. She loves the thrill of the "game," and she's hated my wife for years. His words make me think of Eliza. Her smiling face I will never see again. Her graceful body I will never hold. I'm distracted from my thoughts as the pain increases and picks up speed. At this moment, I feel like the lava has slowly started to spread through my bed. My back arches in pain.

"Ahhh. God." I scream out. We have never done anything to warrant this behavior. I could not believe it.

"You didn't do anything; she's been hunting you for a decade. She saw you in town at your store one day. You didn't notice her. I did. She stalked you to your home where she found the house next to you for sale," he snarled.

My eyes have by now closed shut. I have no more energy to keep them open, and with this darkest night, I cannot see my surroundings. I lie there not knowing what is happening as I feel liquid pour into my mouth. I try to fight away from the disgusting taste that starts to turn sweet. Whatever this is, it fuels the slow-growing fire burning through my veins. The pain increases at an alarming rate. I hear a sadistic laugh as I feel something crack my neck, and everything goes black as I succumb to darkness.

I lie here praying, hoping that I'm dying. I try to use my voice, yet I feel as though my mouth is sewn shut. My lips will not move even for me to scream. The more this fire rages through me, the more I'm immobilized. I know that there is no help for me, no turning back. As my entire body morphs into something else entirely. With each passing hour that the lava rages through me, it feels as if it has turned into a molten spiderweb reaching out and sinking its teeth into every nerve of my body.

At this moment, I feel the pain scorching my veins in my arms. As time moves on, I feel this torture spread toward every vein and nerve ending in my legs. The lava continues to flow, making its way toward my human organs. The more it passes through my system, the more I feel more weight added to my body, as if the anvil continues to grow heavier. While in the same instance, the fire grows hotter.

I feel my core continue to heat up, my kidneys, my liver, and my stomach all changing, transforming into more-than-human organs. I feel the fire in my arms and legs start to cool the more this blazing inferno centers on my upper body. I have lost track of time, lost track of days through this torment. The all-consuming fire scorches through my core. What was once like lava turns hotter, as if rays of the sun have found their way into my body. I feel the fiery webs slowly move through each organ until it rains down daggers on my human heart. I cannot feel my heart as I lie here paralyzed. However, the pain is the worst I have endured yet. I scream for someone in the heavens to end my agony. When I feel my heart jolt like it has been shocked, the searing pain in my head starts to ebb away, leaving my mind clearer that it has ever been.

It as if my human mind was cloudy, like a ship lost in a fog at sea. I know that I'm far from safe. After hours and days of never-ending pain is residing, I know I will never be the same. As my mind clears, I can hear Garrett speaking to me. I continue to lie frozen and in agony. I feel like in this darkness I'm seeing a light, as if I'm waking up into a dream I try my best to focus on the dreamlike light, and I feel like I'm being carried off into oblivion.

Nothingness surrounds me. As I lie there, I see life flash before me. Eliza stares at me from the heavens, a child in her arms. I reach for her. I'm so overjoyed to see my love again that I will do anything to be with her. I feel my surroundings. It feels like I'm standing on rock somewhere. She stands on a ledge directly above me. I begin to climb toward her, only to feel as if hands grab my legs. I look down to make sense of this.

As I turn my eyes back toward her, a great chasm erupts between us. "Eliza." I scream. I use all my strength to attempt to fight off the weight holding me down. I reach for her again. "Come back to me please, my beloved." I can do nothing but watch as the wall continues to build, separating me from what I want most in life.

"God. What did I do to deserve this curse?" I cry out, reaching for heaven.

She shakes her head. "Hunter, I cannot. Our love and life has been destroyed by dark powers we were unaware of."

I drop to my knees, curling myself into a ball of anguish. "I know darling, I know. I did nothing to warrant this." I hang my head as I cry.

Dear God, I did nothing to merit this. Why has this happened?

Eliza speaks to me in her loving voice. "Hunter, I'm not blaming you. You were the greatest husband I could have ever wished for."

I stare at her in this dreamscape. "What should I do? I will never let myself belong to her, this she-demon who destroyed us." I feel the weight leave me in the darkness, and I'm able to move again. Whatever grabbed me has slithered back to its origins.

I start to climb whatever we are standing on in this vast nothingness. She stares back at me with love and longing in her blue eyes. I commit her lovely face to memory, knowing this will be the last time I see her.

"Remember me, my love. Do not forget me." I reach for her sobbing, but knowing I will never touch her. "Hunter, my prince. Please do me one more favor, something I would never normally ask of you."

"What is it?" I ask, desperate to do anything for her, desperate to hear her voice one more time.

"Avenge me."

I cannot believe she could ask this of me, I know how she detests violence, but I cannot ignore her now. I had already planned to kill that she-devil.

Her last words call out to me before she's gone. "Let time heal you. Do not stay lonely. I will always be with you. You have eternity. Find love again." My heart doesn't accept her words at this moment. I'm not sure I will accept it in time, for my heart hurts too much.

"I will in time show you the way. I will send my heart back to you." She blows me a kiss from the heavens before her figure fades away, holding our child. I take one last look as three more little ones peer at me and blow me kisses before they are gone.

"Eliza. Don't go." Everything fades into nothingness as I drift back to reality. All I can feel in this moment is nothingness. Love, life, happiness—all gone.

What is left over is only the seething hate I feel. If I have learned one thing through this darkest night, it is this: life can be a cruel. My love, I will hold you in my heart and face this world with wrath. They have awoken the beast within me, and now the world will know my rage.

CHAPTER 5

Three days later, I awake to a new feeling—my body has been reborn. I feel very light and freed. It is a new sensation that is difficult to describe. There is a new energy. It is as if my mind had been swallowed up inside of a fog my entire life and now is cleared of a thousand different distractions. This immortality, I knew, is from the underworld, with never-ending night and horrors that follow. My throat burns like it has been lit on fire and dry as the Sahara Desert. Everything feels so heightened.

I can smell everything, see everything, as if I have never had sight before. There is a smell of cinnamon mixed with vanilla and earthy grains. It must be from the baker's shop. As I'm adjusting, I hear a male's voice as if it were trying to speak to me. Immediately, my heightened body lets out a snarl of defense as I jump to my feet and press him against the wall.

I open my eyes to see the room with new clarity. I look up to see Garrett smirking at me. I release my hold on him, feeling ashamed and confused.

"Easy, you need to relax. I know it's disorienting, but everything is all right." I'm still out of sorts and unsure about how quickly and aggressively my body is reacting. I just attacked my business partner and mentor.

Garrett sighs in defeat. "I'm amazed that she stayed away as long as she did."

Honestly, learning the truth now, so am I.

It is a game for her, but why did she wait so long to strike now? *Is there something that I'm missing? Everything feels like a blur.* I try my best to remember everything that happened. I still cannot believe how in one night my life can change so drastically. I never imagined that vampires existed, and apparently, I'm now one because of one psychotic woman.

"Garrett, please help me. What shall I do?"

He looks at me and sighs. "Well, right now, you need to hunt. I will help train you. We are going to have to leave London. You cannot just go hunting in the city like she did and be noticed. It is not acceptable. Neither is leaving a victim from this form of attack alive. When she's caught, she will pay the price."

I look at him in surprise. I inquire of him what he means of hunting. I'm used to a musket, but I have nothing like that right now.

Garrett looks at me. "Hunter, hunting is what we do when we are seeking out our prey. It is necessary to satiate our thirst for blood. The thrill of the game is the best part," he says with a wicked smile. "The fear in their eyes before you strike, you will learn to relish this."

I shake my head. "No. I will not kill innocent people," I snarl at him.

He backhands me into the sofa, and before I can move, he's on me, pinning me down. "You will if you don't wish to die of starvation." he snarls at me.

I sigh in defeat and fear at his actions, I am shocked. He has never raised a hand to hit me before. I nod in agreement. He stands and dusts himself off. I decide to inquire about his other comment concerning her actions.

He informs me, "To change someone, we have to have their consent, not a blatant attack like this. She had no right to initiate this situation."

I close my eyes. Yes, she will pay, and I will be the judge and executioner. "You will live and, in time, forget her, but trust me, my friend: in time, you will find love again."

I open my mouth to protest more, and he cuts me off. "Hunter, you need to hunt. Not only that, you need time. I know Bathilda. I hate her as well. She's plain psychotic, as you have learned but very lethal."

The more I think of it, the angrier I become. I don't realize when I grab him by his shirt and shove him into a wall, denting it in the process. Garrett removes my hand from his shirt.

"Firstly, control yourself. You are stronger than you realize because you are a newborn."

I step back, look around, and realize that we are in a room I'm not familiar with. I notice my environment and myself, the paleness of my skin, the smooth yet firm texture. I don't even feel my heartbeat anymore, yet my breath is racing.

"What the bloody hell?" I murmur as I notice my new self. As I examine the room, there are no mirrors for me to see myself. I look around the unfamiliar surroundings.

Garrett informs me that we are in his house. "My house is far away from the city. Being what I am, I need space and isolation so I can hunt where no one can see me."

I nod in understanding. I have heard tales of vampires. "I just never believed the tales to be true," I say to myself.

Garrett nods. "Yes, my own transformation story is quite like yours."

I watch him curiously as Garrett walks over to a painting on the wall of a beautiful maiden with black hair, wearing a medieval dress. "Her name was Liana; she was the love of my life. I would have died for her. It was late one night. I had arrived at home. I had learned from my neighbor that my wife had sent the children to her parent's house and was planning to surprise me with a night alone."

I watched and listened to him, knowing how it feels.

"So, when I came to the house, everything was dark, and there was an eerie feeling. The pungent smell of death filled the house. I found a candle and lit a match. The entire house was destroyed, as if someone had thrown everything around. I found her in our room, thrown on the bed, covered in blood, with her throat ripped out," he whispered in pain.

I sit down and listen to his story, the weight of the other night crushing me again.

"Yes, Hunter, I know how it is. Worse was that the creature was still there. Next thing, I felt a swift bite to my neck, and everything went dark. I awoke the next morning as a vampire." He hangs his head.

I stare at him in shock. "How did you manage?"

He begins to pace around the room. I imagine that he's contemplating what he's going to say. I have no idea how old Garrett truly is. Now knowing that he's a vampire as well, I don't want to imagine how much he has lived through. His eyes look haunted and very far away. He stands by the crackling fireplace looking at the painting that hangs above the mantel.

"I found out a close friend of mine was a vampire, very powerful, with a wife who was a dark witch. Your ancestor, Abner Sloyan."

I fall backward in terror. He bloody knew my ancestor, that insidious person in my family.

I'm completely incredulous at this information, which means also that Garrett is well over five hundred years old. He has been around long enough to know my entire family here in England. I'm at a loss for words. He was friends with that fiend! I have heard stories about him, though I never believed them. How the man was cold hearted and evil, with a wife who was just as vile. We are warned at a young age in my family to always remain faithful and true to God, never turn to darkness like Abner did. It is said that he committed vile acts against humanity, like tearing people apart or butchering young expecting woman, and his wife carried the infant away, never to be seen again. They were very distorted people. Now, learning that he was a sadistic vampire with a wife who was as evil as Satan himself, makes me sick to realize I'm related to such a vile creature. I'm without doubt that his wife didn't want the infant for anything good. May God torture them for eternity for their evil works.

As I think about this information, it leaves questions in my mind, questions that start to plague me for answers, which I feel I will not receive honesty about. *Was he behind our attack? Did he plan my transformation to happen?* I have previously felt watched. Was it him? If so, for how long did he stalk me? Was he the shadowy figure I saw in the alley when Eliza's purse was snatched? The more my mind rants, the more nothing seems to make sense anymore. A small voice whispers that I'm overthinking, overreacting, and imagining things. It says to let it go, and I feel compelled to stop concerning myself with it.

I seethe in anger for some time until I realize that Garrett has continued talking.

"Abner was a good friend and the king of all vampires during that time. He helped me control myself, and she created spells for me in case I went berserk."

I accepted the existence of vampires now that I was one, but witches? "Are all the horror stories true?"

He chuckles. "You will learn they, indeed, are true."

I stare at him longer while I sit down, trying to absorb everything that I'm learning. "Who are you, Garrett? How could you be friends with that insidious monster? Are you that same person, or has time changed you into someone better?"

He whips around to stare at me. Eyes blazing in fury, he hisses at me, opening his mouth to say something when, suddenly, I groan in pain. At that moment, my hand flies to my throat, and I start clawing at it. Noticing my behavior, he pushes me out of the door.

For the next several days, Garrett takes me out hunting and shows me everything that he know. Every trick, every way to stalk, seduce and manipulate my prey. He is so lethal. We go into the hills of Scotland, and we feast on some of the native villagers. My human soul and consciousness scream at me to stop. I try to regain control as hard as I can. However, I feel a beast inside of me screaming at me to satiate myself. This hunger is so crazed that it is a sinister mindset.

I feel like I'm at war with myself constantly. I want to stop; I just have no strength to control this source of evil that is taking over. Garrett sees this and grabs my shoulder. "Hunter, let go. Let it flow. This is who we are. You cannot fight the killer you are!"

I shrug away from him. "Was this your plan the entire time? All along you knew me?" I ask him in anger, wondering why he's letting me become this vicious monster, unless he has a reason. He knows the good man I am. Why is he encouraging this sadistic behavior?

He looks at me, shocked, yet there is a weird look in his eye, as if he's choosing his next words carefully or hiding something. "No, Hunter! I'm not. I know what a good man you were, but you're not human anymore. You need to learn to be a vampire. You need to hunt and learn to control yourself. It takes time."

He continues to help guide me hunting. I have lost track of time. I have asked him when we will be ready to return, and he diverts my attention instead.

The following day we are running through the mountains. I'm growing tired of this man's stalling. I walk away to think. I turn around to stare at him. "Garrett, I want you to be honest with me: How long exactly have we been here? I'm done hunting. I feel in control. I know that have been here for longer than a few days or weeks. Why are you hiding me from the world? I may still be new, but I'm not days old!"

He scoffs at me. "I don't have to explain myself to you."

I snarl at him. Something is amiss here. "You're keeping me here for a reason! Do not play dumb! We have not even handled Eliza's funeral! You have not said a word about it! I *want* to see my *wife*!"

He turns to me with a glint in his eyes I cannot decipher. "Hunter, I took care of everything during your transformation. You had enough pain to deal with, and I could not see you suffer more."

"You had enough time to handle her arrangements in the three days I was unconscious?" I ask him dubiously. I'm shaking with anger. Nothing he's saying makes sense.

He looks me in the eyes. "I had her cremated, and her ashes put inside an urn for you. As far as the house, I sold that for you so you would have no strings to tie you down, and for the time being. I left the store in Fredrick's care."

I sit down, and my body heaves with sorrow, trying to produce tears, which it cannot do anymore.

At this moment, I feel like my soul has been crying for years. My mind is constantly swimming in depression, pain, and sorrow. I do my best to hide it from Garrett, but my heart never stops thinking about the love I once had. Never stops missing my angel. I'm also incredibly furious at his words. That was my life, my marriage! I understand his words. However, it was not his place to handle anything for me. This completely stole away any moment I could have had for grieving and laying my Eliza to rest.

"You still have not answered my question. How long have you been keeping me here roaming and staying in your mountain home?"

He finally meets me at eye level with a smirk. "Three months."

I stare him as he speaks, yet somehow I can feel he's lying. I feel that it has been longer than this time frame. I have seen seasons change more than once. Why is he purposely lying to me?

I have another question in mind that I didn't voice. Where does he disappear to? He told me during my newborn months I needed constant supervision, so why would he disappear at times after we had hunted? He told me to rest. Then he left. I know he will never answer me, so I forgo asking. I walk with him, and he informs me that we are finally going to venture toward humanity.

We are approaching Glasgow, Scotland. I come to learn that his mountain home is about ten miles away from the city. I'm not sure whether to hate him or not learning how close we have been living to humanity, yet he never gave me warning prior.

Time moves on. Garrett and I hunt together, live together, travel together. Time feels like it stands still and stretches on. Every day, I feel as if I lose all conscious sense of time while travelling with Garret. We take what we want. I find myself becoming more and more the monster that nightmares are made of. The beast inside laughs with glee, being fueled into an entity of its own. I feel myself growing more sinister with passing time.

A day came, however, that rattles my core. I feel as if I have been doused in freezing water. I'm hunting. I have gone by myself this time. I think I have ensnared an adult kneeling behind a rock, but I soon discovered it was an adolescent girl, a child who was tall for her age. She screams when she sees me, and I, for the first time, notice my appearance in her glasses. my deathly pale skin and obsidian eyes with a blood-red center. I'm terrified of what I see, not only seeing a child cowering away from me in terror but my appearance. I now understand why Garrett told me to never hunt someone with glasses. He didn't want me to see the truth of what I have become.

Deep in my soul, I hear a woman's cry. I realize it is Eliza crying from the heavens. My lost soul weeps with her. I have not heard her in so long. When I'm near Garrett, he always keeps me distracted. She knew what I would become, yet I made her a promise, and I realize I'm not keeping my promise to her.

I fit the pieces together that Garrett has been keeping me distracted from hunting that evil witch down! I feel consumed by hatred. My burning desire for retribution flares to life. I immediately look at the child and compel her to forget me. She comes to her senses, then runs off into the woods. I decide to find my mentor and confront him. I walk up to his house in search of him.

"Garrett?"

He looks at me with alarm. I think he can see something has changed with me.

"I need to know something. What are we doing? Why are we not exacting justice?"

He gives me a dubious look and asks what I'm referring to.

"You told that I would live to see justice. You told me that Bathilda would pay for her crimes. It has been several years since my wife's death, and her killer is running loose!"

He becomes startled. "Hunter, why are you concerning yourself with that woman?"

I cannot believe what I'm hearing. "Seriously! I made a promise to Eliza, and you said you would help me seek justice! For the evil that she brought to my household, and you are seriously questioning me on this!"

He takes a step back, looking scared and a bit proud. Why, I don't know.

We are standing in the parlor of Garrett's house in Glasgow, Scotland. I glare at him with cold fury. There are days where I wish I have other companions to associate and travel with. I would have left Garrett and his sick twisted behavior. During my human life, Garrett Wilkins was a loyal business partner, and during my childhood, he was a family friend. Since I have become an immortal, I have seen new sides to him that, personally, I want to stay a thousand miles away from.

Last week, he was hunting. He came across a child like I had, but he didn't spare the young one. Instead, he seemed to bask in the child's terror. He sickeningly played with the young one's fear before finally killing the child. I had hidden behind a tree and prayed he didn't detect me. I realized he's just as twisted as Bathilda, only he's a master at hiding it.

I'm in a paradox. I don't want to face this world alone, yet sadly, I don't have anyone else for now. This is all I can do for now. I look into his sinister eyes. "I will hunt her down to the ends of the earth. And if you will not join me, I will go alone," I growl at him.

He immediately starts to walk with me. "No need getting flustered. I will follow you anywhere. Now let us go and find that bitch," he says as I nod with a grin.

He sends a letter to a man who he's familiar with named Carlton and sets him to work on hunting down Bathilda. Finally, I shall have my revenge!

We wait another few days and receive a letter in return, letting us know her whereabouts. We learn that she's somewhere in Paris, France. Upon hearing this, I immediately leave to find passage there. Garrett runs out the door after me, requesting to accompany me. This is my fight not his, but I begrudgingly welcome his company.

I'm really starting to contemplate finding a person who I could change into a vampire myself to have a different companion. I also hate that Garrett has a sire bond on me. That is the reason why I can easily do things his way even if I hate it—he compels me, and I have no willpower to refuse. I figured this out some time ago. I have a friend named Maria who is a female vampire. She owns a tavern and brothel named the Siren's Call. I remember the first time I met her she was traveling through Scotland.

I had left Garrett for a brief time, needing to be away from him. We immediately connected. We hunted together just once, and I noticed how much more humane she was with her hunting. She told me that she figured out a century ago she doesn't have to murder her prey.

"If you leave them alive, that means you can always enjoy them again another day. We don't have to be brutes." I smiled at her words.

This was like providing me an awakening. I hated Garrett's vicious manners, and I felt perhaps I could attain redemption through her lifestyle. We walked to a pub. I was very nervous. Garrett had just started to allow me around people. She took my hand, and I felt calm instantly. She told me to quiet my storm and focus on other parts of my surroundings than human heartbeats. When I achieved it with little difficulty, we were both impressed. I told her that Garrett always instructed me to treat them like cattle, and even if I want to fight it, something about him makes me obey.

She then taught me about the sire relationship, how when you are sired by a vampire, during your early years of life, your body will automatically obey without question because there is like a tether tied between the both of you.

"It's like being a puppet and him pulling strings." I felt as if lightning had struck me when I understood her words. At the same time, I could not accept them. I didn't understand them. I had always been led to believe that Bathilda had turned me into a vampire.

She helped me realize it. It is forever binding unless he releases me, and I don't see that happening. I reflect on that memory of my only other vampiric friend. I have not seen her in what feels like years. Garrett, as I'm aware, has no idea of my friendship with her or how she taught me a new way. I constantly have to fake myself with Garrett. I feel more connected to my humanity when I live my life according to her philosophy.

I walk out of the house to search for a ship. I stop at a local pub. I walk inside to find a captain of a ship we could commandeer. I meet with the man and secure passage. That is when I finally notice the calendar positioned by the wall that reads May 1880. Twenty years have gone by! Garrett has never let me see a calendar or know how much time has passed. I was enraged. I knew it. I had a sinking feeling in my gut that all he ever did was lie. Telling me that we had stayed only three months in the mountains, then, when I had later asked again, he said it was only a few years!

Lies! I turn from the pub and march toward the ship. Garrett walks behind me. I sense his presence, and I snarl at him and shove him off the gang plank toward the ground. He quietly speaks to me.

"Hunter, it was necessary. You are young vampire. Humanity is not your world anymore."

I silence him for a bit with a cold stare. He stands to his feet, hands raised in the air. "I have given you the chance few humans are capable of. You have eternal youth. You have all eternity to live your life and see the world."

I stare at him, flabbergasted! I start to wonder why so long, or does he have an ulterior motive? Reading my thoughts, he suddenly bursts out laughing at my expense. "Hunter, you needed it. During the first several months, you must gorge on your thirst! Otherwise, you could become a savage and blood-crazed. Trust me, my friend." He says this with such conviction, like he's compelling me to believe him.

I start to question if he's correct. After all, he's centuries older than I and has more experience. "Horse hockey! Two decades! That is too bloody long and you know it!"

He looks me in the eye. "No, Hunter, it is right. At this amount of time nearly everyone who originally knew has died."

I feel a pain in my dormant heart at his words. Something, I have never considered. All our friends, Eliza's family, they all have either moved on or died while thinking no doubt both of us were killed. Garrett keeping me isolated around the world has prevented any exposure I might have endured.

I keep on pondering the information that Bathilda is in Paris, France. How ironic, the home of my uncle Hugo.

Garrett reads my mind. "You cannot, Hunter!"

I look at him with fake surprise. "What? Is something wrong?"

Garrett shakes his head. "You are not thinking about visiting your father's brother."

I roll my eyes and shrug at him, walking away

"Hunter, you are a vampire now. You cannot," he yells at me. I walk away from him and leave him standing at the dock. I don't pay heed to what he says. It was just an errant thought.

I would also not visit Hugo. There is a reason why my father stopped associating with him. Hugo is a right arsehole, worse than my father. A regular Ebenezer Scrooge with no hope!

"Like I would visit that bloody prick," I tell him. "He beat his wife, causing her to lose her unborn. I would more like to beat him."

Garrett nods and follows me onto the ship.

I have nothing that holds sentiment anymore without Eliza in my life. After spending more than an hour waiting on the ship for the captain to arrive, we start to depart. I learn from Garrett that they are old friends. The man is a vampire himself, loves the life on the sea. He is a nautical nomad, feels that the sea is better because, if he has something to eat, he can easily throw the remains overboard.

After conversing with him for a little while, we barter passage to France on a ship that is named *Queen Anne's Revenge* docked in the harbor, rather unscrupulous characters boarding with pirates. However, it is not like Garrett and I are saints ourselves. Associating with these miscreants means nothing. If they piss us off, we will just kill them and take their ship.

We meet their second-in-command, John Smythe, after sunset. "Ahoy, mates, where ya be headed?" said the man.

"To Paris, France, to catch a villainous witch!" I say to them.

They all laugh. "Aye, are they not all?" says one of the men with boisterous laughter.

The next thirty days are interesting as well as challenging. The need to feed is growing on us. We have not fed in a while, and I fear the sailors are doomed. The captain was Xavier Teach, son of the infamous pirate Edward Teach. I learned from Garrett that he had pulled into a port off the coast of Portugal where he was attacked and turned into a vampire. Later during that same month, he attacked his crew. Those who were not killed, he turned into vampires themselves. It was a ship of vampire pirates. However, some of the new recruits were mortal.

"Pirates are extremely superstitious. They will not try to anger us. They believe that we are demons from Hades or assassins from Kalypso herself," Garrett explains to me.

The captain welcomes us to feed. "Aye, if ya need the devil's red brew, take from my prisoners. They're dead men anyways." He laughs along with Garrett.

I just sit there watching his men. It feels odd to me how mere mortals can serve on a ship with creatures of the damned. I chuckle, smirk, and walk away to find a prisoner.

"Too bad you don't have prisoners who are women." I laugh.

"Yes, Hunter has quite a taste for the ladies. He loves to play with his food."

I throw a bottle at him. "As if you're one to talk," I say to him as I exit the room.

I walk around the ship and inhale the smell of the sea. I never realized the smell of the ocean could be so calming to me. As I venture deeper inside the hole of the ship, I can hear the cries of the men caged. I let out a sadistic growl that makes them cower in fear.

"Come out, come out, and meet your end," I sing-song to them as I walk along the hallway that is dark to their eyes, but ever so clear to mine.

I find a man praying and shaking in fear, chained to a wall. I can see into his mind. I learned after my first decade, I have the ability to see into the minds. I can determine who has an innocent or guilty soul. I see their hearts in different shades, the darker the heart, the more evil their soul. This man, he's guilty of many counts of rape, murder, and many more sins. He is in here because he tried to steal this ship from the captain.

"Perfect," I purr to the man; he's as wicked as Bathilda herself.

"What are you?" he says.

"Your execution," I say as I sink my teeth into his neck and begin to drink. As I drink, I feel the warmth of his blood flow through my body, and it calms the raging storm that brews inside of me. I take another deep smell of the sea while drink. I feel myself instantly relax.

I throw his body down to the floor as I walk out after satiating my thirst. Before I exist the room, I whisper, "Only two more weeks to go. Pray, you all, for your souls. My partner still needs to be satisfied. Have a good night." I walk out, hearing their fearful whimpers. I lie in my bunk that night and listen to the screams below as Garrett, no doubt, takes his fill.

I notice someone from the corner of my eyes, a young maiden. She smells as if she has been enjoyed numerous times. She cowers in the corner in fear. "Come here, young lady!" I say to her in a commanding voice. I cannot place it, but there is something very familiar about her.

She walks over to me; I see she has red curly hair and green eyes. Her dress is torn at the legs to be a bit revealing. The front of her dress is a bit torn to show her cleavage. She bows her head to me and starts to climb onto my bunk as if it is expected. I still her with my hand, and she stares at me in shock.

"What is your name?" I ask her. She's taken aback, as if no one has spoken to her before.

She whispers, "My name is Margaret McClary, sir."

I nod. "How old are you?" I ask her.

"Fourteen years of age," she says. I had a feeling she was young, but at the right age that most girls in this society would start to marry.

"Where are you from, and how did you get here?"

She sits down. "I come from Dublin, sir," she tells me. "I was waiting by the port with my betrothed. He was paying for some goods from the market when, suddenly, a drunken rabble came upon us. They attacked him, knocked him in the water, and took me aboard ship. I have been here since; I know not what befell him," she whispers, looking around.

I can tell she's fighting back her tears to be strong. I have already understood: they have ravaged her and have taken her away from her betrothed. They no doubt sent her here to pleasure me.

Filthy pirates! I give her a hug. "I was married once; I know what it is like to lose so much!"

She nods and looks away, trying to hide her pain. We spend some more time talking, and she opens to me more. I get to know her better.

I cannot risk Garrett seeing her. He is not like me. He will take his fill in more ways than just lustful pleasure. I contemplate where to hide her. Then I notice barrels in the corner closest to my bunk. I hide her under as much as I can. In the morning, she will have to find somewhere else to be safe. I think through what I should do, then decide, come port, I will dress her in male clothes and sneak her off the ship.

I can provide her with a handsome dowry and provide her a new life in France. I cannot let them destroy her like this. I feel like murdering them all. Garrett wouldn't care about the matter; he has no love lost for humans. I know he tried to mold me that way. However, the vision I had of Eliza one day, seeing her tears rain down from the heavens at the monster I was becoming, was very sobering. It was right before we left Scotland. I saw her in my mind. She reached out her hand to me, caressing my face, and said, "Remember who you are!" It was my wake-up call. I never told Garrett about it. For some reason, something warned me not to.

Our month journey was concluded. We arrived in Paris, France. "Garrett, go ahead and conclude whatever you need to with the captain, I will meet you in the city."

He looks at me dubiously.

"Don't worry about me. I just want to stretch my legs and hunt for a little fun," I joke with him. He smiles and shakes his head, then leaves toward the captain's quarters.

I hunt down Margaret. I follow her scent until I come across a dark corner. I realize she's not alone. She's crying. I hear her begging him to stop. This man has his full weight on her body. Her hands are roughly pinned above her head. Her body is pinned on the cold floor behind a series of crates. She's in the cargo bay of the ship. The man was attempting to hide her from sight. I hear her cry again. I can see her dress torn more. The man is roughly ravaging her bosom as he thrusts into her, laughing at her pleas. I see tears streaming down her face while he's enjoying himself, having his sexual fill. I see red. I snarl in fury.

I move fast and throw the crates away from them. "Disgusting piece of trash!" I growl as I rip him off her. I see the fear in his eyes as I snap his neck and throw him across the room. She immediately tries to cover herself and begins to crawl away from me, from the body of her attacker. She's shaking and crying. I kneel in front of her so she can see it is I. I quickly find a potato sack, wrap her in it.

I instruct her to dress in his clothing so she can sneak off the ship. "Come, we don't have much time. You will have to hold on to me, and I'm going to run at high speed. You'll be safe once we're inside the city. I will arrange for you to have everything needed for a fresh start."

She looks at me, shocked.

"Money, new clothes, everything, and for the time being, a place to stay. You're not going to endure this nightmare again"

She looks up at me. "Why are you doing this? How can I ever pay back this debt?"

I shake my head. "There is nothing to repay. Do you know Agnes McClary from Dublin?"

She's taken aback by the name. "Yes, she's my grandmother."

I nod. "She's my mother's sister. I recognized your name."

She stares at me in shock.

"I'm Hunter Eldridge. You look just like your mother. I remember your grandmother sending us news of her birth, and I remember the day she was married." I stroke her curly hair.

Her eyes fill with tears. She rush in and hugs me. "Damn to the depths whatever evil cursed you to be like this!" she says to me.

I close my eyes and sigh. It would be better for her not to know.

I open my eyes, and we gaze at each other.

"My mother spoke of you," she says. "You were always a very good soul. Your wife was as kind as an angel. I'm sorry for your loss."

I embrace my young cousin. "We're family, Maggie. I will not let anyone hurt my family," I whisper to her. I couldn't let these miscreants ruin her anymore.

I wait while keeping a look out as she dresses in the menswear. After she's finished, I run her into the city. I immediately go to my cousin Marshall's house. He is Hugo's son and hates his father about as much as I do. He was there to witness Hugo's abuse and fought him for the sake of his mother, Gabrielle. Hugo punched him hard, but Marshall also landed a blow, knocking his father out. Marshall was tired of his mother's tears and pain.

We approach the steps. Margaret looks around at the rich atmosphere the house displays. I ring the doorbell. "This is the home of our cousin Marshall Eldridge."

She looks at me, then stares at the door.

"Hunter!" he says as he gives me a once-over, obviously noticing the difference.

I keep my beast at bay. "Marsh," I greet him as we shake hands.

When we step inside the house, he looks over at her. "Is that little Maggie?" he says as he hugs her. "I visited Aunt Aggie's family once years ago and met her. What is she doing here?"

I inform him of everything that has happened to me, and how I met her. His eyes go wide, and his hands clench in fury. He feels as I do, about murdering all those bastards.

"I will take it from here Hunter," he says as he guides her away.

I nod. "I will have money sent to this address in her name so she may have a chance to build a new life here in France," I tell them as I walk away.

"Hunter!"

I turn around.

"I'm so sorry for the pain, you have endured. I didn't know. However, I understand, this will be our last meeting." I nod but don't let my sorrow show to him. "Hunter, given what you are, you are too much of a threat, no matter how much I care about you or my family. Except Hugo, you're welcome to hunt him," he says with a smirk while his eyes fill with sorrow. I'm not sure how he can understand my difference and what I have become.

He sees the questions in my eyes and explains it is familiarity. He has a career in the French government. There is a colleague of his who he had noticed to be oddly different, hypnotic, and so on. The closer he grew to the person, the more he learned of the terrifying secret. They were having brunch one day when the man revealed his secret. However, he warned that if Marshall informed humanity, he would be killed.

I'm heartbroken hearing this news, hearing that he was pulled into a world I never anticipated becoming a part of. I understand why I need to leave my family and never return in his eyes. I nod and walk away, feeling my family and old life slip away from me again.

I move forward into the night to find Garrett and a little taste of Paris. I walk down the street, and I catch the scent of something very luxurious. I decide to follow the appealing scent. I come toward the docks and find many various women. Many of them are dressed very scantily. I can tell they are prostitutes. I decide to indulge. I have not had sex in two decades.

I do love my wife, and I always will. I just need a release, and I need to feed. The women walk toward me with seductive looks. I walk toward them, choosing an enticing blonde. She tells me her name is Phoebe Au Claire.

"Oui, monsieur," she says to me. I take her by the hand and lead her away toward an alleyway. Garrett is not in the area, so I can act as myself. I find a slab of flour sacks to lay her on. I start to kiss her. She's panting beneath me. I lower my lips to her neck and sink my teeth in. She gasps as I begin to feel her warmth flow. I leave her lie there after some time, fully sated. I lick her wound to heal it. I leave her alive.

Unlike Garrett, I have always hated killing. I feel like I do it to answer his bidding. I'm forever grateful to Maria for showing me a new way. After the girl recovers, I lower myself to her and begin to kiss her again. She moans and wraps her arms around me. I roll myself over. I lift her dress more. I release my trousers and ease her over myself. She throws her head back in ecstasy. I begin to gently thrust into her. She screams in pleasure until she comes undone and falls asleep. I pick her up bridal style. I see that we are still near the docks. I begin to walk farther toward east side of Paris until we are near the outer city limits. I come a small town named Claye-Souille.

This is where my aunt Gabrielle's parents' home resides. No one lives here anymore. However, my uncle used it as a country home and kept servants here. I leave her there to hide until she recovers. I compel her to forget and tell her that her name is Giselle La Pierre. I compel my uncle's servants to care for her and help her, let her stay there. I have seen how quickly prostitutes and other people perish on the streets. If I can help her build a new life under my family's care, then perhaps it will help with restoring my soul.

At this moment, I feel like I'm being watched again. I have not had this feeling in a long time. I inhale the sweet scents in the air—sugar cane and raspberry. I turn to find someone behind me.

"Hello, my love!" she purrs.

I growl as the name escapes me. "Bathilda!" I hiss. Looking at her with malicious glee, I realize I can finally end her!

CHAPTER 6

After all this time, Bathilda stands in front of me, as if she's not the reason for my life becoming a twisted nightmare. I cannot hold myself back any further. The moment that I notice her, notice that she has not made a move, I lunge at her, poised to strike. She tries to run. However, I'm quick to grab her and throw her into a building. She snarls, shakes herself off, and propels herself at me. I stand there with a grin on my face, beckoning her forward. She gives me an evil smile and moves to strike, I catch her again. I punch her in the chest, sending her flying twenty feet. A building shakes and shudders at our assaults as it crumbles apart. She's quick to dodge out of the way in time.

Suddenly, I see from the corner of my eye someone hidden underneath a violet robe chanting. Bathilda circles me, and suddenly, purple fog creeps on the pathway. I feel like I cannot move!

"What sorcery is this?" I snarl. Suddenly, hidden in the shadows is a small figure cloaked in a deep-purple hooded robe, waving her hands. She notices me stare and slinks out of sight.

I immediately start to panic. The closer the fog creeps toward me, the more frozen I feel. I start to feel dizzy. My body is trying to collapse and fall to the ground, yet I feel as stiff as a statue. This is another form of torment. It has to be a bloody witch!

"Run, little girl! Before I find you!" I snarl. The more I struggle, the more it affects me.

Bathilda laughs in delight. "Oh, Hunter! I have missed you so much, my sweet." She grins at me.

I snarl at her as I fight my bindings. I look down at my feet, and the purple fog has crept up and wrapped around my legs. "What dark magic is this?"

She laughs as she wraps her arms around my neck and licks me. "Hunter! Lighten up and join in on the fun! Stop with this moral code! I know that you were rescuing that little delicious damsel! Whatever she's to you! Why do you concern yourself with a mere human? We are gods Hunter! Start acting like it!" she says as she kisses my neck.

As I'm frozen, I feel Bathilda's hands roam over my body. She softly moans as she licks and kisses my neck, reaching toward the apex of my thighs.

"No!" I snarl at her.

I begin to fight for control. I snarl, and it is then I notice that the hooded girl is gone. I feel I can move again. I swing, grab her by her throat, and throw her into a nearby building. She grunts, falling. "Guess again, witch! You ripped apart my life, yet you gloat at me to lighten up? Yes, I will—when you are dead!"

I growl. She laughs and then jumps into the water, swimming out of sight. I roar in agitation.

Garrett finds me a moment later. Looking disheveled, with blood on his collar, I ask, "Where have you been?" He stops and looks at me when I notice his messy situation. Then I also notice her scent on him. I glare at Garrett. "Why do I smell Bathilda on you?"

He steps back. "I was lustfully feeding, and she came out of the shadows. We just talked before she inhaled your scent, smiled, and ran in this direction. I tried to stop her."

For some reason, that sounds like a load of malarkey. "You're a vampire. How could you not stop her, no matter who your male appendage was thrusting into?" I grit through my teeth.

I walk away seething. I don't want to accuse him of anything false. However, it is highly irregular that every time we think we have her, she either is not where we anticipated, she has already left, or I find her by myself, and she escapes!

I feel him run to my side. "Well, now, what do we do?" Garrett says.

I shrug. "We keep looking. I don't care how long it takes. Something has to give, and I find that bitch!" I snarl at him and then walk off toward the French countryside. Last I heard, Garrett talking about was Germany, so I asked Garrett to lead the way as we make chase and run toward Germany.

I love the feeling of running, the wind in my hair, the feel of the earth under my feet. I hear the sound of a bee collecting pollen. I can hear the sound of a spider stabbing its prey and spinning the web. I can hear the sound of a distant waterfall splashing on some rocks. I rush past Garrett and signal I want to race. This feeling is so freeing, so fun. I take off at full speed and don't stop as I sail over a canyon. I enjoy the scenery that comes with running through the wilderness. I marvel at the earthly beauty and pass a castle that is so majestic I wish I could have shared the sight with Eliza.

I feel a sense of power and believe that I'm winning when I don't see Garrett in the area. I lose my confidence when I see him standing twenty yards in front of me. I slow myself to a stop and curse my chances that he somehow gained a lead and won. Garrett is laughing at my expression. He is lounging by a tree. I kick my feet in sour disappointment. He walks toward me and informs me that, since this is my first time in this area, we will stop at the European regent's house, which apparently, we should have done in the beginning.

"In Europe, every vampire that comes for an intended purpose must meet with the regent and be granted permission. In order, to search this area of Europe for Bathilda, especially after losing track of her again, we will need his blessing," Garrett says.

After running through the various countries and cities in France, Luxembourg, Netherlands, and Germany, we finally arrive in Bremen, Germany. It is a port city just outside of the country called Belgium. One of the best things about being in Europe is the fact that the countries are so linked together. When you are a vampire, it makes it very easy to travel from one country to the other swiftly, with little delay. The only thing we had to do was meet with one of the European coven leaders and be granted passage through.

I learned that, in America, there is something called a coven council with elders and a vampire king. However, apparently, he was killed in the 1700s during a war with the Lycans, and they had yet to appoint another king. The whole council elect were friends with the king, had been for centuries, so it was all one giant clique. In Europe and England, there was one king who was head of the entire region. It had been this way for centuries longer than America had existed. The court consisted of the king and his three appointed elders.

I didn't know for certain where they were located, and Garrett wouldn't grant me that information. He did tell me these three elders were responsible for the entire European region, and the king was responsible for that region, plus the region of England. Garrett informs me that, once upon a time, the true real king was my ancestor Abner, and he reigned in Romania. After his execution, the king in England was appointed as his replacement. Garrett says that someday there needs to be a real king to take the rightful place. I have a sinking feeling in my bones that he's referring to me. I'm not sure how I feel about this at the moment. Could I really be a king? The thought seems so foreign to me.

After arriving, Garrett leads the way through the country, and we are brought to a mansion. The house was built on the border of the black forest, and I can tell was very ancient. It had no doubt been rebuilt a few times. Overall, it is still very beautiful. As we approach, Garrett informs me that the regent's name is Herr Fredrick Von Hofer, reminding me to be respectful in his presence and only speak when spoken to. I was annoyed with him suggesting this as if I am a child. I only nodded my head in understanding. A young woman emerges from a gatekeeper's cottage. I can tell that she's human. I can also see fear in her eyes as she observes us. She knows what we are and is terrified. This is enough to tell me that the regents do have respect for human life.

I know. However, I cannot speak on such things. I'm still young to this world. These men are, without question, very ancient and have no doubt given up their humanity after years of adjusting to their cursed immortality. Garrett steps forward and talks with the maiden. She introduces herself as Petra. She opens the gate for us and walks us toward the vampire lord's mansion. She opens the door for us and ushers us inside. She leaves us as a housekeeper named Gertrude comes to collect our coats.

After we are settled. Gertrude guides us farther into the residence and directs us toward a door that she informs us is his study. I take a chance to look around at the grandiose German mansion. I can smell the scent of roasted sausages from somewhere outside, lilies blooming in a nearby garden, freshly baked pumpernickel bread cooling on a stone somewhere. I detect the scent of horses in the livery stable close by. I take a deep smell to explore other sensory treats. I then smell the succulent aroma of blood. I hear something being poured into a glass. I now can imagine the glass filling with blood.

Garrett knocks on the door, and we hear a grunt from someone standing up to answer our call.

"Eintreten," we hear a deep gruff voice call out.

Garrett stops me before he opens the door, he informs me to mind my manners, and always bow in respect. I remind him that my wife's family was connected to the royal court in England so, I know very well how to show appropriate manners to royalty. Garrett nods his head in understanding. Upon entering the room we bow our heads in submission to the vampire regent. He walks toward us.

The man is tall, broad shouldered. He wears a fine tailored suit coat the color of the midnight sky, with soft material along the collar that is blood red. His pants are in matching with his suit coat. His skin is very pale, almost translucent showing how ancient he is. He has wavy blond hair which flows to his shoulders, and piercing blue eyes with a blood-red center. Very different from my eyes which are grey with a black center. He has a superior aura that nearly makes me want to bow down in fear. I dare not show this however, I want him to see me as strong and confident, not weak. Weak men do not last well even in human society. touchy feely hugging men even in human society, are seen as weak in nature and are prevailed upon. I stand next to Garrett appearing strong, and sure of myself.

"Wie schön, dich zu sehen?"

Garrett embraces him like an old friend and speaks fluent German with him for the next hour. I decide to take a seat on a sofa and listen to their conversation without actually knowing what they were saying. Sometime later, Garrett acknowledges me and explains that he was welcoming us. He asked who I am, and what is our business in this area, since we come from England?

I learn that night that Garrett originated in Bulgaria, lived in Romania during the time of my ancestor Abner, and served on Abner's council. I'm starting to feel more and more like the Garrett I grew up knowing was a lie. I'm not happy about this. I understand that, being as old as he is, he has a history. Yet I'm growing to feel like the Garrett I have known through the years, even as a vampire, is a facade. *Did he evolve, or is everything I knew a lie? Who is Garrett Wilkins?*

The conversation shifts when the elder asks a question that makes Garrett pale. I ask for a translation and am left seething.

"What did he say?" I ask quietly when I hear the term *sire*.

The elder answers for Garrett. "I will answer that for my longtime friend. You see, Herr Hunter Garrett is your sire. He turned you into a vampire. Without our approval, I might add."

I glare at Garrett questioningly. My mind cannot come to terms with what this vampiric delegate has informed me of. I know a part of me suspected it but, I did not want to believe it. "It cannot be true! You were not there that night of my attack, Bathilda Morris turned me. She killed my wife and turned me into this creature that I am. Garrett saved me! I don't mean to offend. I just cannot believe it," I tell the German regent. No, it cannot be! I know that Maria explained to about the sire bond, and she believed it was Garrett. However, if I'm honest, I cannot confirm.

"Herr Hunter, do you remember the night this happened?" says the German delegate.

I still my head and close my eyes as I try to recall the events of that night so long ago. "Everything was so dark that night. I only have assumed circumstance and what I have been informed."

I grab my head in frustration, trying to recall. "I remember, taking a moonlight stroll with my wife. The streetlamps had been mysteriously snuffed out. Suddenly, I heard someone running in circles around us. It could have been one person or more. The situation was nightmarish and will forever haunt me. I could not see anything with how dark the night was, just hearing and feeling everything that transpired."

I feel my soul cry as I relive that night. I close my eyes and see my wife take my hand.

Herr Richter puts his hand on my shoulder. "I'm not offended. However, I can smell the scent of Garrett's siring venom. I have been there myself in previous centuries when he helped sire new recruits for Lord Abner's army. I know better than anyone. I also know that Bathilda, to my knowledge, has never sired anyone. She's too much of a loose cannon who would no doubt kill the person instead."

I nod, trying to contain my rage.

"No, Garrett is your sire, now why did he lie? What are you up to, Garrett?"

Garrett is speechless and pale.

I glare at him, daring him to finally tell me the truth. He finally speaks again. "I know that I lied, Hunter. That night, you were very disoriented. You had been brutally attacked by Bathilda. She killed your wife, and she had started to try to sire you. However, the wounds that were inflicted nearly killed you instead. I bit you more, fed you my blood, and sealed the wound in order to complete the siring. I didn't want to see you die so horrifically." I turn to him befuddled "I distinctly remember Bathilda licking my wound closed after she whispered her love to me? why are you lying? were you even fighting her like I thought I heard?"

I'm seething. Herr Von Hofer looks at me, hearing my words then turns to him with curiosity. "Herr Garrett, nothing you have spoken makes sense. By Herr Hunters account it was Bathilda who was a part of this, what are you hiding?"

Garrett grows still and refuses to answer.

I'm too angry to listen to any more of his lies. "I would rather have died that night and joined my wife in eternity. You know that!" I growl at him. He stands to confront me as the regent orders him again to sit. Garrett gives me a look of warning. I stare into his eyes, refusing to back down, and give him a hateful glare. Before he can utter a word, I turn and storm out of the room. I cannot stand to stay here with him. I take off into the night. I need to find something or someone to kill. I can feel the beast inside me wanting to be unleashed. I start to run away. I run so far that I completely exit Germany. I cannot be with Garrett right now. I feel betrayed. I'm hurt and infuriated. I continue to run without a thought to where I'm heading.

I realize that I ran to Russia. I laugh to myself at the uncharted territory. I have never hunted anything but human. However, I really have the desire to fight. I reach the Ural Mountains and stumble on a tiger. It growls at me, hunching its back, its massive paws swiping the air. I'm so angry. I need to let out my frustration. We start to circle each other. The tiger bares its teeth at me. Its looks are deadly, sensing the predator that I am. I stalk the weaker predator. I'm not craving. I would never drink animal blood. I just need to release the beast inside me before I go insane. I launch myself at the tiger. I match its strength at first. I'm just toying with it until I'm tired of stalling, and I unleash vampire strength. I take the tiger down within minutes. I drag its carcass to some polar bears and present my gift to them. I turn from the mountains and decide to continue running. I spend a few hours running in a new direction. At this point, I'm loving the freedom of being this loose. I now understand how nomad vampires feel and live. Nomadic vampires are constantly roaming. They never have a place to call home. They live anywhere they run. I know this is not going to happen for me. However, it is a fun thought.

I continue running until I come face-to-face with Garrett, who went in search of me. I stop, stare at him, and walk away. He follows me while calling out my name. I don't stop to listen. I continue walking until I arrive on the outskirts of a small town. It is in a different language from German or Russian. I recognize that I ran from Russian all the way to the Netherlands. I continue on as if I don't hear him. He is now screaming for me in my mind, and I decide to block him out. I need time away from him still. I find a ship called the *Sangria*. I want to visit Madrid and then board passage back to England alone. I need time to think. I'm so confused about everything that has been going on since my wife died. Garrett turned me for a reason, and he's not telling me what it is.

CHAPTER 7

Time continues to move forward when you are a vampire scouring Europe searching for someone. We had so far been searching for what felt like years. I arrive in Madrid Spain within a month of leaving Garrett in the dust. I find an inn called the Conquistador and stay there for a time while I hunt the area. While I'm in Madrid, I continue to search for Bathilda. I speak with Spanish vampires to discover her whereabouts. I meet with a man named Ricardo Delavega, the leader of a small circle of Spanish vampires. He runs a tavern, and he also trades in marketable goods to humans and spiced blood wine to high-society vampires.

I highly doubt that Bathilda would be seen with him, considering her crimes. However, he could know of someone who spotted her. I explain to him who I am, who I'm searching for, and what she has done against me. I snarl, and he stares at me with fury in his eyes. He tells me, as Garrett has, that it is against vampiric laws for the attack that she committed to happen.

"Yes, we do feed on humans. However, we don't premeditate an attack so aggressively with the intent that she so obviously had. She intended to tear your marriage apart to claim you for herself. There are plenty of vampire males for her to choose from, without deliberately changing a human so cruelly." He shakes my hand. "I'm sorry this happened to you."

He tells me that he has not aware of her being near his territory but informed me that he will make inquiries. "Meet me tomorrow night at my establishment, the Blue Lagoon. I will share with you what information I find out."

I hate the idea of waiting. But I don't want to burn any bridges in this town. This man is willing to help me with a possible lead on someone who I have been hunting for quite a while.

The next night comes, and I arrive at his place of business. I find that it is a tavern for vampires named La Laguna Azul. The place has an aristocratic aura. The flooring has a carpet runner that is the color of garnet. The walls are black-plated wood with intricate carvings of roses with crowns ingrained in the wood. There is a prominent bar counter in a corner of the room with engravings that match the walls and a winding wood mahogany staircase with garnet carpeting. I continue to walk around and take in the luxury of the place.

This place befits a place where vampires would desire to not only socialize but also quietly sate their thrusts while filling sexual pleasures. Much like my friend Maria's tavern, this place holds a higher sense of royalty due to the Spanish vampire lord who resides here.

I hear moaning in rooms upstairs. I see scantily dressed women dancing on tables. Some are vampires, and some are humans. I see in a dim corner two people engaged in sexual desires. One man is a vampire, and I can tell he's lustfully feeding on a woman.

I walk through the place, trying not to become affected. I'm just about near the bar counter when some of the women start to walk toward me. They start trying to move their hands around my body. I can tell the human girls have been indulging in something to make them sexually intolerable. I'm doing my best to decline their advances. But they are insatiable. The vampire women are worse. A few start to remove their clothes, tempting me. I'm so thankful when I see Ricardo by a stairwell. I immediately walk toward him and away from the vixens. We walk up the stairs. It is quiet in the section.

We come into what appears to be his office, and he closes the door. He offers me some of his spiced wine. Instead, I ask for spiced scotch. He smirks and fills my glass. Then we sit down and, throughout the night, discuss the information that he found.

It turns out Bathilda is wanted in Romania and several other places for criminal acts. "Glad to know that I'm not the only one hunting her." He laughs and assures me that several people want her dead, along with whoever she's working for. "According to my latest findings, she has escaped to America. Where, I'm not sure. I have people there who are in search of her." I close my eyes and pinch the bridge of my nose. This is becoming to be a hassle finding her.

I bid him farewell, and he wishes me success on my journey. This entire stay in this city has turned into a waste of my time. I decide to board a ship called the HMS *Spartacus*. It takes me about six weeks aboard to reach the shores of England. I breathe in the cool London air.

Many years have passed, and I'm back where everything started. I had once inquired of Garrett exactly where my wife is. He has never told me, nor has he let me see her. I decide to go and search. I went to Garrett's house, and there on the mantel above the fireplace was an urn. It has to be hers. I fell to the floor and cried as I held it.

I heard someone approach me from behind. I was not expecting him to find me after three months apart.

"See, this is why I was not sure about informing you, Hunter! Still, human emotions cloud your judgment!"

I snarl at him and shove him, not taking his guff. "Do not give me your shit, Garrett! She was my wife! My everything, you know this! Yet you are treating her like it doesn't matter!" I yell at him.

"Hunter, it shouldn't you are no longer human. These are human memories! You need to stop this rubbish!"

I growl at him and throw him into the wall. As I walk out, I hear him laughing. I shake my head, walking away from him.

"Where will you go, Hunter? I'm your sire! I will always find you and bring you in. I'm trying to help train you to be strong, to be powerful, Hunter! Embrace what you *are*!"

I turn and growl at him. "*No!*" I roar as I leave him behind again. I start to run away again.

I head to my shop. It has been so many years. I need to make sure that everything is going well. As I walk inside, I'm greeted by a new face I have never seen. Considering how much time as gone by, I'm happy to see the store still a success.

I inquire with the young man whose name is Richard what became of Fredrick Potter. The young man informs me that Fredrick has been tending the store for several years. He recently this last year decided to retire. Upon his departure, he promoted Thomas Dersley as store manager, leaving the store to his care. I'm impressed, happy, and shocked at the news.

I never expected Thomas to stay working here. Did he not attend Oxford? He aspired to attend college. I'm very proud of Thomas for being such a loyal employee.

I see him in the backroom, tending inventory. "Hello, Thomas," I say to him.

He nearly falls over in shock. "Mr. Eldridge?"

I walk up to him and shake his hand. "I know it has been many years. I have been travelling and touring the world in different areas with idea of opening more stores." I lie smoothly. "I'm very impressed with everything you have done."

He shakes my hand, still shook up. "I'm sorry, sir. It is just that Mr. Wilkins told everyone you had died, that you and Mrs. Eldridge were attacked by an animal and killed."

I stare at him and chuckle sadly. "Yes, but not I. It was Eliza who had died."

He looks down while muttering his apologies to me. I clap him on the back and make my way back toward the office to see how everything is managing. To my shock, I see a photograph of Thomas with a certain red-haired woman I know very well. He walks up behind me.

"Oh, my beautiful wife Margaret."

I stare at the photo. I have not seen her in decades after I rescued her. I, at times, wondered where she was. I'm glad that she found a good man.

"Where did you meet her?"

He looks at me. "It was thirty-five years ago. I was still working here. I just began to close up shop for Fredrick. I received word that my sister had returned from Paris with her newly betrothed. His name is Jameson. He is a physician. She returned with him and a friend who she had met at a dinner party. She met Maggie through her betrothed. Maggie worked as a governess for a family in association with the physician."

I nod, thinking back. I remember Maggie, and she did talk about wishing for that.

"We met, and it was like we clicked. Her wealthy stature has helped me manage the store. She loves this place and contributes to everything so it is prosperous."

I smile and embrace him. "Should I say, welcome to my family then?"

"Sir?"

I laugh lightly. Evidently, he's not aware. "I recognized Maggie. She's my cousin."

Thomas sits down in shock.

I assure him that it is absolutely fine. I'm very happy for him, and I feel at peace leaving the store in his hands. He is a good man. I feel at peace that I can leave London, as I'm considering, and my store will continue to be in good hands. I leave my shop and walk around for a while. Already deciding what I'm going to do, I connect with a carriage and take it to Garrett's house. I was so angry at him this morning for his callousness.

I also know it is my triggered reaction to being back here in this city where everything happened—my love, life, family, and our demise. I need a change. I need somewhere new. I know exactly where to go, where, once upon a time, I had dreamed of relocating to with Eliza, a place where I can lay her spirit and ashes to rest. I arrive at the house and inform Garrett that I'm relocating to America if he wishes to come along with me.

I walk out the door, feeling finally free and excited to be taking on this new adventure completely of my choosing and for myself. I walk out the door, feeling like I don't need to return very often. I will stop in from time to time. However, with the store still somewhat remaining in the family and in the hands of Thomas.

I feel good relocating to America. I go for a long walk. I notice all of the changes in the area as time has moved on and continues to evolve everything around it. Thomas informing that he has been married to her for thirty-five years is like a dose of cold water to me. That means the year is 1915. This means that, being completely distracted from society, I have been travelling Europe and various other places for over three decades. I stop walking at the thought, and I realize where I am. I'm on the path by the opera house. It is the same place where we met our demise. The park is still present. However, there is now a confectionary store nearby that was not there years ago. As I look around, my mind starts to wander back to that horrific night.

I run away from the area and block everything out. I know that I will break, I will crumble, and that is not what I want right now. I decide to just leave England, possibly for good. I leave the shores of England alone, feeling completely alone.

I didn't ever go back to Garrett. It is my first time completely by myself. I have a feeling, though, that Garrett will figure it out and find me. A part of me knows I will never completely be alone with him in existence as my sire. I board the HMS *Darrington*, and I was right. I'm not sure if it is coincidence or planned, but waiting inside of a first-class cabin is Garrett, as if he were expecting me.

I shake my head, drop my belongings, and shut the door to the suite. I'm not even going to ask how he knew. I'm just not going to. Instead, I go to the ship's office and arrange for a suite for myself. Once I have it, I settle myself in and place Eliza's urn on the fireplace mantel. I give her a kiss goodnight and lay on my bed to relax while waiting for the voyage to end.

It takes six weeks for the journey. I tell Garrett that I need time and space away. I don't leave this open for discussion as I take my wife's urn and, also, my finances from the sale of my house, which I found in his office, marked with my name. It is more than enough for me start over here.

I purchase a beautiful country home in Ithaca, New York. I bury Eliza's urn inside the rose garden located in the back of the house. It is lovely and perfect; she always loved roses. With still plenty of money, I go into town and purchase a store near the local university. There I set up an Eldridge Books, which becomes a rousing success. I decide that, within a few years, I start another in Syracuse, New York. My business starts to grow more successful.

After ten years of living here and seeing how successful everything was becoming, I decide to venture to Chicago. It is crazy how fast time can move. We left England in 1880. And I realized that for all the time we were traveling, searching every single country. We spent a decade in each area in Europe we searched, including Spain, Africa, and various areas of the Mediterranean. So, by my calculation, we spent fifty years, searching the earth.

As my store continues to grow and I can hire more people, that means less time I'm demanded to be there. This gives me more time to scour the country looking for her. I have now been living in Chicago for ten years. Today is a day that I expected to happen but am not ready for. I'm in my office when I hear the chime of the entryway door. I hear my store clerk Robert greet someone. The voice is a man who I knew would one day seek me out but who I was not sure I wanted to tolerate as of yet.

I arise from my desk and greet my former mentor. "Hello, Garrett Wilkins," I say with a dry smile.

He smiles. But it doesn't reach his eyes. He whispers in a low voice, "You should remember I will always find you, Hunter."

I softly growl at him. "As if I wanted to be found by you!"

He laughs and grips my hand in a shake. "No matter. A sire cannot hide from its creator."

I glare at him while my employees don't hear anything. I have developed more abilities. And I put up mental blocks.

Only supernaturals can hear us. Normal humans will not hear anything. "Let us discuss things in private. Away from mortals," I suggest.

We walk toward my back office. I pull out some glass bottles of blood from my ice box and offer one to him.

"So, this is what you are doing now rather than enjoying a warm vein? Bottle feeding?" he said with a scoff.

"Garrett, I spent several decades thanks to you isolated from society. I intend to stay around here and work for a while. I go on hunting trips during weekends when I take the time off," I say coldly.

He raises his hands in surrender.

"As you can see, I no longer need you," I retort at him.

His eyes harden at my comment, then he admits that I'm right.

He informs me that he has also opened his own business. He has finally taken initiative for himself. He tells me he was furious when the bookstore didn't pass to him, and he had a disagreement with my father but enjoyed working with me. Now, in this new era, he has established himself and doesn't need to be my partner anymore. However, he made me aware that he's still willing to assist me.

He informed me that, over the last decade, he took college attendance to become an attorney and is working toward being a judge. I'm very happy for him. I inquire if he has been searching for Bathilda. And I'm furious when he speaks as if he has forgotten. I'm pissed at this revelation. He has completely moved on. Honestly, I cannot blame him after that fight we previously had, and it is not his wife.

I continue my search against his advice. One day, he comes to visit my Chicago riverside home. I have just returned to my personal office when I found him searching my desk. I hold him against the wall. He dares to intrude on my privacy. We snarl at each other and then engage in fisticuffs. I punch him several times and throw him around the room while he does the same to me. It goes on for a while until he compels me to stop. I fight against it and win. The look in Garrett's eyes is pure shock and fear. I have never realized how much stronger I have grown to be until this moment. This causes me to go on a vengeful rampage. For the first time in my existence, I resisted my creator's controlling bond. This proves that the sire bond is damaged or broken, and I'm finally free of him. Though in my heart, my human side will still love him as family, I no longer will belong to him.

I stop fighting and throw him on to the lawn, demanding to know why he's searching in my desk. He informs me he noticed my mapping information with Bathilda's coordinates.

"So, what of it? I now have vampire colleagues, some who are familiar with her and hate her who are assisting me with my continued search since you gave up!" I shout at him.

He snarls at me. "Not this again about that human filth! Hunter, it has been nearly fifty years!"

I kick him in the face in rage. "I no longer abide by your rules. Know this! I will hunt her down until my last breath. And everyone who refuses to assist me with capturing her meets a bloody death." I snarl and slam the door.

CHAPTER 8

Today is April 15. The year is 1925. It is a full cloud cover, the perfect day for a vampire. During the time in which I have been living in America, I have become associated with the American Coven Council of Vampires, a bunch of filthy ingrates. I'm quite popular with the women in the council. Many try to fall at my feet as if I were a god. Female vampires are so insatiable. Many are true sirens of the night. The council elders who are male hate me. I'm quickly rising in the ranks for becoming an ambassador to the vampiric people.

Every time I hear someone speak of this, it makes me roll my eyes. I'm honestly not fond of them either. There was a time during my stay in New York, right before I relocated to Chicago, which I was hunting in the Canadian Mountains. I came across a native village, werewolves, which I had never encountered before. I had fed on some of the maidens and caused an uproar that I settled by killing them all. Now, the council thinks I'm doing it for the glory of vampiric kind. They think I'm intent on purging society of everything but vampires! What fools! I laugh to myself at their ridiculous gloating.

Their entitled nature makes me cringe. Garrett spoke to me in my office this morning about curbing my bloodlust. I have started to become angrier on some days. When I sink into my thoughts and memories of my wife fill my mind, I crave Bathilda's blood. I start trying desperately to find her. When I cannot find her, I start to take my anger out on humanity. Today, I'm feeling the heat from local newspapers.

I'm busy in my office when Garrett walks in, fuming angry. I know he's seething because of my feasting I have been doing.

"Hunter, we need to leave Chicago."

I stare at him in confusion. "Why do you feel we must do that?"

Garrett scoffs. "Because if you continue with this killing spree, you've been on lately like a mafia leader, the humans are going to become suspicious!"

I roll my eyes. It has not been that bad. "I have not been on a killing spree. It's only been fifteen men." As if he has not done worse!

Garrett shoots me a look. "Exactly, Hunter, why?"

I shrug. "Maybe because I have been bored outside of work, or perhaps, they shouldn't have pissed me off!" I glare out the window.

Garrett shakes his head, "Still, we need to leave. At least until the heat cools down."

I turn and face him. "I thought you wanted this? For me to be more ruthless? To be a cold-hearted beast?" I say coldly.

Garrett looks at me curiously. "Hunter, I have given up trying to help you become greater than yourself. I regret siring you! You are too weak, soft. You have never moved on from that filthy bitch! You let her memories and human emotions become fog in your brain!"

I growl at him. I punch him right in the face and then walk out of the office. After spending a few hours walking around, I head back to my house in Riverside to gain some time to think. I need some fresh air. A trip to the country might just be a good thing. I decide to call Garrett at the office if he's still there.

"Yes, let us get out of here. I need this," I tell him as I hang up the rotary phone on the wall. I briefly look over my documents. I hear someone running toward the house. I stand up from my desk, walk out the door, meet Garrett outside, and we both take off toward the northern woods in Wisconsin.

I'm not going to forgive what transpired in my office. He was completely out of line. I just need to go hunting with him one more time before I leave him permanently. I know now that he's going to continue trying to control me. I know he's lying when he said he gave up. If he did give up, why did he still follow me to America? Why doesn't he just let me lead my own life? He knows I'm doing well. How dare he talk so insultingly about my wife! A woman he knew and claimed one time that he loved like a sister.

Lately, through my separation from him, I start to see through his lies as time moves forward. I started to suspect a long time ago. It just took separation to fully let me see. I realize he never truly cared for me as he said. He used to tell me that he loved me like a son. Now I'm questioning everything he ever said.

I know what I'm going to do. I will not let my thoughts known. I will go on this trip with him, acting as devoted friend and follower until it is finished.

CHAPTER 9

We left Chicago a few hours ago, Garrett has informed me there is a cabin located in the northern Wisconsin woods near Superior Lake. He first built it years ago when there were only Native Americans who resided there.

"We are getting away into the hills because I have also heard that the council is looking for you."

I shudder at the mention of those fiends. "I know. Though surprising. I have heard whispers some are wishing to grant me a place amongst them."

Garrett laughs. "That's only because the few women want to jump your manhood."

Garrett laughs with me.

"Do not worry, Garrett. I don't give attention to succubi," I tell him.

He sighs, knowing I'm right.

I do not know why, but something deep within me tells me that Garrett is planning something for me. I decide to play nice and fake friendship.

"Garrett, I want to apologize for all our quarrelling. I have given it thought. I know that you are only looking out for me. With you being my sire, I should be more supportive."

Garrett's eyes grow wide, and an evil smile plays on his lips. "Well done, Hunter. Finally. It took you so long. Welcome to the vampire world!"

I close my eyes, lay my head against the window, and inwardly cringe at the notion of allowing him to think he has won my sadistic allegiance.

I'm plotting my escape away. A part of me still loves Garrett like family. I have known him all my life, no matter our situation now. It will be difficult to completely leave and never return. I'm immersed in my thoughts as we arrive at the cabin. I push the thoughts from my mind. I can smell the fresh air; we can also smell the scent of someone in the forest.

We take off running into the northern woods. Right away, we catch sight of a black bear. It senses our presence and hunches its back in attack mode, sensing another predator. Garrett, at times, tolerates this sort of thing, surprisingly, considering he pushes me hardest toward a human diet.

"Garrett. I'll let you do the honors while I hunt somewhere else."

"Thank you," he says as he disappears into the woods.

I run in the opposite direction into a different area of forest. I catch a wonderful scent. It's sweet and rich. I already know she's human. Just as I crouch, I look up and see her. She's beautiful. She's kneeling, looking at plants as if she's studying them. I stand up. I run into the woods, coming around her other side, facing her. I walk slowly toward her, and I greet her, making her feel comfortable.

"Hello there," I say in a charming voice.

She's startled. Her head snaps up, and her eyes meet mine.

She looks like a deer caught in a trap. Her eyes glaze over, and she looks at me with carnal appreciation. I know I'm good looking. I'm going to use it to my advantage.

"What are you doing out here, beautiful?" I watch her. She's such a beauty. I would say about five eight, wavy dark hair, amazing green eyes, full pink lips. Her smell is amazing, a combination of jasmine and honey. If she were a vampire, I would instantly take her to bed and bury myself in her. She's a human, who is undoubtedly in the wrong place at the wrong time.

"I'm a researcher, a scientist. I am studying wolves." She's still staring like she can't look away—she's affected.

"I would love to research you, angel," I whisper seductively into her ear. She's dazed, and her lips are parted.

"You're so beautiful," I whisper to her as I snake my arms around her waist. I can smell her arousal. I start to kiss down her throat. She moans and purrs as I continue to work my magic with my lips.

"Do you have a place we could take this?" I ask her.

"No. It's too far away. We can stay here," she tells me with an alluring voice.

"Oh. I'm so going to enjoy you." I continue giving gentle caresses. I bite into her neck. I drink in her warmth as her moans turn into weak whimpers, and she's laying limp against me. I can feel her pulse still going. However, it is a bit weak. I bite into my wrist and leak some of my fluid into her mouth so she will heal.

I carry her while searching the area for her scent. I find it and follow it back to her campsite. I place her inside the tent and walk away. I'm starting to feel better about myself. I don't have to kill everyone while I drink. I can leave them alive to see another day. Garrett would have my head on a platter if he knew what I have been doing. This is one part of myself I will never share. I have never wanted to be a killer. I killed enough in the military. I know that I have killed humans. I'm not sinless in that regard. Every kill I ever made was Garrett compelling me too. If he knew how much I hated it, I would have been in a dangerous situation with a sadistic mentor.

I'm thankful that I'm finding ways to sedate the beast inside without ending innocent lives. Suddenly, I feel as if I'm being watched. I look around. All I can see is an owl hooting in a tree. I feel it is my imagination, so I decide to head back toward the direction we arrived. I search the area to pick up Garrett's scent. I come upon the wooded area where we parted ways. His scent was here but is now becoming faint. There is no sign of him.

"Garrett!" I call out, yet I hear nothing. "What in tarnation is happening?" I suddenly feel that something is not right. I continue to search for him.

I know that the bear wouldn't have overpowered him—that's impossible. As I start searching, I find the bear's carcass, just as I knew I would.

"What the devil has happened?" I whisper to myself. "Garrett!" I scream. "Where are you?" I'm starting to lose my mind. I hear the short cackle of woman. I look around and run in the direction that I heard the laugh. I still don't see anyone.

As I'm about to search again, I catch another scent. It's earthy with a twist of sour mud. My nose wrinkles in distaste. I see a bear larger than any I have ever seen come out of the woods. I stare at it in horror. Three more join it. They are as big as mountains! I have no idea what was happening. But I take off faster than any speed I have ever used.

I hear them close behind me, so I instinctually jump into the trees. I jump from tree to tree while finding a way around to search for my old friend. I sit in the tree. I'm at a loss for words as to what has happened. I can only imagine that the universe has taken another loved one from my life.

Just then I see this monstrosity of a bear morph into a man. They praise each other with high-fives. I listen closer.

"Nice takedown, Darius!"

"I had to. And I don't regret it! I saw that monster killing natural wildlife on our land! That disgusting filth! Now, I will have to care for those cubs that black bear left behind."

The men talk to him. "I have only heard of such a creature from myth. The humans call them vampires."

They start looking around, wondering what happened to me.

The leader answers, "He jumped into the trees. He'll come down, and we'll be waiting."

Bugger off on that one! I think. I have had enough of this. I'm not going to attack three gigantic, mutated creatures and commit suicide.

It is evident they killed Garrett. What I cannot figure out is where the hell they put the body. He was the last bit of family I had left. After I relocated to America, I tried to search for my brothers and sister, only to learn they have passed on to heaven. All I have left is Garrett, now. He is gone too, thanks to these shifters.

I run away from them where they cannot see me. I search the area for any sign they buried him. This is frustrating and confusing. There are no indicators of any burial or charred remains. It is as if he completely vanished. How is this possible? I heard them confirm that they slayed a vampire. My heart hurts, and I start to become swallowed up by my emotions.

I cannot continue thinking about this. The pain is too much. Is it enough to lose my wife and then later find out that my entire immediate family has passed on. They have all gone to heaven. And I'm left here on this earth alone. I jump through the trees and dive into the lake, completely baffled how this weekend has gone so wrong. We came up here for a time of hunting and fun, only for Garrett to completely disappear as if he never existed. Not even a scent is in the area.

In an ironic thought, fate granted me my wish. I left Garrett, moved on. I just welcome him back in the hopes we could be friends and business colleagues. His sudden departure racks my brain and eats me alive. I never got to say goodbye to him.

I spend the next week busying myself at work. I try everything that I can to not think of what became of Garrett. My employees know that something happened. I'm very bitter, and my temper is out of control.

I lose control of my temper one evening when a vampire meets with me as the council ambassador. He seeks me out about allegations that his mate is cheating on him with a lycan. The miserable sack is very whiney and nearly crying. I decide to become the deciding judge when it is proven true. I snap her neck and torch her, to the horror of accusing vampire. I bitterly tell the man, "Honestly, what were you expecting? We are vampires not humans! Find a new mate that will be loyal!" The man, who cowered away from me, is the embodiment of a shriveling mess. Disgusting worm!

This whole week, I'm trying to bury myself in either human work or my ambassador duties. However, I cannot overcome my anger for what those shifters did. The beast inside craves revenge, worse than Bathilda, whom he still wants to rip apart. Those bear shifters need to pay! I return to the woods a week later.

I arrive after the sky had fallen into pitch-black darkness. I stalk their village. "They're all asleep, perfect." I remember my years as an assassin in the king's army. They have already grown to recognize the vampire scent, so I go into the woods and find strong earth scents such as wintergreen. There are six different huts that I can count. I'm going to make each of them suffer for Garrett's death. They will boil in hellfire after this night. These abominations will feel my wrath! Moving as quick as a wraith, I come upon some guards. I cover their mouths as I rip their hearts out and they fall to the ground. I sneak into the huts and unleash my fury on the sleeping males. I stalk each shifter that I find. A woman wakes up, and I bite her neck and drain her before she can scream. Another person wakes up at that moment and runs out of the tent, screaming, before I backhand them into a tree.

More come out of huts I didn't see. The people are running and screaming. The warrior men left over shift and charge toward me. The warrior lunges at me. And I dodge his attack. He growls as I jump onto his back, wrap my arms around his throat and crush his neck. I continue through the night battling and dodging attacks from these mutant creatures. Some of the men have already shifted into bears.

I dodge their attacks. And I break their necks before they can take me down. Most of their men, I have already killed while they were asleep, so their numbers have dwindled. I swear that by the end of this night this clan of bear-shifting monsters will be ended. As I run from the scene, I notice a small fire outside one of the huts. I create a torch and set fire to the village as I run away from the land. I look behind. I'm now yards away. I perch in a tree, and the whole area turns into a blazing inferno.

I run from the area before the fire can reach me. As I leave, I walk away for the first time in a long time covered in blood, looking very macabre. Once the rage dissipates, I feel hollow inside. A small part of me feels satisfied with my rage. But another part of me feels empty. It is like there is a hole punched through my chest that will not close. I'm left with a question: *Where do I go from here?* I have no one. It feels as though the universe is determined to take everything from me. Garrett was like an uncle to me. He was connected to me and my family nearly all my life. He always felt like a guardian to me after my father's death.

Through the years, I found out so much that caused me to turn and hate him. He was still family to me. I walk into a clearing, fall to the ground, and let out a gut-wrenching scream in agony. "God! Why! Is this what you saved me for! Is this all that I am! Can I not find love and happiness? Am I meant to suffer?" I used to struggle with my belief. Now I struggle more. God has taken my entire family into eternity. Why did he not take me with her? Why! Am I cursed to be like this!

I fall over, lying on the ground, trying to cry tears I'm no longer capable of achieving. I lose count of the hours I lie here lost in this sea of torment. I roll over and stare at the night sky, wishing more than anything to see Eliza or to see my mother. Mother was so kind and wise; she would know the right words pull me through this moment.

I know that I cannot stay here in this field any longer. I'm still covered in blood. I need to do something. I need to get away in case there are any more shifters in the area. I stand up from the ground with a heavy heart. I need to be strong and move forward, no matter how painful it is. This grief, this night, is so much. But I need to move on before I find myself dead as well. I get up from the ground where I'm kneeling, walking back to Garrett's cabin. I decide to leave the car and just run back home. I need to run. I need to escape. As I leave my heart, my past, the piece of my life in the field of carnage and sorrow.

I leave the north Wisconsin woods in the aftermath of my slaughter of the freakish shifter clan. If any in the nearby area see the smoke and learn what happened, they will know to never again mess with a vampire! As I run back to Chicago, I'm not certain that I can return to the store at this moment. I'm thankful for the decade we had spent separate. It gave me time to grow and move forward away from Garrett.

He was, is, and will always be my friend, uncle, and mentor. Though we spent time apart, the decades we were together will always stay with me no matter how much I grew to despise parts of our relationship. Right now, in this grief, I would do anything to see him again than face this world alone. My mind is sinking into depression, whispering for me to join him, to join Eliza and my family who have gone. It says, *No one cares, no one would miss you.*

I feel the ever-crushing weight of despair trying to lure me into its blackness. I fight against its calming sensation. I need to step away and rebuild myself in my current life. I need to do something or meet someone, to keep this emotional tidal wave at bay. Running at top speed, feeling the wind in my face, helps a bit of my soul feel free. I run like this for what seems like years until I hear the skies roar and see the rain pour down.

Rain pours down cold. If I were still human, I would be freezing. Luckily, I arrive home, drenched but in one piece, within an hour.

As I walk through the front door of my house, I head straight up the stairs to my bedroom toward my bathroom en suite. I step into the shower. As I discard my soaked clothes, I don't even bother to dry off. Completely naked, I enter my bedroom and lie in my bed.

I let the shadows that I'm feeling engulf me. I don't know how long I lie in my bed. Since Eliza's death, I have only been associated with Garrett. I would meet others of my kind. But I would stay tied to Garrett. Once upon a time in my human life, I was socially active. Even after marrying Eliza, we still interacted with friends and family whenever we could. My wife and I took care of my father. We socialized with Eliza's family, since mine was not available. How did I become such a hermit?

Days, weeks pass. And I wallow in my grief. I tried so hard not to let it affect me. Coming back here to the place where I spent my last months with Garrett is pulling me under. I close my eyes, and it's like I'm transported into another realm. I look around to see I'm back in my previous house in London. I see Eliza. She stands in front of me. Her beauty is more radiant. She wears a long pearl-colored gown. Her hair flows wild like the wind.

Her eyes sparkle with desire. "Hunter, come to me!" She stretches out her hand in acceptance. I'm so tempted to take it. My mind snaps me out of the decision. I look at her more clearly. I realize that it is not her. My wife doesn't have eyes black as charcoal. The realization of what is happening is staggering and terrifying. I understand immediately what this is! I jerk my hand away and take a step back.

She smiles at me, and the smile twists into something sinister. "Hunter! Come with me!" she purrs.

I try to force my eyes open. At once, I feel trapped. I jerk away from her. "No! Alethia! You will not capture me!" I scream at her. She steps back and gives me a sadistic smile. Alethia. I have heard of her and her kind. An Algea. A demon of despair. If I accepted her hand, I would have become an empty shell. The physical body is paralyzed as she feeds on the despair through someone's mind.

"Bravo, Hunter! You are the first one to resist me. Your despair smells delicious. I can feel it. It smells so good. Let me taste you," she says in a seductively sweet voice as she tries to come toward me.

For a fleeting moment, I feel frozen. And I feel as though I'm being pulled forward. I shake my head, grit my teeth, fighting against the powers against me. Coming to my senses, I punch her right in the throat. She lets out a shrilling scream and disappears in a cloud of black smoke. I feel as if the weight binding me has lifted. I snap my eyes open.

Out of nowhere, I feel a gentle nudge like a soft spirit pushing me. I feel a sense of peace and happiness trying to fill my senses. I feel as if a soft hand grasps mine. I feel something caressing my face, pulling me upward. I close my eyes. And I almost think I see her. Eliza is willing me to get up and do something. With this feeling, I compel myself to get up, dress, and leave the house.

I start to drive into the night. The rain pounds harder on the road. The wind howls like an alpha wolf. For a human, it would almost be impossible to see what direction to go. As I'm heading down the road, I pass a macabre scene. I hit the brakes on my car and pull over to survey what has occurred. A car appears to have veered off the road and wrapped around a tree. It is a grizzly sight. I stop the car and make my way toward the wreck. I doubt anyone in this scrap heap is still alive.

Walking around the car, I find a woman. Half of her body hangs out the window. There's a child inside who looks pinned under the seat disturbingly. Both mother and son are dead. I notice a man on the driver's side. He mumbles and fights to free himself. This man has great inner strength. How he's still alive is a miracle. I cannot let him waste away and die. I don't think his wife would even like it.

I try to think about what I could do. Should I run him into town? To a doctor? The local police officers will not get here in time. And neither will the local ambulance. "Stupid, moronic humans!" I say to myself. Why do they take irresponsible risks? I wish there were seat belts in the back end of cars for children. Who knows? Maybe someday someone will become smart and install the damn things.

This is irresponsibility of the car manufacturer, and the mother here not wearing her belt cost both their lives. "Martha! Titus!" the man screams. "Oh God! No!" He continues to scream as he starts to stir and notices his wife's condition. "Titus! Where are you son?"

I approach cautiously, not wanting to startle him. "Sir," I address him. He tries to look around, startled.

It is pouring rain. They shouldn't have been driving in this weather. "Who is there?"

I raise my hands and walk toward the car. "Sir, I was driving and noticed your accident. My name is Hunter Eldridge," I tell the man as I kneel close to the car so he can have a better look at me.

The man looks up in my direction. I can see the instant shock on his face. "Hunter Eldridge! The man who is considered America's fastest-growing entrepreneur?"

I lightly laugh. "Yes, that's me."

The man stares at me as if I were royalty standing in front of him, even as he looks at the brink of death.

"How can a man who is clearly in pain and could be on death's door be talking to me in this manner?" I ask him, a little perplexed that he can talk and think so clearly given the situation.

"I'm in agony. I'm trying not to concentrate on it or wonder why my son is answering my call. Oh God! My Titus! My Martha!" The man screams in pain and sorrow.

Suddenly, a thought occurs to me. I can be his cure! "I can help make sure that you live. You'll be better and stronger than ever. You can live on so no one forgets them," I tell him as I figure out how I can open his door without causing more harm.

"You can? How?" he asks me in pain.

"You will be reborn into a new life. You will be powerful, stronger, and will be able to live forever."

The man looks at me dubiously. "I don't know if I want that. I want to see my love again," he says, shaking his head.

"I know. But I'm sure it's what she'd want. I don't think she'd want you to end yourself and forget her?"

He turns his head to stare at me, looking me in the eyes. "Please, help me. Take it away. Take me away from here."

I lean down, rip the car door off, and move to remove him from his seat. "As you wish," I say to him.

While no one is looking, I pick him up and gently run back toward my car. Once I have him inside, I make sure he's secure. I drive him to my house. By the time we arrive, it is near midnight. I have never attempted to transform someone before into a vampire. But I cannot let this man die. I cannot continue alone myself.

I help him inside the house and lay him down on my sofa. I clean him off and clean his wounds. I don't want any filth to get in when I start to change him. I bite into his neck deeply, mimicking the actions that I assume happened to me. I hear him scream in pain. I then cut myself and let my blood leak into his mouth. He starts to resist. But the attempt is weak because of his health. I pin him down and cover his mouth so he cannot spit it out.

Once I'm finished restraining him, I see the color of flames forming around his wounds. I know that the venomous fire is spreading. When it closes, he lets out a guttural scream in pain. At this moment, I knock him out. The fire will spread. But he will be unconscious while he completes the transformation. I pick him up and head upstairs to one of the bedrooms.

Waiting three days for this man to revive will be unbearable. However, I need to have hope that he will pull through. This is my first time attempting anything of this magnitude. I also pray that he doesn't hate me. I still remember the painful memories of my transformation, the pain and black pit of despair. I remember the soul-sucking agony of that dream I was living in while I watched my love float to heaven and I was pulled into black nothingness of hell. I try to never think of that nightmare again.

The man lies completely still, as if he's in death's clutches. I pace the room. Deciding I cannot sit in this room anymore, I quickly go for a run to ease my nerves. A few hours later, I walk back into the house. I head straight for the room. Victor still lies on the bed. Time ticks by. When I fear that something went wrong, he opens his eyes and flies off the bed as if he's been struck by a bolt of lightning. He jumps in the air, lands in a crouch on top of the sofa in the room, his eyes scanning his surroundings. A guttural growl leaves his lips. He locks eyes with me and lunges at me, no doubt sensing another predator. Thanks to my years of experience in combat, I catch him by the throat at the right moment and slam his body to the floor, without breaking it. He is panting and writhing for a short moment. I order him to relax and focus on me. He straightens up and moves to stand on his feet.

After this altercation, I was grateful for my thought of hiding all the mirrors in the house just as precaution. Victor would freak out if he were to observe the physical changes to himself. Our skin is pale as the moon. All signs of impurities have dissolved away, leaving behind an ethereal glow, transforming even the most beautiful humans into a godlike form of perfection. The eyes of all newborns are sinister black with blood-red centers.

Being decades older, my eyes have cooled back to my original color when I'm not hunting. Those eyes freaked me out when I first noticed them. I had spent a lot of time in the wilderness. However, it was at Garrett's cabin. He never considered I would notice my reflection in a bowl of water as I tried to wash my hands one day. I freaked out and tore the room apart.

I take careful steps toward him so as not to startle him. "My name is Hunter Eldridge."

He looks at me curiously.

"We met last night; you had a terrible night. I found you lying in the road, and you were begging me to save you."

He stares at me in thought. "I remember I had an accident."

I nod for him to continue.

"Hunter, thank you for granting my request."

I'm surprised by this and relieved that he's so calm.

"This feeling, I feel so different, so new!" he says with his eyes full of wonder, as if losing one's soul is an exciting feature.

I know some may say that it was wrong of me to take his soul from him during his hour of death. I know that it may be selfish. But to wallow in despair. Contemplating everything that I have lost which I once had held dear? That will indeed take me to places of darkness I fear to venture. And I fear I will not return. I don't want to live my life like some vampires I have met, those poor souls who lost a mate and let the dark abyss of despair suck their lives away.

"You will become familiar with it; everything right now feels fresh and indestructible."

Just as I say this to him, pain crosses his face. He grabs his throat. And his eyes look wild. He snarls and thrashes as I try to pin him down.

"You need to hunt. Now!" Before he destroys the entire town, I take him out and show him everything that I know. Much of it is superfluous, honestly. Some it is very valuable. The inescapable pheromones that our bodies give off. It creates an addictive scent that few humans can ignore, and like an alluring siren, they are drawn in, ensuring no escape.

Our voices are sweet and seductive. Our attractive looks make them believe they are gazing at a deity who demands worship with an inevitable sacrifice. Garrett taught me how to use every skill to my best advantage. Looking back, during that time when I was with him, I knew that I not was being myself. I have not been myself in a long time. But I could see Garrett was trying to turn me into a savage monster. He wanted me to forget my humanity, forget my wife, to just embrace being a dark creature, just as he was. I became that for a while, only to placate him. I thought it worked. I never knew that he saw through me. I was young and naive to think I fooled him.

I know who I have always been, and I never want to forget my wife. I fought very hard through the years to hold on to every memory that I had with her. I made sure to burn them into my brain. I remember asking him one time why he pushed me so hard.

And he said, "It makes it easier if you try to forget it all."

I told him that I had a good life and I didn't want to forget it. He looked at me with a scowl, shook his head, walking away. If he thought that he completely altered who I am, he really should have known better. Victor, I will never do that to him. He is a good man, as I was. I will never strip away what is left of his soul.

CHAPTER 10

Year 1940

Over the next several years, we hunt and live together. I provide him with a place in my house as we grow to be close friends. I sired him, and I feel it my responsibility to help care for him until he is able to stand on his own. Spending time with him, he becomes a brother to me and my wingman. I'm thankful to have a friend like Victor. I'm never melancholy anymore. We travel the world together just like I used to with Garrett.

Victor, on the other hand, is much better company to associate with. He is talkative and always finds a way to lift my spirits, make me laugh. The man is the life of the party. Life has been very entertaining with his friendship.

This week during our stay in Syracuse, New York, we overhear some humans discussing the Second World War that looms around the world. A man says it is already rampaging through Europe and England. I hang my head in sorrow for my homeland. I have heard the stories of how torn apart the country is. I have heard how this war will be worse than the previous one.

I want to join the forces. I once served in His Majesty's military. I could be a great asset, especially now. The old London I knew is long dead. My cousins have perished. Their children or grandchildren are all that remain. We leave the room and walk a considerable way until we're on a country road away from humanity. We take off running. It has been a while since we hunted. Sure, we traveled everywhere. And we hunted. But we took a break after we spent time in Louisiana and ran into banshees, which I didn't know existed! Hidden creatures live in those swamp areas.

After that experience, we came back to Chicago and stayed still for a few months before leaving again. Before my departures, I made arrangements to hire new staff who had extensive experience and good credentials. These individuals will be acting store managers in my stead. I made sure with the advanced telephone technologies that I do weekly check-ins with the store to determine its progress and be assured that everything is running smoothly.

The blessing and curse about being a vampire is that it's difficult to stay in one place very long without humans becoming curious. I have always used the excuse of traveling for business. We find a wooded area. The smell of human is in the air. There must be a town nearby. We find a hiding place, being careful so no one will notice. As we walk around, we find a neighborhood near the woods. Perfect, people will think that the person simply got lost in the woods and suffered an animal attack. We find an opening in the forest. I inhale. I can smell a luscious scent. Victor's bloodlust is worse than mine. After so many years, he still struggles to control it.

I learned a long time ago that each vampire has different abilities that make them unique. Mine relies on the mind. Most vampires can read thoughts and manipulate the mind through compulsion by looking into someone's eyes. I notice with myself that I don't have to have to lock eyes with someone. I can not only create a mental wall that blocks mortals' senses but also project myself inside their heads. They believe they're seeing themselves talk, like a conscience. And they obey everything they're told.

I can create movie-like scenarios. For example, a woman could believe that she has met her soulmate and we are passionately making love while I feed.

Victor has a heightened sense. Some groups would use him as a tracker if they knew about him. He has difficulty controlling himself once he gets a scent because of his advanced sense of smell. It drives him wild. Currently, it is bothering him. He looks at me with wild eyes.

I tried to distract him by carrying on conversation. However, it was a failure. Now, it's after dark. The humans will be starting to turn in. I find a young woman who is letting the dog into the yard. I came from the woods; she looks at me. I know what she will see: six four, black hair, piercing gray eyes, strong bone structure, firm body, and attractive looks like the gods of old. My eyes shine, sweet, dangerously seductive, wild with a desire she's not aware of.

She walks toward me, completely forgetting the dog, which is growling at me. She doesn't notice, already enthralled. It's so easy; she has no idea what I am. She stands right in front of me as if she's waiting for something.

"Hello, my, you're beautiful!" I purr as I walk toward her.

At this moment, her heart rate picks up. But she's still beside me, ignoring the warnings her body is sending her. She's completely captivated. She looks like she's in a trance. I pull her into my arms, and she moans. I whisper to my friend, "Now."

We both bite her in the neck, draining her rich, warm, and addictingly sweet essence. I stop my tasting and let him finish while I find someone else. Shortly afterward, I find a man and drain him before he's aware of it. I find another man and bring him to Victor before he can utter a word. He drains the man but gives a sour look. I know: when we drink from men, it makes us feel empty. Women give us a lustful craving, and we desire sexual interaction.

Victor smiles and looks up at me. "Are there any female vampires?" I know what he's thinking. After this experience, he needs somewhere to seek release. I nod and tell I know of some.

"Oh? Where?" he asks me as I smile.

"An old friend in Kenosha Wisconsin. Her name is Maria. She's a female vampire I had the pleasure meeting once while I spent decades traveling through Europe. She helped me become the man I am today. I owe her a lot."

We arrive at the Siren's Call. It was made to look like a tavern. However, Maria has a complete upstairs floor dedicated to fleshly desires for the supernaturals. As we approach the building, a woman in her thirties meets us, standing on the steps with a smile.

"Well, as I live and breathe! Hunter!" she says while pulling me in for a hug.

"Hello, Maria," I say nicely to her.

She's a good friend. This is just not my scene. "It's about time you came to my place after so long! Who might this be?"

I give her a brief hug and gesture to my partner. "This is Victor Nelson. Vic, this is my old friend, Maria Carmelo."

She smile, warmly.

"Victor and I have been on the hunt for hours; he's wearied and needs company."

She looks at him appraisingly. "Well, welcome to my club. I have something for you I believe," she says with a purr. And I see his cock start to stand up.

I laugh, shaking my head at her lustful temptation. "What do you want, doll?"

I shake my head at her.

"When will you let down your guard?"

I lightly laugh. "I don't know, Maria. Someday, not now."

She shakes her head and turns to walk back inside. I call out to Victor and wish him well. I know this is what he needs. And I hope he finds some peace of mind tonight. I walk until I find a suitable hotel in the city.

It has been a long time since I have settled down. My friend Charlie has been managing my company in Chicago. I met him while we were in Philadelphia, visiting my brother's grave. He was there visiting his wife's grave. She had been murdered. I learned that he was turned into a vampire by Garrett. I had never heard of it. Considering all the lies and secrets kept, I was no longer surprised. So, we had a bit in common and struck up a friendship. Now, he's one of my closest friends next to Victor.

I spend the night talking on the phone with him about my business until I hear a woman's voice in the wee hours of the morning. I look outside the hotel window and stare into the alley below me. I see a silhouette of rich, dark, wavy hair that's strikingly familiar, joined by another similar figure that's encased in shadows with a cloak on. They're feeding on a human man. I shut the window, feeling like I'm hallucinating, that it could be the scientist I left alive. I ignore the idea and return to my phone call with Charles.

After we hang up, I receive a phone call from Victor telling me he has some news to share. I leave with haste as soon as morning arrives. I stepped out of the hotel. And my first stop was to the back alley where I observed last night's vampiric feasting. Damn, that got my bloodlust going, hearing them carry on in the alley. I was highly tempted to jump down and join them. It was torture. But I didn't leave my room. Preferably, I don't choose to indulge in men. That is how I knew very well they were both vampiresses. Females tend to be more aggressive and attracted to human men. They become extremely lustful as they satiate their thirst. Many can become violent. Men almost never survive without becoming savagely ripped apart.

I reach the alleyway. And I'm shocked at what I find. There's a pool of blood in the alley. And the victim is still there. His neck is deeply ripped open, and his chest is ripped apart. He's missing an arm. Someone needs to get these so-called vampire lords at the council off their asses to handle this mess! Seriously, they don't do shit! They sit on their ivory thrones and act like rulers over us, yet lately, they have done nothing when a situation like this occurs!

Disgusting ingrates! They better hope and pray I never become king! Their days will be numbered! I walk away from the horrific sight. I quickly go in search of a payphone to call the council, hoping they will handle this situation. I rather doubt it, but if they don't want human scandal, they better! I briefly make the call. Ingrid answers. She's one foxy lady. From what I understand, she previously was born of nobility in Austria to the Weidhaus clan.

"Hello, this is Hunter Eldridge. I need to report an incident I found."

She speaks to me asking about the situation, then puts me on hold to alert Lord Langford. I roll my eyes at the waiting.

After sitting here for what feels like hours, we end the call with her thanking me for making them aware. She promises that they will send some aid within minutes to clean up. I roll my eyes as I hang the telephone up and walk away. I meet Victor at a local park. And I can see that he's not alone. He introduces me to her, says her name is Elizabeth. She was his entertainment last night. She's a vampire, turned at the age of seventeen. And that is all she says. Victor informs me that she's attending a local university, studying for a degree in library science. Victor tells me about how he felt a click with her. And they both feel they are meant to be together.

I feel sad, knowing that I will be alone again. However, I'm very happy for him to find a mate. I pray someday that I can do the same, which I can finally move on from the loss of my wife. I will always miss her. But I don't feel I can love again yet. I embrace them both and wish them happiness. We part ways as I feel my heart slowly tear at the loss of my friend. I know he's not truly gone. However, I don't know when I will see him again.

I head back to the hotel. I'm glad I thought of driving to Kenosha. After our hunting trip, we return to my house in Chicago, cleaned ourselves, and made the drive here. I retrieve my car and make the trip back to Chicago. I stop at my little bookstore in Evanston. I need to keep occupied to take my mind away from the departure of

Victor. I walk behind the counter into my office, and I see my store clerk Cornelia Williams attending to the books.

She's a hardworking employee. "Good day, Nelia," I say to her.

She turns around. "Oh! Good morning, Mr. Eldridge. How was your trip?" She smiles at me as I sit behind my desk.

I respond to her that it was pleasant and well needed.

I start to check over all the annual paperwork. She comes in addressing me. "Mr. Eldridge?"

"Yes, what is it?" I ask her without looking up.

"May I have a day or two off next week off? My daughter Meredith is not feeling. And I want to be home with her." She looks a bit timid awaiting my response.

"Cornelia, take the week off. I don't mind. I will have Bridget mind the shop; she's due back from her honeymoon."

Her eyes light with happiness. "Oh, thank you, sir!" she says as she walks away toward the front of the store.

After I dismiss her, I'm pleased to see the store very successful. I instruct my manager Bartholomew to continue tending the store and be sure to close shop in a few hours. He nods and continues his work on his typewriter while looking over documents. Man, I remember being in his position and using a quill with a fountain of ink. I sometimes miss those days. I walk out and head for my home. My friend and sired individual has requested permission to start a new life, and I'm very happy for him.

CHAPTER 11

Three months pass without my friend to keep me company. The only blessing is that Charles has returned. He helps me with my business and my thirsty adventures. It's so good to have him back here in the city. He has been traveling the world as a tracker on council matters. He loathes the council leaders as much as I do, yet he does their bidding, so he's not seen as insubordinate.

There's little we can do, however, since we're not honorary representatives, although he did point out to me once that I could easily take up the mantle there or even go higher. It's in my blood and birthright to be the ruler. But that's not something on my horizon.

All I want is to avenge Eliza, have my business, and in time, find love again when it feels right. Speaking of that slippery little she-devil, I need to see if Charlie has any news of her. I go in search of him, and I'm surprised when he comes up to me.

"I already know what you are going to ask of me, Hunter."

I smile and shake my head. Damn, he read my mind.

"Yes. I do know of Bathilda's whereabouts."

I grip his shoulders. "Where?" I demand. He looks at his shoulders, and I release my hands. I have been trying to track her for years now. And this is the first solid piece of information that I have received.

I know I should not have gripped him in such a manner. I couldn't help myself, the rage that boiled up inside me at the thought of her. My anger is ready to seep out like hot lava, and I take a few calming breaths to control myself. He gives me a measured look, telling me to calm myself. Then he speaks.

"It is a bit far from here, near Canada on the border of New York State. I need to warn—no, beg—you to really consider what I'm about to tell you and think carefully about make this choice."

I'm listening to him but growing impatient. I look at him for a measured moment before tell him to continue.

"She's in the witch's kingdom."

The minute he tells me this, I feel myself turn to ice. Damn! This is not news I was expecting. No one enters there and survives. Those witches are evil to the core and more dangerous than a vampire, some possessing elemental gifts. I cannot let this opportunity pass.

"Hunter, you need to really consider this. I understand how long you've searched. These witches are sinister creatures. Stories say they eat the souls of any man they don't welcome. I don't want to die!"

I can hear his fear. Vampires are immortal to an extent. We can live for eternity, providing another supernatural creature doesn't kill us. There are ways for a vampire to die. It's highly difficult. Only a supernatural hunter or a supernatural itself can do the job. A mere human doesn't have to ability to do damage. Human horror stories are bedtime tales concocted with myths and imagination.

These witches are indeed deadly creatures who would relish the chance to kill a vampire. They are Wiccan and hate my kind. They are very reclusive. If we don't seize this chance, she could hide there for years without being harmed. I can't help the grin that spreads across my face. Charles looks at me questioningly. A brilliant thought comes to my mind. I can tell it's the monster speaking.

"Burn them to cinders."

He laughs sinisterly. Sometimes I fear demonic creature inside me. It is everything Garrett wants me to be, which I fight to contain. He whispers, "Everyone knows the witches were rotten to the core." He's suggesting this interesting idea. I feel it fill me with glee.

"What are you planning in the wicked brain of yours?" Charles snaps.

I laugh. "Very simply, my friend. We burn their kingdom to the ground if they don't surrender her to us." We both grin. We decide rent a small plane, and Charles flies to the mountains where the witches live. This will be easier and quicker than driving or running. We land in the closest area to the mountains. We decide it will be better to travel there on foot. It's a treacherous path up those mountains. Humans would likely fall to their deaths. The witches can easily teleport in and out of the kingdom.

"How much longer until we find this place?" I ask him as we continue to hike up the mountain.

"Another thirty minutes, we're almost there."

Not too long after, we arrive at a large gate. There's a beautiful crest on it—a creature with two heads on it. One head is of a black wolf howling at a moon; the other is the head of a lion. And both creatures are connected to what looks like a dragon's body. The lion has vampire-looking teeth.

"They are called the Luna-fire coven," Charles whispers to me. "From what I understand, they're one of the oldest covens in the world. And they're rare."

That piqued my interest. "What do you mean?"

He shrugs. "What I mean is they're the only coven of their kind that are immortal."

The shock is apparent from my expression.

He further explains, "Legend has it that the first king and queen were hybrids. The queen was the cross between a lycan and witch. The king was the cross between a witch and a vampire from a royal bloodline out of Romania."

I don't let my emotions show how much that information knocks the wind out of me. He was speaking of my evil ancestor and his abhorrent children. Well, I guess I know what became of them.

Abner the Vile, according to my family history, was the wicked brother of my fifth great-grandfather. It was said that this great-grandfather was being forced to become an immortal by his brother Abner. When he learned of this, he smuggled his wife Hilda and their children out of Romania in the middle of the night and arranged passage to England, where she changed her last name to Eldridge to avoid being discovered. Great-Grandfather Vilheim ignited the people in rebellion and committed suicide before Abner find him.

Abner's wife was a dark witch, so it makes sense she would find a way to birth evil spawn. "Are all of them immortal?" I ask of him.

He shakes his head. "No, only the royal family and not completely immortal. They can live for eternity if they are not killed. Much like any other supernatural being."

I nod. This information also leaves a sick twist in my gut, knowing that Alania, that dark witch, must have smuggled her children and members of her coven out before their execution. I praise God my own great-grandmother escaped unnoticed.

Either way, that's good news. We near the gate and knock. Just then, a voice as beautiful as a siren calls out. "Who is there? Who dares to invade our land and disturb us! Speak or I will cut out your tongue!"

We both laugh when we hear this. I decide to answer her. "Hello, we are travelers. We are looking for someone. I heard reports that a woman who I have a history with named Bathilda Morris has come to your land."

Minutes pass as we wait for their response. "I don't know of whom you speak!"

"Then let us enter, that we may search for ourselves." We look at each other. We can smell her lies.

We wait for a long time. As we stand there, a group of women come to meet us, radiating a powerful aura. I stretch my senses to test it. The female guard's powers feel like invisible, hot, flaming daggers poised to strike on command. I tense myself to prepare for battle if they should decide to attack us.

Not long after we approached the castle, a woman came through a door. My only thought is that she's beautiful beyond belief—long, flowing, curly hair dark as midnight, skin as pale as the moon soft and perfect, eyes green as emeralds. Her body looks like it was designed by the goddess herself, with long legs, an hourglass figure, and voluptuous breasts. I stare at her appraisingly. Power radiates off her in waves, with an elemental feel to it. It's very dark, though there's an ancient feel to it. I look into her soul at her heart, using my other gift. It's dark as midnight and oozes darkness as if it has been gifted from Hades himself. If I could put it into colors, I would surmise dark emerald-green like her eyes with a black mist as a shadow. Any human would die of fear.

This woman, I can tell, relishes the darkness I feel. I continue to gaze at her. I can slightly see the familial resemblance. I have no knowledge of her age. But she is much old than I was. Her power level speaks of her age. It's like being face-to-face with a goddess. One look and I know I will do anything to spend an evening with this rare beauty. I'll make her writhe, moan, and scream from pleasure. I will relish her body all night long if need be. She's distantly related to me, but not by blood, not anymore. I was an Eldridge. That family line is long dead. Abner only had two daughters and a son. It's apparent that one married and kept her maiden's name. I can only hope the son is long dead. If he was anything like his father, he would be walking nightmare.

Just as I'm staring at her, trying to hide my carnal desires, she speaks. "I'm Queen Minerva Sloyan. Who are you, and what is your business here?"

Charles and I bow in respect to her. "Your Majesty, my name is William Barrowcliff," I tell her, lying about my identity. "We seek an audience with your greatness." I bow as I address the Witch Queen, who happens to bear the last name of my ancestors. She's a descendant of that monster. I don't sense vampire in her, though, so perhaps they are not completely hybrids anymore? There's no way that I'm giving her my real identity. If Bathilda is here, I can't afford a chance that she'll recognize either of us and vanish again.

"Very well, how may we help you?"

I pull out a picture I took of a painting done with Bathilda and Eliza sitting together. The only one I have from my human life. "This woman has committed serious crimes against my kind. It has been reported that she was seen entering your kingdom. We wish to collect her so she may face the consequences."

I notice a flash in her eyes briefly.

"I know not of whom you speak. But you have permission to search my kingdom for her."

We bow toward in reverence. "We thank you very kindly for your hospitality," I tell her as we bow again in respect.

We walk into the castle. I notice the carnal looks on several of the witches. As they appraise me and Charles, I speak so only we can hear each other. "I don't know about you. But I'm planning to enjoy my stay."

He laughs and agrees with me. "If these witches don't cooperate, I already know you're planning retribution."

I smile. "You know me so well, my friend."

He looks amused.

"I'm very attracted to that fiery queen."

Charles shakes his head. "You do know how to smooth your way with the ladies."

I laugh out loud, causing some of the residents to look at us. I clear my throat and act as if nothing has happened. The guard's hold is in the foyer. They pat us down, searching us to make sure we aren't armed. Once their search is complete, we're shown to our rooms. And before I close the door, I wink at our tour guide. She blushes and giggles as she walks away.

Another woman approaches, and before she says anything, I speak. "You need not fear us. I'm only here to claim a vampiress who has broken our laws so she may face justice." I lie smoothly.

The witch guard turns to me and says, "We don't care why you claim to be here. Just be aware: if either of you attempt to harm our queen, we will not hesitate to kill you!"

I just shrug and walk away. I'm not going to abide by anything these harpies have to say. I'll just wait and bide my time. We wait for a little while. Then we decide to walk around the town.

I decide it would be best if we split up to search better. As we walk around town, they know why we are here. There is no need to sneak around about it. The town is very small, villagelike. We exit our rooms and walk down the palace corridors. Charles has the guard's directions toward the community. They sharply show us the way out. After we exit, they aggressively shut the doors.

The palace sits on a hill overlooking the village. We descend the valley of steps that stop in the center of the town square. I begin my search on the east side of the town. Charles tells me he will cover the opposite end. We plan to meet back in our guest chambers once we have finished. In every store I see, I do my best to pick up her scent. I've been searching for so long now. It has been hours, and all I've done is hit dead ends.

With the somewhat modern times, I'm surprised, looking at this town. These witches really must be isolated. Everything in this town has the look and feel of something straight from the Middle Ages. I feel as if I'm inside of a J. R. R. Tolkien Book. There are small craft shops, baker shops, butcher shops, and an alchemy store. The roads are either cobblestone or gravel. It is as if this town were built centuries ago before America was founded, and preserved over time.

How in the hell have they stayed so well secluded and away from the public eye? How does the US government not know of their existence? They aren't magically sealed. If they were, Charles and I wouldn't have been able to walk up here.

It has been a long time now. I have combed over every store in this place. If she's here, they must be using a disguising spell. Who is she to these people that they would protect her if that were what they are doing? I'm honestly growing weary of this cat-and-mouse game. I know, as a vampire, I cannot physically tire. However, this hunting her with no positive results is starting to mentally strain. I wish Garrett were here. I pray that he's at peace. And I'm thankful to have Charles with me. Charles is a great friend. I'm starting to consider that we may have to devise a way to let her come to us.

I almost decide to leave this kingdom and search elsewhere when I smell it just as I'm starting to give up hope.

I catch her scent as I walk inside a shop. I observe the attendant is busy with a customer, so I start to walk around the place, trying to hunt down the scent.

The shopkeeper stares at me with a look of disgust. "What do you want leech?"

I stop and look at her. "Well, that is no way to greet a customer. If you were working in my store, I would fire your ass," I tell her as she glares at me in revulsion before walking away.

I hear her say, "Just don't touch anything, bloodsucker!" But I don't miss the look of panic in her eyes. I realize she knows something, and she's not willing to share it. I'm just about to approach her when my feet step over what is obviously a door. We lock gazes. And I see the fear in her eyes.

Crouching down, I notice a door; she immediately runs toward me, intent on stopping me. *Too bad*, I think. I rip the door off its hinges. Bathilda's scent is very strong below. The woman throws her hands up, and I feel her magic about to be released. I'm quicker than she as I jump inside. An energy ball hits the spot where I was. She looks down, hissing at me as I snarl and run away from the entrance.

I discover that I'm in a tunnel. The scent is so strong that I feel as if she's all around me. I give her a smirk, yeah. I follow the path until it arrives at a small but luxurious room. I observe the room in awe and fury. There is a large bed, a comfortable sofa, a table with a kerosene lamp, fluorescent lighting, and a wardrobe. Bathilda's scent is all over this room. I snarl. I knew they were lying! As I'm leaving the room, I hear voices. I search for the source of the sound. I feel the breeze through a crack. One of the walls slides easily out of the way to reveal a door. I crack the door slightly to see where the passage leads.

With shock and amusement, I realize that it leads to a dark hallway. I easily notice this is a part of the castle. So, Bathilda was here, as I assumed, and they used this passageway to sneak her out when we arrived. She must have noticed us coming and fully alerted them. I recognize the voice; it is the servant I flirted with earlier. Well, what a naughty little witch! I chuckle to myself and listen to the voices.

"Do you think Ms. Bathilda escaped all right?"

A different servant answers her, "I don't know. It was smart for us to conceal her and smuggle out the secret room."

One maid tells the other, "What do you think those men want with her?"

The other servant scoffs. "I don't know, and I don't care honestly. I just wanted her off our land."

This surprises me. Apparently, she's not welcomed here by everyone.

The other maid stares scornfully at her friend. "How can you say that about her? Have you forgotten who she is?"

The other maid snarls back, "She's disgusting. That's what she is! She was turned into a bloodsucker! She'll never belong here again!"

The other maid looks in horror. "Don't talk that way about the princess!"

That left more questions in my mind.

"I don't know why our beloved queen continues to allow her back!"

The maid with the black wavy hair says, "I'm sure Her Majesty has her reason. And I would watch my tongue if I were you. We are but maids. If the royals hear you, we'll both be in great danger."

I stay in the room until they're gone. Once there's no one in sight, I take it as my chance to escape. I'm lucky that the secret room led to section of the palace. I can hear Queen Minerva in one of the rooms, so it apparently is located in the royal wing. I keep myself hidden as I find my way back to the guest chambers.

I rush inside Charles's room and share with him all the information I have just uncovered. He is as shocked as I am. "If the servants knew her so well, and if she's royalty here, we need to tread lightly. The last thing we need is a war between species."

I look at him and agree.

Charles shoots me a glance and says, "I think tonight we need to get our answers and then leave this place."

I agree with him. Either peacefully or not, tonight is going to be a wild ride. And I cannot wait to see how everything unfolds.

Hours pass, and it is nearly nightfall. I know that soon we'll be escorted to dinner. Charles and I prepare to attend dinner with the queen.

The door swings open, revealing a royal guard. "The queen requests your presence at dinner."

I nod. "Very well, we shan't keep Her Majesty waiting," I reply. I already expected this. I look over at Charles as we walk down the corridor. We know that tonight is going to result in a bloodbath in some form. We're furious that they lied and concealed her. If they had been open, this wouldn't happen.

We stand in the great dining hall, awaiting the queen. Once she enters, we sit, and dinner is served. I stare at the feast presented to us—roasted elk, butter rolls, and various garden greens served with a glass of red-tinted liquid. I can already surmise what it is. I notice in the corner of eyes the revolting looks on everyone's faces. But none says a word to us. However, their thoughts are shouting at me: "Monster!" "Freak!" "Bloodsucker!" is all I can hear.

I expected this. Our species have never been at peace.

Everything looks very delicious. If I were still human, my mouth would be salivating. We dine with the queen and exchange pleasantries. The evening lingers, and dinner winds down. Everyone is escorted into a parlor to socialize. I have the feeling these formalities are nothing but a stall. These witches are not known for such welcoming hospitality. It is well known that witches don't like us, and we cannot tolerate them, especially dark witches like this coven. I start to let my emotional fog slip to her when she's not expecting it.

My emotional fog will seep into her mind, make her feel relaxed, letting her barriers fall. And the fog will make her desire me. Once I'm successful, I can use my projection into her mind to get the answers I need. I could easily conjure up a movie-like scenario in her mind of us being a happy family and her giving her trust to me to obtain what I want.

She's talking with Charles. I know that he's distracting her. She's completely unaware. I know that she's stalling so Bathilda can escape. And this needs to end now. I start to feel her emotions and thoughts. My fog is invisible to the naked eye unless you have the gift to see invisibility. Since I can conjure it, I can see it. I watch the fog take the color of a white cloud forming around her. I see her start to feel at peace. I see the awareness in her eyes. She knows something is happening to her but hopefully doesn't know what. I'm projecting a desire into her. She's fighting the desire. I let my emotions flow through me. I was already aware that she wants me by the flirtatious eyes she was showing me when we first met. I have not wanted a woman in a long time.

This will be only a night of passion and persuasion. I need her to open up about where Bathilda is. She's not going to give in easily. I keep my eyes on Charles as he's speaking like I'm doing nothing to affect her. I see her from my side glance. She's starting to flush. She stands to leave.

"If you will excuse me. I'm feeling out of sorts. It must be the wine."

Charles and I stand, then bow. "Of course, Your Highness, shall we wait here?" Charles asks.

She replies, "No, you may leave, except for you, Sir Hunter. Please walk with me."

Charles and I exchange a look. He mentally says, "Good luck," as he walks back to his room. She takes my hand as we start to walk. We talk over many things concerning her kingdom, concerning my human life, my time in His Majesty's royal court. We turn out of the gardens and start back toward the castle.

Suddenly, she presses herself against me, and I can tell this is more than just my seductive ways. She has a plan in her mind as well.

"Hunter. I want you. I can't stop craving you!"

I act as if I'm stunned. "My lady, this is so sudden. I'm a guest!"

She throws herself at me. "I know. I just need to be with you! Take me now!" she says with urgency.

I smirk. "Anything you wish, Your Majesty."

She whispers seductively, "Please call me Mira."

We walk toward her bed with our bodies barely separated. We kiss passionately as we remove our clothes one piece at a time. I run my tongue through their cleavage. We fall onto her bed within seconds.

I lock her wrists above her head in my hand. She's panting in anticipation.

"Let's make this more entertaining," she says while a pair of handcuffs magically appear trying to trap my wrists! Not on your life, sweetheart. I catch them before they lock. Her eyes widen in surprise. I start to kiss her again. I flip her over and lock her own wrists. She's shocked, terrified, and furious. I dodge her spell and use the handcuffs against her. She tries to lock eyes with me while muttering words. I keep my eyes and head down. I cannot allow her to look into my eyes. It will complete whatever spell she's trying to use. I know she's powerful; I knew she would try to thwart me.

I kiss her, plunging my tongue in her mouth. She tries to scream in frustration as I continue to distract her. She's falling apart in my hands.

"Mira, you're so sensitive!" I kiss her neck while she's writhing.

"Ahhh!" Her back bows off the bed. She smells amazing. She starts to scream and moan in pleasure. She has already orgasmed, more than once. And I'm not stopping. I'm going to make her scream.

"Scream, Mira! Scream for me!" I whisper in her ear.

Her eyes are wide and staring at me. "Oh Goddess! Oh, Hunter!" she finally screams my name.

I stop kissing her. I use this moment to sink into her mind before she can sober up. It works like a charm. *Tell Hunter where Bathilda is. You can trust him.*

I hear her mental words. *Bathilda is my sister. I hid her in the safe room when I heard that two vampires were looking for her. I don't give a fuck what you think. I will not turn in my sister! Hunter, go fuck yourself!*

My eyes turn black with rage as I hear her thoughts. Then she smiles at me and starts to laugh. I know full well this moment she was not affected by my charm and told it to me out of spite.

She starts to wrestle with me and fight me on the bed while she cackles like a sadistic demon. "Did you really think I didn't know who you are, Hunter Eldridge?" She grins wickedly. "Did you really think I was just going to hand over my sister to you? I don't give a shit if she killed your filthy nomagia wife! Disgusting pathetic humans! You have been hunting her all this time over a dirty parasite!" She starts maniacally laughing.

I see her eyes go black. I decide to act fast. I flip her over on the bed and pin her down. Her words have filled me with rage and a sharp pain in my heart, thinking of my lovely beloved who was gruesomely killed. These witches are wicked and don't respect any form of life but their own insidious selves. I hate being cruel to a woman. But these women, sadly, are purely evil and will kill a human for sport. I have heard stories about them kidnapping human men to mate with, then killing them for pleasure.

She starts to laugh maniacally; her eyes turn red like fire. She looks at me with an evil grin. She glares at me maliciously. "Rot in hell vampire!" she snarls.

I feel her power starting to swirl around the room. I'm thrown off the bed, but at the exact moment it happens, I'm quick to latch onto her. I snarl at her in full fury. "You made the wrong choice!" I bite into her as I'm being thrown, and she goes with me. I'm no longer holding back my rage; she realizes what is happening. She screams, trying to shove me away from her with no use. I'm too strong. When a vampire drinks from a witch, the vampire absorbs the witch's power. I now feel more powerful than ever.

Her body goes limp on the floor. To make sure she doesn't rejuvenate, I tear out her heart and crush it in my hand. It breaks like porcelain. I pick her up and I throw her so hard she crashes through a window. I see her sail over the castle walls. I hear people start to scream in horror. I rip the doors off the room. Guards come at me. I move with twice the speed. With the new power in my body, I launch them through walls. They shoot lightning bolts at me. I catch the powerful blasts and fling them into the witches who are attacking from all sides.

Their eyes widen in horror, realizing what has happened. We have killed their queen. This means that we have just declared war on the witches. We laugh with glee as more warriors start to charge toward us. I am in battle yet again, except this time, it is a different, powerful kind of battle. This is so exciting. Charles finds me during the chaos that has erupted. And we duck behind one of the walls that was broken, which provided a perfect hiding place. We kept watch, avoiding attacks of magic as I wait for the opportunity to strike back with the powers I have absorbed.

We continue like this, warring against the entire palace for quite some time until I grow sick of it. I decide to really test these dark powers and call forth the elemental power of fire. I start to throw flames at them. Some are fireballs. Others come out like flaming discs. It's truly incredible. After a short time, the castle is burning, and all the Wiccan royal warriors have fallen to our powers. I can see Charles on the other side. Using his sneak attacks, quick as lightning strikes, he approaches them from behind and tears their throats out one after another while I fend off the magic attacks. After everything is finished, we walk out into the town square.

All the villagers fall to the ground in surrender, cowering at the rumble of my voice, with the power that I currently hold. Their eyes look at me in horror. They now are beginning to realize that I killed their queen and absorbed her power and they are as good as dead.

Charles chuckles. "Let us teach them a lesson they will never forget!" he says as I lift my hand. The earth starts to shake, and the walls start to tremble. I watch, amazed at this power. I turn a building into rubble. I raise the remains in the air and drop them as people try to run away. Everyone around screams and runs in fear. I raise my other hand and watch as fire extends from my fingers. I smirk. I throw the fire toward all the buildings, engulfing them in flames. Charles is laughing in amazement as the town starts to burn.

We quickly run toward the gate. Passing through, we close it and place a boulder in front of it, sealing their fate. I hate doing this. I feel like a piece of my lost soul is turning into obsidian. And Eliza is crying. I know in my heart I have fallen farther from grace than I ever was. It is like darkness has taken over. The monster and assassin inside of me don't want to stop. It still craves Bathilda's blood and vengeance on whoever stands in our way. I have become the symbol of death and destruction in my quest to find her. I don't know if I will ever be pulled back to the light.

The flames rise high into the night as the kingdom is scorched as if it is consumed by dragon fire. I still have not found Bathilda. I still feel nothing. I thought that killing her sister would bring me some form of satisfaction. She took the one who I loved most, so I made sure karma was repaid. I took her sister's life and her entire kingdom.

"I thought that I would feel something at least with the knowledge that I just destroyed her family as she did mine." I sigh and hang my head in remorse.

Charles puts his hand on my shoulder. "Hunter, nothing is going to help take the pain away, finding her and getting revenge will be justice."

I shake my head. "Well, now, she can live with the pain I have been feeling," I say darkly. We start leaving the area, intent on heading back to Chicago. I need to go home and wash this disgusting place off me. At that moment, we hear the mournful screams of a woman. The pain she's in and the wailing sounds cause the entire forest to go quiet.

Out of nowhere, the sky turns pitch black, thunder cracks, and rain pours harder than anything I have ever seen. If the rain pours any more, it will cause a flood in the mountains. She sounds insane with grief. We walk toward the sound, fighting the winds and pelting rain. We stop dead in our tracks. Fifty yards away, Bathilda is holding the queen's lifeless body in her arms.

"What happened to you, Mira!" she cries. She lifts her head and stares at us in surprise recognition.

I smirk as I look at Mira's naked body.

She seems shocked to see us. "Hunter!"

I bite back a growl.

"Hello, Bathilda," Charles says.

She's stunned to see Charles. "What are you doing here? Wait! What's wrong with your eyes, Hunter?"

I look to Charles, wondering what she's speaking of.

"Hunter, I didn't know how to say this. But your eyes are glowing like fire."

I look at him in shock. I should have expected this with the amount of witches' power flowing through me right now. But I didn't consider it.

She continues to stare at us, trying to piece everything together. She looks back toward the mountain we just came from and sees the smoke rising high into the night's sky. The screams of the townspeople can still be heard in the distance. Her entire form shakes in rage. Fire shines in her eyes as she realizes what has happened and who is responsible.

I can't help but torture her. "She was so good tonight, screaming my name, writhing in pleasure," I taunt.

Bathilda is beyond enraged. Her eyes are wild. She's thrashing against the cold ground like a banshee being tied down.

I chuckle darkly. "Karma is a bitch!"

She pulls on her hair as she screams, "How could you!"

I smirk at her as she positions herself in a pounce position. "You destroyed my family. Now I just destroyed yours. How does it feel, bitch!"

She screams and barrels through us. I sidestep her and catch her around the waist, throwing her into a tree. She propels herself back as the tree snaps in half. She soars through the air. Charles catches her by the ankle. She spins around with the other foot and kicks him in the nose.

We snarl. She swings at me. I predict her attack and dodge just in the right time. I see an opening and deliver a hard kick to her gut, sending her soaring through the air. She collides with the side of the mountain. This causes a rock slide. Charles and I quickly jump away from the falling rocks as we watch her become buried. If I were a human, I would be exhausted. This is most battle I have done since I fought with the Lycans. She truly is lethal, as lethal as Garrett used to be. I have so many emotions filling me right now—sorrow for my painful memories, rage for the torment I endured, frustration from the countless years we have been chasing her around the world, only for her to make fools of us.

I poise myself defensively for attack. She's too crazy to be held down by a pile of rocks. The pile bursts open, and she lunges toward us. Charles lunges toward her throat. He grips her firmly while I punch her in the face. We think we are the victors until she breaks Charles's hand and backhands me hard to the ground. He screams in pain as she shoves him hard into a tree. I spring to my feet and stand to square off facing her for another round as we dance this deadly game.

She snarls at me as I sink into a crouch. "I gave you life, Hunter! We were meant to be together!"

I growl at her. "Lies! Garrett gave me life! You stole my life, you demon!" I run toward her, and she kicks a shower of dirt right into my face, temporarily blinding me. I shake my head to rebalance myself when she catches me off guard from behind and hugs me around the neck.

"No! I have always been meant for you. But Garrett stole you away before we could become one!"

I snarl, "Bitch!"

She licks me on the cheek, letting out her own breathy moan.

I'm trying to shake her off until she drops down and kicks me in the groin. I fall to my knees before she picks me up and throws me into the side of the mountain. I turn with the right velocity and somehow manage to cling on to the mountain rather than colliding with it. I use my stance on the side of the cliff as a springboard and launch myself back at her again.

We continue trying to take each other down until I decide enough is enough. I look at Charles, who had to set his broken bone quickly before it healed wrong. We try to corner her; we start backing her toward to cliff's ledge, intending to force her down. She gives a sadistic grin and charges through the center of us, knocking both of us to the ground.

A sandstorm stirs unexpectedly, and we realize that we are cornered in front of her. What we don't expect is her raising her hands. I feel an energy surge in the earth. She throws her hands down and slams the ground. Her eyes also glow like fire, then turn like obsidian. She stands and a pillar of fire corners us on the mountain. I glare with a malicious smirk as I close my eyes, inhale, concentrate on my new gifts, and extend my hands, channeling the new magic. I conjure a tornado between my hands. It instantly starts to pull the pillar of fire in. The funnel consumes the fire and passes it into me as I absorb her magic.

She stands there, frozen. Her face becomes pale, and she's shaking in fear. She's trying to understand how I was able to do steal her magic, being only a vampire.

I chuckle darkly. "It's quite simple. I absorbed the queen's magic. Aside from my own gifts, what does that make me? Nearly all powerful! Try that again! I dare you!" I stare her down as I let myself settle with this new feeling inside me. Charles, who was rendered unconscious after being knocked head first into the rocks, is starting to awaken.

We both start to move toward her again. I really want to end this here and now! She laughs maniacally and creates a strong wind. A tree flies toward us. We have to dodge its assault. We knock the tree aside to keep it from falling on us, just in time to see her take off running faster than a bullet.

She jumps off the mountain into the water below, and we watch her take off swimming like a shooting star. I roar in fury, "We had her, and she got away again!"

I hear her voice in my mind through the magic. "Until next time, Hunter! Oh, and stop looking for me unless you want to accept me, lover!"

I snarl at her through my thoughts. "Never! I would rather enjoy your death!"

I feel her laughter, then silence.

I'm shaking with rage. I cannot believe everything that has happened not only tonight but also in my life, everything that she has forced me to become, through her sick, twisted mind.

She dared to become sexual with me after I killed her kingdom! How deranged is this woman? How far will she go?

If I ever find love again, will she return and repeat the knife in my heart as her disgusting way of claiming me?

Will I ever know peace in my life?

CHAPTER 12

We walk away from the mountain. I continue to feel the rage consume me. It seems even with Garrett gone for so many years, some of his ruthlessness stayed with me, waiting to rear its ugly head. I really wish I had Eliza; she always finds a way to keep the darkness at bay. I thought I would feel the joy of sweet revenge. But I felt absolutely nothing. My only short-lived joy was knowing I had finally caught Bathilda, only for it to die after our battle. Her sly maneuvers that outdid me, only for her to disappear into the water below.

We are both exasperated. So many years looking, we finally find her only to completely lose her again!

"Honestly, if she had not pulled that little trick throwing a tree in our faces, she would be a pile of cinder right now! Nice work absorbing that power," Charles says to me.

I shrug and nod at his comment. I'm too furious to speak.

Charles continues talking, "If we had known who she was and just how powerful, we could have planned a better strategy. Now, we need to be careful."

I nod in agreement and respond. "I don't know how long I will have this power; she was born with it. Her family has hybrid genes."

He considers what I'm saying. "Plus, she was also turned into a vampire, usually the power disappears, the turn must have triggered her hybrid DNA," Charles says.

We walk for hours before we reach a small town. I need to find a car we can drive back. After that battle, I need rest. Charles turns toward me as I step into a payphone booth. "Hunter. I really think you need to consider resting. All of our attempts have been for naught. I know what Garrett and Bathilda did to you was cruel. It appears that someone in the universe is telling us that we are not meant to catch her, yet please walk away and rest."

I lean against the booth, listening to him, thinking about it. It has been so long, so stressful trying to track down one damned woman! I didn't think I would feel it as a vampire, but I almost feel exhausted. How much more can we continue to play these cat-and-mouse games with her? She knows we are tracking her; how much longer will this continue?

"I agree. I have spent so much energy in my existence chasing her." We both nod.

"So, what is the next strategy?"

I ask him to bear with me a moment. I look in phone book for the nearest car salesman. I find one not too far from our current location, we start to walk there. I tell him that I need time away. I need him to be a friend and mind my store. I have not spent a day relaxing and being normal with my life in ages.

Charles sighs. "I feel what you are saying. This merry go around is ridiculous."

I tell him that I would also love to travel back to Europe to check on everything that is in London.

"You're thinking about what I said about taking a holiday?"

It feels right to do. "Yes, when was the last time I was in London and visited the store?"

He nods in agreement. "That is a great idea. We both need to rest. I will write to the storekeeper and let him know of your arrival."

My smile is evident. "What will you do with me on holiday?"

Charles laughs. "I suppose do something which I have not done in centuries—fool around."

We both laugh. "I will be happy for you if you find love," I tell Charles.

He grips my shoulder. "I will be happy too. And for you, my friend, I hope you find peace," he says as he clasps me on the shoulder.

I shake my head. "No. I don't think that will happen as of yet." I'm about to speak when he interrupts me.

"Give it a chance, Hunter. Let your heart open again. I know you miss her. But even in the human world. There has been enough time that has passed. Remember your dream? When she spoke to you? I think she would want you to move on."

I sigh, look at him, and walk away in thought. I know she would. But I don't feel it in my heart yet.

We found the car sales business. It is small, not much of a selection. This will have to do. I find a 1935 Studebaker Packard. It's red with running boards on either side of its four doors, a bit used but in good condition for eight hundred dollars. Usually, these cars brand new would cost at minimum $950. I need to find a local bank and make arrangements for a loan. Charles informs that he will wait at the lot.

I walk around the town. And I'm happy when I find a Wells Fargo company. I immediately enter and request a loan. I'm fortunate to be carrying my driver's license. This provides proof of identity. Once they understand who I am, they immediately grant my loan with no questions. I collect the sum and head toward the car lot. We pay for the car and head on our way. I park at an Amoco gas station to fill up on gas. I'm in no mood to deal with anyone, so we request full service. We keep the windows up, and the attendant comes out, fills our tank, and cleans our windows. I ask him to put the cost on my tab and drive away.

We drive toward Ithaca, New York. I have a thought. I cannot wait to return to Chicago, though I know I will be leaving for London first. Firstly,. I want to check on the estate. The last time I was in this area was five years ago. I make sure my secretary handles all the maid services for the Eldridge Estate in New York and my services in Chicago as well. I drive to the estate where my wife lays in rest.

I have not been here a while, and after recent events, now that I have come to the mind of leaving for the old country, I need to visit. Charles whispers that he will wait in the car. He knows this is something I must personally do. I walk around the property. I step inside to see its status. Everything looks the same. Everything is still well managed. However, I can see the caretakers here are starting to become worn. Mrs. Heckler is now gray haired. Her once red hair has aged. Her face shows the wrinkles of her years she has seen.

She's cleaning the house. And I watch, take a seat. I hear her grumble, "I don't know whatever happened to Mr. Eldridge. I pray God be with him."

I hear a man speak. "I thought when he bought this place he would have lived here to stay. It was only about, what, ten years he stayed here? Why keep the place?"

I stepped into the house. "Because he buried his wife here."

They stand up, startled. "I apologize. My name is Alexander Eldridge. I'm Hunter's son." I lie smoothly.

They shake my hand. "You are a dead ringer for your father, my boy," the elder man says to me and, ironically is, very right.

I smile and thank him. "His wife, his only true love, died due to a vicious attack before he moved here from England. It was her dream to come here to live."

They hang their heads and offer up a prayer for Mrs. Eldridge, saying their condolences and wishing my father well. I nod solemnly and make my way toward the garden where my Eliza lies. I bow my head on the ceramic bench that acts as her headstone. I pour out my heart in grief and speak to her, knowing that she can hear me. I feel a presence with me, and a soft hand brushes the tears away from my face.

"I'm so sorry, my love! I have constantly failed you! I failed to protect you. And I have continually failed to avenge you!" I say as I hang my head to cry tears that I can no longer shed.

I close my eyes, and I feel like I'm transported back to that precipice. I see Eliza, standing far off from me. I reach for her again. This time, the wall moves us closer. I jump toward her and wrap my arms around her.

"Hunter, my darling!" I inhale her scent that's still there, feel her beauty all around me.

"My love," I whisper to her.

"Hunter, I have called you here. You need to stop, my love! You weary yourself and have driven yourself mad with rage, revenge, and grief." She takes my face in her hands. "I will always love you. Do you not recall what I told you? I said that one day I would send my love back to you for you to cherish. How can I possibly do that when all you do is fill your heart with hate and plot revenge?"

I didn't know how to respond. "Yes, Bathilda was a fake friend. Yes, she played a part in ending the life we knew. This is all water under the bridge."

I look at her dubiously.

"Do not give me that look, Hunter Eldridge! You have let your heart become consumed with hatred and bitterness; you have let Garrett form you into a savage beast! You are not the man I married anymore. I don't know who you have become," she said with tear-stained eyes.

I fall to my knees and onto my face. Everything she said was the truth. I have changed into such a violent creature. I feel as if my soul had been marred black with sinister stains. I look at her.

"You're right! I'm so sorry, Eliza! I have fallen so far from grace. I don't know what to do! I want to be the man I was. But I fear Garrett has corrupted me too much."

She smiles at me. "Oh Hunter, you are not lost. Look what you did for your cousin. Look how you have altered your hunting so you don't kill. You are better than he is! Never forget this. All I ask is for you to let go, stop hating, stop hurting, stop holding on so I can one day return to you. Live and love again my darling," she says as she kisses me.

I feel myself falling into the dark abyss around me. I wake up and notice I have been sent back to reality. I feel a gentle sense of peace overcome me. For the first time in decades, I feel like my soul is clean.

CHAPTER 13

World War II

I bid my farewells to the caretakers, with the mind to arrange for their retirement, fully compensated and a new staff to oversee in a few months. I reflect on our conversation. My head hears his words. But my cold dead heart yearns for someone who is beyond my reach forever.

Somewhere in my mind, a small voice whispers, *This is the reason why every woman you've ever fed off you inevitably craved to be with. Admit it, Hunter: you're craving to be loved again.*

I shake my head. As much as I want to deny it, I cannot deny the vision I had of Eliza still is fresh in my mind. The voice whispers again, *Hunter, Admit it: your heart wants to feel again.*

I push the words from my mind. I don't need it. I don't want or need anyone else but the one person I can never have again. I need to get away from here. I need to distract myself. And suddenly, the great world war comes to mind, my homeland under siege. I know what I'm going to do. Once upon a time, I was a soldier in the king's army. I have a duty to defend my homeland against this Nazi invasion. Foolish humans have no idea what they are up against.

There are rumored talks about Hitler's mind control and so on. There is a reason for that. He is being influenced by one of the three vampire elders. He is an Anorial. Humans would never realize this. This is a human who has a birth connection to dark power that one of the three vampire royals possess. The human is willingly controlled by a supernatural being who is very powerful. Most of the time, they are like a keeper to a vampire's dark presence. That dark form is a silent influence in that child's life so that, when they grow up, they will be completely subservient to the vampire lord and do his bidding naturally.

I may be a vampire, but England is my home, and I will not let them destroy it over whatever sick games they are weaving. I heard whispers that they were creating this war, to see how many new sires they could create because they are bored and want to increase the vampire population. And there was also talk that they wanted an elaborate hunting game if other vampires would join the war. It would become an ultimate vampire feast around the world.

I will join. I will fight, only to defend my home country! We continue to drive back to Chicago. I drive Charles to his high-rise flat. I inform him that I'm leaving tonight for England, and I'm going to enlist in the royal service. I want to do my part in the war to stop evil powers from consuming the world. He wishes me luck and happiness.

We bid each other farewell, and I drive home to my riverside mansion. After so much time doing nothing but trying to satisfy my taste for revenge, this feels right.

The following day, I call a taxi and make my way to the airport. I board the plane that will take me to England, my true homeland. The flight takes several hours. And I'm glad I hunted last night before I left. I was tired of pacing around my house and decided to hunt to prepare for the trip. I ran toward the Indiana border and came across two humans. They were stranded on a back country road miles away from society, perfect midnight snack. That midnight trip will tide me over for the next month.

I'm happy when the plane lands so I can stretch my legs. I immediately make my way to the recruiting center; it is mind numbing to wait in line here as a human persona when a vampire could have me out of here within seconds. Finally, after what feels like hours, I step up toward the attendant and give her all my information. I sign it with my middle name.

"Lionel Eldridge," I lie smoothly. I'm praying that I will not have to start from basic.

That would be brutal. A military man calls me forward with a questioning look. I step forward to shake his hand.

"Dear fellow, are you at all related to Hunter Eldridge?"

I smile and laugh a bit, someone remembers me. "Yes. I dare say that I am. He was my great-grandfather," I tell the man.

He eyes me with a look of amazement.

"Did you know of him?" I ask him.

"I do know of him. My grandfather spoke of him. Apparently, they were in the group together. He saved his life."

I look at him now with interest. "Is his name Wulfric Proctor?"

The man smiles. "Yes. Do you know of him?"

I smile. I do remember that time. I did save his life. I'm glad he found a happy ending.

"I heard my father share stories which my great-grandfather had shared with the family. He had a high code of honor and protecting one's family as well as country," I tell the man. I still do, which is why I'm here.

The man nods with a smile. "That sounds like the right man. Well, now that we are acquainted, and you are an Eldridge, I'm not going to let you suffer the basic training, especially your age. You will obviously have to train a bit. But you will not start out from scratch."

I'm grateful for this.

"Report next week to the Allenby Barracks."

I stand and salute the man in the traditional British form. I walk out of that place, ready to fight in WWII. That following week, I measure myself so I won't appear nonhuman. I am very fortunate that none suspect what I am. I decide that I will save my appetite for the battlefield during cover of night. I can help the war effort by preying on whatever enemy force we will be fighting. I pray that it is Germany.

After several weeks of training and preparing, we are finally heading toward combat. I have had combat experience previously. However, this type of combat is very different than it was in 1840. During that time, we had muskets, swords, cannons, and other weapons. In this modern society, there are rifles, grenades, and cannons. The choices of weapons are much more advanced, less related to battles that would require swordplay. There is no honor left in war anymore.

I walk into the officer's club and listen to their conversation for a safe distance.

"So, Charles, how are things looking?" asks Colonel Albright.

"I would say they are shaping up rather swimmingly," replies Lieutenant Commander Reilly.

"Splendid, how are the new recruits? Any notable progress or promising prospects?" says another officer, who I believe is Colonel Watson.

"I would say everything is going very well. We have some favorable recruits. I think my best promising one is Mr. Eldridge," I hear one of the officers' comments.

"Yes. I do have to agree. With the way he fights and trains, you would think the man has decades of experience in war?" says Commander Beasley

"Did I hear something that he's the grandson of the late lieutenant Hunter Eldridge?"

All the men look at the man who just spoke. I look over that the man slyly. I realize that he looks familiar.

"Commander Striker, I didn't hear you enter the club," one of the men address him.

I realize why he looks familiar. Either this man is a grandson as I'm pretending to be, or he became immortal because. I'm looking into the eyes of my commanding officer from the previous war. And if memory serves right, he didn't like me. If it is him, I will know. I continue to listen to the men.

"Yes, from what I understand, his name is Lionel Eldridge," the captain says.

"Is that not the same name as Hunter's middle name?" Striker says with a smirk.

"My God, fellow, are you trying to say that it is *the* Hunter Eldridge? Preposterous, the man would be over a hundred years old. And this man is merely twenty-five years old. What in the devil are you trying to imply?" The men scoff at him. He walks away with a devious smirk.

I need to keep my guard up. I didn't realize that he noticed me and headed my direction since I was looking downward at a paper.

"Greetings, Hunter," he says to me. I go to speak, and he stops me. "Do not even bother lying." I stare at him in shock, so it was him. How?

"How? How is it possible for you?" I said in surprise.

"How is it possible for you? Do not ask questions which you already know the answer to," he says as he took a seat next to me.

"Who turned you? And when?" I ask him out of curiosity.

He studies me for a moment. "I was on the field one day. If you recall, it was the day when everyone in the regiment thought I had died." I did remember that day. We all mourned for him. "I was lying on the field. I thought for sure that I would die. Then a man by the name of Byron came to me and offered me a second chance. He promised me new life, so I took it. Three days later, I awoke to my new life, killed the doctors in my thirst. Lord Byron took me under his wing."

I scowl as I listen. I didn't like Byron.

I'm nervous; we have never gotten along. It's jealousy on his part of skill in combat and coveting Eliza. He wanted her, yet I met her first. I'm coming in as an officer recruit. He has seniority.

"Do not worry, Hunter. Whatever animosity we had is in the past. We are both gods among sheep now."

I was not sure I agreed with his statement.

"The only thing I still despise is your easy adjustment to anything that relates to command." I chuckle.

"What is it about you that makes people bow down?" he asks me with irritation.

"Honestly, I don't know, perhaps I'm that talented, who can say?"

He scowls, calls me an arsehole, and walks away.

I continue to listen to the colonel's table. I learn that the regiment is being deployed to Normandy, France. I smile with excitement! We're facing the Germans! I receive my recognition, my new rank as an officer. I have once again been positioned as a sniper due to stellar marks in long range gunmanship. During wartime, this is what I'm born to do!

We board the ships and start the journey toward Normandy. I meet with Montgomery; I learn that he oversees the secret vampire garrison I have been training with. There is only a handful of us. But it is enough. Ten of us could eliminate the entire enemy fleet.

We have been on this boat for weeks traveling toward our destination. The atmosphere is very cramped. Human emotions are starting to become elevated. Fights had begun to break out, and tensions were running rampant. Some men are starting to show they signs of cowardice, and some men are craving this fight like a drug. There are nearly a hundred men on board with us. I'm fortunate to be an officer. I received my commission of lieutenant again, so I will be in charge of my own garrison. Thus, I'm able to have my own accommodations for a room. This is preferable than bunking with the recruits. I walk the ship and check on the men.

The barrack area of the ship is overcrowded with bunk beds and dozens of sleeping enlisted men. Once I make my way through there, I walk the narrow corridors until I reach the captain's cabin where Mr. Montgomery is awaiting my presence. He sent word an hour earlier that we had been requested for a meeting to discuss land tactics on the day when we are ready for invasion. We discussed the information the Allies decoded, and prepared ourselves for war.

It's the next morning that I begin to see land in sight. I cannot mention this to the humans because their senses are duller than a vampire's sense. When a human asks me why I'm packing. I just say that I want to be prepared. I see guys roll their eyes. They have no idea, poor souls. Most of them are going to die. I could save some. However, that is not why we are here.

Two more hours go by, and we hit the beachheads. I can already hear the cannons being prepared, the clicks of Nazi rifles being adjusted. I rally my men that I'm in command of. I order them to stay down, keep their helmets on, and don't be stupid. Tonight, all hell is going to break lose. So many of these humans are just kids, not much older than I was when I first served in the king's army. I was sixteen years old when I first enlisted. I served His Majesty for four years until I was twenty years old. It was after I returned home that my life truly began. I look back on those years with love and longing. Now I'm back behind the lines again, and I'm proud of my service. My leadership experience will help try to keep some of these kids alive.

We start to charge off the landing cruisers. I see Montgomery's crew charging forward. Several of them have been shot. I manage to get more of mine off the beach. Some have fallen, and their souls have gone to God. We give the sign of the cross and say quick prayers for our fallen, then continue to charge forward.

I have a handful of people left. We find the trenches and dive in, awaiting the other troops to arrive. I take out my rifle and, with vampiric sight, shoot off several rounds, hitting each target, to the amazement of the men in my command.

"My eyesight is my strongest advantage," I tell them. And they look a bit dubious. But start to fire themselves. I just knock him off utilizing my vampire eyesight among humans. This continues for several hours, until both sides feel exhaustion. The humans take rest and take cover as this bloody night lingers on.

We wait until the humans fall asleep, then we start to really move. Montgomery, Ajax, Warren, Thurston, Reginald, and a handful of other vampires I have become acquainted with.

We spend a minute organizing then we take off into the night. We all cross the lines with ease.

We jump into the German bunkers and let loose the mayhem. Montgomery takes two men, pinning them down. I join him as we start to drink.

Afterward, I break their necks. I look over as more Germans are beginning to pour into the area in retaliation. Montgomery and I grin as we start to tear them apart. Their screams feed the beast inside of me that craves blood, mayhem, and destruction. We continue through the night destroying the German army and satiating our insatiable thirst. The following day, we move the troops forward with little difficulty.

As we moved onward, I started to see something I was not expecting. There are members of our own soldiers who were just as savagely torn apart. I look at Reginald. "You understand what this means?"

He nods. "The German armies have vampires on their side."

"They were sent from that bloody elder! They are trying to even the field, or they are spicing up their life-and-death game." Ajax growls. It's time to end this soon.

We need to end this assault so the human allies can do their part. My vampire comrades and I continue to tear through the German army until we are all clear. We return to our trenches and guide our troops into the closest town square. We find a position to take as we wait for the Germans to come. I send most of my men to Ajax and Montgomery to station as I take a handful with me.

It feels like hours. The German garrison starts to enter the area. I take my aim and start firing from the tower position where I'm situated. The German start to scramble becoming aware of my presence without knowing where I am. I continue to quickly kill each German that I can shoot. It lasts for a while until one of them figures out where I am. I jump from my tower, knowing that it will not hurt me.

Thurston meets me. And we look over to find most of the troops dead. I see my second-in-command still alive and struggling. I know that I shouldn't. However, his wound is fatal. I quickly sire him and leave him to complete the process. I will come back for Adam in a few days, God willing any of us make it through the night.

We continue to march through hell and high water as we fight for king and country. Bodies of young men lay scattered all over the French countryside. The scene is grizzly as we continue to move onward, advancing during the day. At night, we continue to feed on the German army until we come face-to-face with the German vampires. They attack us in retribution. And we start to rip each other apart. I realize these vampire soldiers are inexperienced. Montgomery and I tear through them easily. I feel the hurt when I see Archibald being torn apart, then burned. Thurston, Richard, Montgomery, and I start to fight harder until we finally subdued the enemy threat. The battle rages on until finally we reach Paris. We reclaim the city and free the French people

When all hope seems lost, we receive the news we prayed for: Germany had surrendered and Adolf Hitler has committed suicide, the war in Europe had ended. Reginald asks if he can take Adam as his apprentice. I'm happy to grant him this. I learned that he has been alone for two centuries. No one should be alone for that long.

I return to England and helped them pick up the pieces. I wire Charles to remind him I decided to stay in England and help with the reconstruction. I spend several years in London, assisting them with aid until staying in the city began to be too much. I decide to relocate to somewhere else I had never been. I chose to explore Liverpool and see where my life takes me.

CHAPTER 14

Twenty Years Later

It is hard to believe how fast time can go by. However, that's the one constant with time. It's ever evolving. I have moved my main store from London to Liverpool. I'm really enjoying it here. I didn't think it would happen, but I feel like I'm finding myself again for the first time since I became a vampire. To my great surprise, I have found someone to care for.

Her name is Lucinda, a woman who works for a bakery next to my shop. She has a lovely daughter. When I first met her, her daughter, Molly, had a condition that crippled her. Physicians didn't believe that she would live very long. Lucinda worried constantly about her. Her husband left her shortly after conception when she told him the news. He never returned. If he ever does, I will personally kill him for abandoning his family.

One day, Molly fell deathly ill. And Lucinda was fearful of losing her. She has no idea of her recovery; I could not watch the child die, and neither could she. I called it a "special medicine." It's a medicine that I brewed with magical ingredients. I was overjoyed when she came to me and informed me that whatever medicine I had given her completely cured her daughter. Lucinda questions what I gave her. However, I will never tell her. I just want her to be at peace and happy Molly is well. I'm happy to be with her. Today I'm planning a surprise for the two ladies, and we will be sailing on my yacht

"Hunter," Lucinda calls me from the doorway. She makes me feel so happy. I never thought I would feel this way again. She's a stunning woman, long, curly, black hair, emerald, green eyes, and amazing curves. Her daughter Molly is growing into a fine young woman. It's amazing that it has been five years since I first met them. I'm proud to be her father figure. She's now approaching the age of graduating school. She will leave for college soon.

She has not let us know where she's planning to enroll. I know, wherever she goes, she will excel. She's very smart. I'm mulling over this when Lucinda approaches me.

"Hunter, Molly wanted me to ask you if we could all go camping at the end of the month? You know she's been itching to experience the outdoors."

We both laugh. "Nothing would make me happier. The outdoors is wonderful and very educational."

She beams. "It is settled then! I will go and tell Molly."

I sit here staring out the window as Lucinda talks with Molly.

"Lucinda, what are you doing to me? Where are you leading me?" I walk out the door to join the ladies. It is a beautiful August day. I plan to take my girls sailing. It is something I have always loved since I was a child. Luckily now, I have prospered enough that I have bought my own yacht, something that I have not made Lucinda aware of.

"So, you girls ready?"

They turn around and look at me. "For what?" says Molly.

I smile. "I have a surprise for you both," I say as I walk away.

I step into my car, wait for them to climb in. I have only ever spent time with them at my guest house. It is smaller than my mansion in Ellesmere Port, which is a half-hour drive from Liverpool. I hear them coming out of the garden gate. We drive for the next thirty minutes. They are shocked at the grand gate that closes off a property. I enter in the code, and my seaport estate comes into view. It is a grand and beautiful house. Being here really makes me feel like I'm home. I head toward my garage which I made sure is ample space enough for each of my vehicles. I park. And they gawk at the line of cars that I have which I have kept hidden.

"Welcome to my home, loves," I say to them.

I lead them into the mansion and go to find my keys for my yacht, *Tesoro*. Lucinda is in awe of the house. "Hunter! This place is amazing."

I hug her and thank her.

"Wow. What a surprise!" Molly shouts from a different room. "Thank you."

"This is not all. I know we have spent many years together, but I have yet to show you some fun things I have."

"That is because, when you are spending time with us at the house, you are work or in meetings," Lucinda says in a scolding voice.

I sigh. She has a point. Even in my marriage, I just could not stop working. I realize I'm making similar mistakes, which is why I planned this weekend.

"Let us go for a drive and have some real fun!" I tell them as I hold up my keys. I chuckle as they smile.

We drive down the road toward the marina where my yacht is kept. I have grown to care about her, spending time with her has helped me start to feel normal again. She's given me a sense of belonging that I have not felt in so many years. As we exit the car at the shoreline, both look around in awe at the docks.

"Where are you taking us?" Molly asks.

"You will see." That is all I say. "There is also a small café here. And they serve the best food. Their spotted dick is good. However, my favorite is their homemade blood sausage."

Lucinda pinches me and says, "Of course, it is," with a laugh.

She knows me so well. I informed her a few years ago what type of creature I was. I decided that if we were going to be together, she needed to know. I was surprised to hear her tell me that she met some vampires before, so it's not a shock to her.

We are sitting in front of the marina café, enjoying our food. I relish my blood sausage for obvious reasons also. It reminds me of my youth. I remember my mother's favorite dish to make for breakfast was a scotch egg, Eton mess, and toad in the hole. She used to serve blood sausage on holidays when we had Christmas parties the jellied eel and black pudding were highly popular nibbles. I remember and miss how happy those times were. I can only hope, with Lucinda by my side, it will be again.

Lucinda looks up from her lunch and addresses me. "So, Hunter, what are we doing today?"

I smile at her. "What if I were to tell you that I own a yacht, and we are going to go sailing?"

Both girls beam with glowing smiles. "Oh, Father! That is amazing!"

I look at Molly calling me father for the first time. Lucinda looks at her questioningly as well.

"What? Is he not like a father figure to me? Has he not been by our side for countless years?"

Lucinda and I both sigh in understanding. After all, from her perspective, she was correct.

I am the only father figure she has ever known. Bloody hell, this trip just got awkward. We finish our midday meal, and I lead them toward the yacht. I walk over and spot Fredrick, my boat hand, tending to the yacht. "Hello, Fred!"

He looks toward us. "Hello, Mr. El! How are you doing?" he said while waving at us. "Why, I had no idea you had a family, sir." He smiles at the three of us as I help the ladies climb aboard.

"Yes, this is Lucinda. And, Molly, girls, this is Fredrick Bishop, my right-hand shipmate on this vessel."

They smile and make conversation with him. After introductions are made, I walk the ladies around the yacht and show them everything in the cabin. Molly takes off to find a room of her own as I continue to walk Lucinda around.

"Here is the lounge. There is an open bar in it. There are bathrooms."

She looks around with awe and a happy face. I can hear Molly jumping up and down shouting in excitement. I walk her to the master cabin.

"This will be our room." I feel butterflies fill my stomach with anticipation for later.

I kiss the back of her neck softly and wrap my arms around her waist as I breathe in her scent. I hear her soft moan, and I feel her body start to vibrate. "I cannot wait to christen this bed with you later," I softly tell her as my hands lightly roam her body.

I see fire fill her eyes, and she clutches my coat in her hands. I pull her deep into my arms as I kiss her. She doesn't fear anything from me. Before we left for our trip, I fed. And even at the restaurant, I had some of the black pudding and blood sausage. I'm fully prepared.

"I would love to get started now. But I need to help Fred push off. Come up on deck when you are ready." I give her a deep kiss. I leave her in the room and go up the deck.

I check the ship and look over at Fredrick. "Everything ready, Fred?"

He gives me a salute. "Everything perfect. She's firing good and ready to head out."

I give him a nod. "All right, let us take her out for a stretch." She pulls out of the dock and gracefully sails through the water. I love the feel of the sea on my face. Lucinda comes out from below, and I can already see Molly on one of the lounge chairs preparing to catch some sun.

"Where did you learn to sail?" Molly asks me.

"At the nautical school in London."

Molly looks over at me. "Wow! Would you be willing to teach me or send me there?"

I'm happy to hear she's interested. "Sure. As long as your mother is all right with it," I tell her. She gives me a thumbs-up gesture and lays back down.

I look around. I close my eyes as I feel the wind in my face, the smell of the sea filling my black soul. I feel a hand slip into mine. I turn to see Lucinda caressing my hand while smiling at me.

"Thank you, Hunter."

I wrap my around her and kiss her forehead. I have not felt this content in decades.

After a few hours of sailing, I whisper to her, "Come with me." I pull her toward the lower level. Her eyes fill with desire but nervousness. She glances at Molly.

I turn toward my soon-to-be stepdaughter. "Molly, we'll be back in a little while," I tell her.

She smiles, waves, and continues to lay down. I pull Lucinda downward; I can't stay away from her anymore. I pull her into the cabin and lock the door.

"I cannot stay away from you anymore, watching you soak in the sun the last hours have been tormenting me."

She's deeply panting. Her gaze is locked on mine. She has a fire in her eyes as if she's slowly burning inside. I pull her into my arms. I push her gently against the wall. Our eyes lock as my lips descends on hers. Her arms secure themselves around my neck as I grip her waist. I plunge my tongue into her mouth and keep a conscious effort to keep my fangs from slipping out as we embrace each other in passion. I'm very thankful I have super self-control, or else I wouldn't feel so relaxed.

When a vampire becomes aroused, if he's not exercising good control, it is very easy for us to become overwhelmed and give in to our desires. The result of this can cause our fangs to slip out, and we go into a frenzy. Therefore, while hunting, it is easy to get aroused as I finish a meal. I will admit there have been times with Lucinda where I feel like the beast inside me wants out, to claim her. However, I have known the feeling of loss, and now that I have found my second chance, I will not let the monster within harm either of them.

As I think this, I'm already pulling her onto the bed. I tear her blouse open as I trail my fingers down her stomach. She writhes and moans as I caress her soft skin with my fingers. Heading her most sensitive area, I slip my fingers into the moistened cave and start to move them. Her back bows off the bed. Her mouth is open in a silent scream. As I caress her heated core, I start to kiss her neck and move down her body. She's trembling.

"Oh, bugger!" she breathes.

"You like the feel of me?"

She moans, "Yes!" She breathes as I continue to excite her.

"I have not even let you fully feel," I tell her as her eyes widen with what I just said.

I slowly move my head down her body to her heated core. I latch my mouth onto her tender bud and start to ravage her with my tongue. She lets out a soft wail as she arches further off the bed. And I'm so thankful I made this room soundproof. I decide that she's been aroused enough I climb up her body, position myself and slowly enter her. Her face twists into a silent moan as I stretch her inner area while my hardened member fully becomes sheathed inside.

I wait for a moment for her to adjust and start to slowly pump into her. I bury my head in her neck as I continue to pump myself into her.

"Oh, Hunter! Oh, crikey!" She starts to pant and writhe in ecstasy.

"Lucinda. I love you more than anything." I kiss her deeply with all the emotions that I'm feeling. "You've freed my soul," I tell her as I continue to move inside of her. I continue to move as she continually climbs her passionate high.

Reaching a peak that neither of us has ever had before, as she screams, I unload inside of her. My emotions feel like they are as high as a mountain slowly falling. I have not felt this alive in a long time. I knew deep in my heart that she would become special to me. However, I never imagined it would be this good, and she gave me the gift of fatherhood after waiting so long. She has given me my life back. And I cannot imagine anything better. I know what I am. I know that there will be dangers. My world is very hazardous. And I will do everything in my power to keep her hidden from it or fight whatever storms may come at us.

CHAPTER 15

It is a beautiful morning; I cannot contain the happiness I feel. Ever since the yacht cruise I shared with them. I feel as if I have developed a deeper relationship with Lucinda and Molly. Being with her, sharing every experience and every passionate moment with her, has awoken my long-dead heart. Her fierceness, her strength, her love call to my soul. I start to think of marriage again.

As I'm lost in thought, Molly walks toward me interrupting my reverie. "Hunter. I have been wondering something."

I turn toward her. "Yes, Molly, what is it?"

She looks at the ground shyly. I gaze at her, trying to compel her to continue.

Honestly, there is something very special about Molly. I don't know if it is the result of her taking some of my blood to heal her, no matter how small amount. But I cannot hear her thoughts. And none of my gifts work on her. She's like a psychological shield.

"I was wondering if you are ever going to marry my mom?"

I turn to her in shock, then compose myself before she notices. "Molly why would you say that? Has your mom been speaking of it?"

She becomes embarrassed. "No. It's just we all seem like a family. And I want us to be one."

I give her a hug. I'm speechless. "Molly. I think that is something your mother and I should discuss."

She looked very hopeful.

"Molly. I do want you to know between us that I do see you as my daughter. And I would love to marry your mother. However, she must have the same desire of me first."

Molly was in tears looking at me. She hugged me tighter. "I'm so happy to hear this. I hope that Mom has the same wish! Could I be your adopted child if she does not? You are like a father to me."

I feel so elated and happy. I felt the same way and already considered her a daughter. "Molly, nothing would make me happier."

She grew a big smile on her face. "I will go talk to her." I laugh as she scurries away.

I walk toward to front of the car to start it so we may leave. Suddenly, a figure appears from the corner of my eye, yards away, watching us. It happened so quick, and I was so preoccupied with the conversation I just had with Molly that I was not able to fully see who it was. Whoever it was, they were blindingly fast. All I saw was a fan of blond hair. I have no idea who it could be. Whoever it is is gone.

I shrug off the chilling feeling that I have traveling up my spine. I'm determined to enjoy this trip.

"So, I hear Molly is asking you to marry me?" Lucinda says as she steps through the mansion door.

I chuckle. Leave it to Molly to not beat around the bush. "Yes, she did mention something like that."

"What did you tell her?"

We are within inches of each other. "I told her that is a discussion for you and me to have. She's adamant about us becoming a family. She wants me to adopt her as my daughter."

Lucinda is slightly taken aback.

"I swear. I didn't encourage it."

She seems slightly relieved. "Hunter, I will admit. I love you. I know you love me. I also know your history with marriage, so I don't expect it. When someone has lost love like that, it's difficult to find it again. I would love to be family with you. You have been so good to Molly. You are the only father figure she's known. I do worry about your condition."

I sigh and embrace her. I'm so thankful she understands.

I care for her. She's a rare and amazing woman. I know what she means by my condition. We've just never told Molly. She doesn't need to learn about the supernatural world of vampires. I don't want her life to change. I look into Lucinda's eyes.

"I understand. Really, I do. And I know what you are saying. I don't want anything about my life or past to affect her." I take her into my arms and hold her until we hear Molly walk out the front door of the house.

"Are we ready to leave?" she says.

I turn to Lucinda smile, kiss her deeply.

Molly makes gagging noises as she climbs into the car. We drive down the road. Molly is chattering happily, talking about her schooling, her dreams, her future, and she reveals to us that she's applied to Cambridge University. She also shyly lets us in on a little secret.

"What do you mean you have met someone? Is it a college roommate?" Lucinda turns to look at her daughter.

Molly answers her mother. "No. I mean I have met someone I may be attractively interested in."

Lucinda stares in shock and I nearly slam the breaks. "Explain yourself!" we both say to her at the exact same time.

Molly sighs deeply before addressing our questions. "I met a young man last week while I was on the college tour with Barbara. We were sitting inside of the café at Cambridge when he walked in. He was so amazing, very good looking. He was from Scotland; his scent was amazing! I don't know if it was cologne. But it was mouthwatering—sandalwood and fresh mint. God, I wanted to embrace him!"

I stare at her dumbfounded. She's describing the man as a supernatural would, but she's human!

"Anyways. I met him. His name is David Lennox. He's amazing. A bit weird. But very sweet. And pleasant to associate with."

Lucinda is beside herself. "Just when were you going to tell me!" she huffed.

Molly rolled her eyes. "I just did. Anyways, I really hope that I can see him again. He said he'll be attending Cambridge for medical studies." We just stare at her and each other in shock.

I wonder when she was going to tell us this news. Right now is very sudden, and not a proper time to reveal this. I am concerned what her mother could do. Molly, that I know of, is not aware, but Lucinda is acting odd lately. Last week during Molly's achievements dinner, she blew into a fit of rage and abandoned us at the restaurant without saying why. I do not want Lucinda becoming unhinged with Molly right now.

"What do you mean by weird?" I ask her hesitantly.

She replies, "I don't know how to say it. I just thought I heard him mumble, 'Mate.' But I could be hearing things."

I look at her in the mirror. "Are you sure?"

She nods. "I might be hearing things. But at the same time, I heard an inner voice inside of my head say the same thing. And I felt like that same voice was singing for joy and dancing in my head." She sat back, looking confused and conflicted as to if she was trying to understand what was going on.

I stare at her in shock.

I whisper to her mother, "You wanted to guard her against my world. Well, I would start working extra harder at it because it's about to come closing in and this is not my doing."

Lucinda stares at me in shock. I lean toward her.

"Is there something that we don't know about her? Or is there something that you are not telling me?" I inquire with a hard look. Molly has to be part supernatural! No human has these reactions!

Lucinda turns her head away from me.

"Who is her father?" I ask.

Just then Lucinda's eyes are wide with worry and fear. She's never mentioned anything about him, which makes me question what she's hiding.

This revelation is not a good one. I'm starting to question, after five years of dating, how well I know my girlfriend. She never mentions Molly's father. She never mentions her own family. Does she have any? Where are they? Questions that I have considered before but never concentrated on start to make their way to the forefront of my mind.

I keep my thoughts to myself as I glance at her from the corner of my eye. She looks out the window, ignoring me, so I just continue heading toward our destination. A short time later, we arrived in the Highlands of Scotland. I'm looking forward to the weekend of camping with my two beauties. Thanks to Molly's new and unsettling information in the car, my mind is buzzing with questions I will need answers to. I now know that I'm not going to marry her unless we have no secrets. We need transparent honesty. She needs to share everything with me, just as I always have with her.

I park on the familiar path that I know. Lucinda and Molly exit the vehicle while I continue to think. I watch Molly from the front seat of the car as she walks off. She's grown into an elegant young woman. It is no wonder when we are out in the public eye. All the men watch her every move. As her supposed stepfather, it is difficult to watch. I want to protect her from the world. I want smash those gawking men to powder. But I don't want her to hate me.

I exit the car and follow the ladies into the woods to start setting up the camping gear. I love the smell of nature. This is also a perfect opportunity to later go hunting. I detest animal blood. However, it is far smarter than losing control in front of them. As my mind is thinking of this, Lucinda comes toward me. I embrace her and kiss her just as Molly skips my way. I know I need to talk to her in private. But it will be difficult right this second with Molly being so close.

"You ready, Dad?" Molly asks.

I look at Lucinda. She's staring into the trees. "Lucinda?" I call to her.

She looks at me. "Why did we come to the Highlands?" she asks me sharply.

I look at her bewilderment. "Where else would we go camping?" I ask her, and she shakes her head at my comment.

"Is there something wrong, darling?" I ask her as she keeps staring at the trees with a worried look on her face.

Suddenly, she turns to me with confused look. "Wrong? No, nothing." It's as if she's trying to keep a poker face on.

I say into her mind, *You do realize. I can see through the bullshit you are pulling? What are you hiding?*

She starts to walk forward into the forest. I want to ask her about it. I can smell her fear. I feel her heart beating a little harder. This tells me that she's not as composed as she pretends to be. As we continue to walk forward, I start to become anxious myself. I'm getting the feeling that we are being watched. I sniff the air; I sense the smell of the earth and something else. It smells like pine and sour eggs. This smell is revolting.

I continue walking. Committing this scent to memory. I approach the trees and start to look around myself, feeling anxious. I notice the girls have stopped in a clearing away from me. I head to join them. And we start setting up camp. Molly is so excited. I walk forward and wrap my arms around Lucinda. I start to kiss down her neck. I hear Molly making a gagging noise. When I raise my head, she walks away.

"What? I thought you wanted me to be with her?" I tease her.

"Just because. I'm fine with it. Doesn't mean I want to see it!" Molly snaps at me.

I chuckle and continue kissing her mother when I hear Molly groan, "Ahh!" and start to walk away.

I start to laugh. And Lucinda regains her senses, then elbows me in the side. "Hunter. Don't taunt my daughter!"

I look at her. "Molly declared me her stepfather, so she's also my daughter."

Lucinda leans back. "Don't I get a say?"

I smile. "Of course. But I thought the consent was implied considering she mentioned it to you a few weeks ago and you didn't shut her down or completely say no."

She stands there speechless. And I know that I have won as a huge grin spread across my face.

We go into the tent. And I distinctly hear a growl that makes me look around. I don't see anything, so I proceed with my desires. Once in the tent, I pull Lucinda into my arms. I start to kiss her neck. "Hunter," she breathes my name. "Molly could—"

I don't give her the chance to finish her thought as I claim her mouth with sweet kisses. Molly already is aware of what we could be doing. That's why she went inside her tent, to get away.

She smiles as I tell her this. She starts to kiss me back passionately. I start to unbutton her shirt as she undoes mine. My mouth falls to her breasts as cover them in sweet kisses. Lucinda is moaning in ecstasy. I lay her down after removing her skirt. She removes all of me, and I slide into her sweet heavenly center. Her head falls back in bliss. I raise her hands above her head and kiss her deeply. For the rest of the night, we make sweet music together. After a few rounds of hearing her soprano voice cry in carnal bliss, she falls asleep.

With the sky turned to darkness of night and the moon shining bright, I decide to go for a walk. All day, I have been feeling a presence here, and I want to confront it. As I head toward the woods, I see Molly's tent light is on. What is she doing awake? I walk over quietly and notice from inside the tent she's inspecting herself. Then I see it. Her eyes are shining brighter than they were this morning.

I'm very convinced that Molly is a hybrid of something, and she has no idea. She's only starting to realize.

Just as I'm pondering this, Molly notices me. "Dad?"

I walk forward. "Hello. I was just going to take a walk alone. I love the smell of the Highlands."

She nods her head and lowers her eyes.

"Molly what is the matter?"

She looks at me, broken, like she's trying to hold back tears. "I don't know what is happening to me. Every day. I feel different. I feel strange."

I sit by her. "Strange how?"

She shakes her head. "It is like there is a part of me that has been dormant or locked away for a long time is to break free. I'm scared. Will I be a freak? I don't know how to share this with Mom. Will she hate me?"

I pull her into my arms. I rock her back and forth as she lays her head on my shoulder. "Of course not. She's your mother. She loves you. Whatever this is is completely new."

She nods.

"Molly, I have known you a long time. I have always treated you as my own. I'm being honest. This is something I have noticed recently with you." I turn her head toward me. "Look at me. It is okay. Everyone is different, and it is okay to be different. You just need to figure out how to handle it. You're still you. Nothing will change that."

She quietly cries in my arms.

At this moment, I hear the growling again. I look up to see something standing by the trees in the darkness, eyes glowing at me. Whatever this is, it is huge and exchanging glances between me and a sobbing Molly. She lifts up her head. Her eyes glow purple in the moonlight. Its eyes lock on her with a shocking awareness. I hold her tighter and glare back it. I call out in my mind, *Whoever you are, stay away from my daughter!* It bares its teeth at me and disappears.

I knew I could feel it earlier. We are not alone. The need to protect my family now is very strong. I stayed awake all night while my family sleeps. I continue to watch the trees for any sign of our intruding visitor.

Morning comes, and I straighten myself up when I hear one of the tents open. Molly walks out of the tent; we exchange morning pleasantries. After the scenario last night, I want to make sure she's all right. Within a couple of hours, Lucinda wakes up, and we all spend time together. But there is something off with Lucinda. She is not herself. I feel a dark presence faintly near her. There is a powerful aura about her I have never felt before. As I ponder this, I feel someone's presence lurking in the trees again. Whoever it is has returned. I know I will soon find out who it is. Judging by Lucinda's reactions, the way her eyes keep on darting into the trees and denying that something is bothering her, she knows exactly what might be going on. And I don't know how to make her tell me without using my mental abilities.

I know, though, if she saw through that, she would hate me. I'm left waiting for her to open up. But with Lucinda, that could be never. As night falls, the girls start to prepare to retire into their tents to fall asleep. I, however, don't necessarily need sleep. I will rest with Lucinda. But sleep is not a necessity. During this time, I decide to go hunting. I'm frustrated lately with Lucinda, and I need to relieve tension.

This trip is revealing things to me about Lucinda that I really don't want to question. I may not let it show, but I'm growing dubious of Lucinda's behavior. I have seen things that I don't even voice to Molly. As a supernatural creature, as far as I'm certain, Molly doesn't know I'm vampire, so how I do I tell her that I have a strong sense her mother is possessed? I really feel it in my bones. There is something very off about Lucinda that I never mention. I do my best to act as if I'm unaware. However, I'm not clueless. Lucinda owns her own home about a twenty-minute drive from my small house in Liverpool but a ten-minute drive from our work in a quiet neighborhood almost outside of the city but close enough to still walk into town. The drive is a nice lane covered with trees. Every time I go near that area, I get a feeling of evil that chills me to the bone, as if nature itself is trying to escape its energy.

Two weeks ago, I drove by her house to see if she was home. I needed to speak with her. I had tried to call. But she was not answering. I drove toward the house. I decided to stop and park across the street. I was glad I did because what I saw was alarming. Lucinda was in her piano room, yet her behavior, the way she was acting, the way her lips were moving, was as if she was talking to someone. But there was no one in the room. I then saw her slap herself hard across the face. I saw her eyes go black as midnight for a second, then become normal again. When what happened, it's like I almost saw a shadow in front of her. I heard her hiss. I heard her shout, "Leave Hunter alone!" I eerily heard an evil cackle. I saw her acting as if she was fighting herself to keep from being choked, then she dropped to the floor.

Molly ran into the room to check on her right before the windows magically shut. I was bloody freaked out. I don't know how long this has been going on. But it is clear this only happens when I'm not around. I then understand why she becomes nervous with the idea of getting married. This could also widely explain her irrational behavior. I swear some days she's a sweet, loving mother. The next day, she's acting like a cruel, vindictive person. I need to speak with her father at some time about these mood swings of hers. As of right now, I play my role as the very-in-love boyfriend. However, I have determined I cannot trust her with my life. She's dangerous and psychotically unstable. I still love her. But if my theory is true, I'm starting to wonder what version of Lucinda I have really been with.

Everything is so mind boggling. If we are no longer together after this weekend, I will accept it and carry her with me with love in my heart. I just pray I don't lose Molly. I need distance and fresh air to think straight on where I should go from here. I drive to an area right outside of Glasgow, Scotland. All I smell is human, so I get into my hunting crouch and spend the next couple of hours satiating my thirst.

Once I'm finished hunting, I sneak into a store and find new clothes to appear better. I don't want to give them a heart attack finding me in my disheveled state. I'm entirely messy. I try my best to stay clean but still have stains on my collar. Luckily, I drove an hour away, and it takes at least thirty minutes for my eyes to return to their natural color, so the girls hopefully will not suspect anything.

When I arrive, it is already late at night. I still notice someone's presence. However, this time, it is different, stronger. I can feel a powerful aura lurking around in the shadows, and I have no doubt that it is the alpha. I have no idea who they are or what this alpha wolf wants. But I intend to call him out.

I stare into the shadows with an intense glare. "I don't know who you are. But we're merely trying to have a family weekend, and you prowl around us in the darkness of the forest! Come out and face me!"

Just as I'm losing my patience, I hear a voice. "Family camping! What a joke! You're a vampire! How do I know you're not planning anything?"

I growl into the darkness, and I slightly chuckle. "I can assure you now that no one here is planning anything except perhaps you. If you truly knew me, you wouldn't utter such nonsense. This is my girlfriend and her daughter, who I have loved for several years!"

The alpha growls when I say this.

I challenge him. "Instead of cowering in the shadows watching us like a creeper, come out and stand in front of me. Otherwise, get lost!"

I hear a growl at my words. I see a shadow move in the darkness as the alpha comes and stands before me.

Looking upon him, I recognize him from the tales I have heard. "Alpha Rydon. It is a pleasure to meet you."

At this moment, I hear a gasp from my tent. Lucinda has awoken. She has come out and stares directly at Rydon.

"Lucinda, my love did I wake you? I'm sorry," I try to apologize.

She continues to stare at Rydon. She is pale, as if she is seeing a ghost.

"Hunter, you're all right. I was awake." I hear the stutter of her heart. And I know she's lying.

"Lucinda, long time," Rydon says as he glowers at her.

I try to understand why he's so angry at her.

"Yes, long time no see."

I instantly make the connection when they both stop talking and glance at Molly's tent. Bloody hell! This is her father!

As I connected it, he speaks in a loathing voice. "So, when were you going to tell *me*!"

She pales. Molly asked her in years past about the identity of her father, and Lucinda blatantly ignores her.

"You're a fucking piece of work, Lucinda!" he roars. "You deliberately isolate her from me, then allowed her to be raised by this bloodsucker!" He snarls at me.

I'm in shock at the raging storm that is brewing right now between both of them. My mind is spinning. All my assumptions are being revealed. I never truly knew my girlfriend at all. She acted all sweet and innocent, yet it seems she has an evil siren hiding behind that beautiful face. As much as I'm starting to grow angry at her, I attempt to rein in my temper.

Lucinda yells, "You abandoned us before I found out I was pregnant. I don't give a shit if you met your mate. I deserved a proper goodbye." She growls at him. The way she's acting right now is completely selfish. If she went to bed with a werewolf, and she seems very informed about their society, she has no excuse. If she knows about his mate, it means she has met her. This means he may have tried to say farewell, and she instead banished him from her life. She banished him from Molly's life. What is worse is isolating her own daughter! My God, this means she knows exactly what her daughter is. She's purposely denying Molly the chance to be prepared for her transformation.

I interrupt her. "Does that make it right? For years, Molly has asked about her father, and you blatantly ignored her!"

Rydon looks at me incredulously. She's glaring balefully at me. And I know after this we might be finished. The thought is breaking me inside. But I need to say my peace.

"All you ever will do is look at her, then walk away without saying anything. It is her heritage. She's changing. You know she's part werewolf."

She's shaking her head, not wanting to hear me. "You're sheltering her. What happens when she shifts? How do you explain that to her?" I growl at her.

She glares at me. "Shut the fuck up, Hunter!"

We both look at her in shock.

"You're supposed to be on my side. You're turning on me!"

I cannot believe what I'm hearing. "How am I turning on you? By speaking the truth. You know she's more than human!"

She shakes her head. "No, she's human!" She's in complete denial.

Rydon is watching our interaction, and I can tell he agrees with me. I don't stop. I'm on a roll. "How do you explain the graduation then? When that bratty girl was picking on her, when she stood up to her, her aura was so strong. All the other humans and werewolf teens that were there nearly bowed to her!"

She shakes her head, and Rydon stares, stunned. I hear him whisper, "My daughter is an alpha female?"

"Yes!" I answer both. "You were there, Lucinda; you were shocked. And I was damn proud!"

She looks at me in disbelief. "How can you be proud of that?"

I chuckle. "Proud that our daughter is not only smart enough to be voted valedictorian but enough to defend herself and the other students that brat was humiliating? Yes. I'm damn proud!"

I hear Rydon growl at me. I turn to him. "I'm not denying that you have been wronged. But I will not deny the right for Molly to proclaim me her stepdad after all the years I have been here for her."

Lucinda chimes in. "She came up with that on her own!" she shouts at me.

I stare at her in disbelief. I cannot believe her words. "Are you going to deny me too? Do you forget how much I have helped you both? Your little baker shop developed into a bigger enterprise. I helped provide Molly with that treatment for when she was crippled!" I hear a sharp gasp from Rydon. "I helped pay for her to be in a better school. I just made arrangements for her to be accepted into Cambridge without being in the honors program because she couldn't tolerate those snobby kids. Tell me how I haven't earned it!"

I growl at her, "I have done everything that I could of for you both, so you had a good life!"

She pales at me as her eyes start to water, realizing everything that I'm telling her is the truth.

Rydon snarls at her, and he's shaking with fury. "What the fuck, Lucinda! This is what I mean! It should have been me! I should have been there for her! I admit I should have come to you and told you the truth. But you had no right to hide this from *me*!" His frame is starting to blur.

I stand in front of her. And this makes him spiral out of control. I snarl at him, "Don't you dare hurt her!"

His dark eyes glower at me. "You dare order me around! Leech!" Then he lunges toward me while shifting. I sidestep him, grab his tail, and throw him into the trees. He snarls back at me as he barrels into me, knocking me into the woods. I growl back at this wolf, its teeth inches from my face as I continue to hold it back.

The wolf turns to approach Lucinda. He's too angered to see reason not to hurt her for what she has done, the nearly eighteen years she has denied him his daughter. I throw myself in front of her again, protecting her just before he pounces. We fight face-to-face.

I'm doing my best trying to hold him back. I get him in a headlock and attempt to make him shift back without hurting him. Lucinda is near the tent on the ground, crying as she watches us fight over her. He finally shifts back to human form and glowers at her.

I'm standing still, watching to be sure he doesn't snap again.

"I want my daughter Lucinda! You didn't even consider that, since I'm a werewolf, she might be as well. How blind or heartless can you be?"

She's shaking and looking toward the ground.

I speak to her as well. "I love you. But haven't you hurt her enough?"

She glares at me. "I never hurt her!"

I shake my head. "You have denied her the right to even know her own family. She never knew anything about you. She met your dad for the first time last month!"

Rydon stares at her, flabbergasted that Lucina has kept Molly so hidden.

It is so cruel. At his moment, we all hear Molly talking in the tent. And I pray she didn't wake up.

Rydon stares at Lucinda. "I want to meet my daughter before you all leave here, or else, I will come to find her!" He shifts and jumps into the shadows, leaving Lucinda and me alone.

"Mom? Dad? What was that?" Molly asks.

I look at Lucinda and whisper, "Truth, or I dare you to lie to her again!" I walk away and leave them alone to talk.

I'm not sure if Lucinda is the true person for me anymore. I loved her so much, yet how can I trust her? The image of that day in front of her house replays in my mind. I continue to be baffled. Which Lucinda is the real one? If she's possessed, who or what is it that has taken hold of her? How long has she been captive? I'm terrified now for Molly's safety with her. Has she done anything to Molly when I'm not around her? Would Molly tell me? I feel as if I'm standing at a turning point in my life.

Should I walk away from her, or should I find a way to free her from this demonic hold? The magic too. I have a sense telling me that she's a witch. Yet I have never seen her practice anything in front of me or show me any inkling of power. I have limited experiences with witches. The last witch I encountered was the sinister coven I killed in America. That was so long ago. I have not met one since. I still have the feeling in my core to not trust her.

As I return from my run, I spot Rydon by the trees near Molly's tent. I look at him questioningly.

"Now that I know I have a daughter, my wolf is not letting me stay away anymore."

I nod. "I understand. I would be the same way."

He looks at me in surprise. "When I was human, I was married. We tried for so long to have a child. But each pregnancy turned into a failure and heartbreak for my Eliza as she watched the child go to heaven away from her each time." My voice is thick with past emotions.

Rydon stares at me with sorrow. "I'm so sorry, Hunter. I had no idea."

I shake my head. "It is not something I willingly talk about, so I do empathize. I know how it is being kept away from your child. What she did was cruel not only to you but your daughter as well."

Rydon holds back a growl while looking at Molly's tent.

I take the time to tell him about her. "Molly is a wonderful girl. She's sweet, kind, and she's strong. She stands up for herself and others around her." I glow with pride. "She thinks she might have found her mate on a college tour to Cambridge. She said he's going to be a student there as well. He is a werewolf too; I'm sure of it."

Rydon looks at me. "How can you tell?"

I tell about their interaction, how Molly called it weird, that they both whispered, "Mate," and the weird voice in her head that did a happy dance when it happened.

He smiles. "So, Molly has a wolf?" I nod. "I thought so as well. She reaches her eighteenth birthday next month. Her wolf will come out by then." He grins. "My daughter is about to shift!" Then he frowns. "I just don't know what to do. My pack hates humans and hybrids."

I stare him. This worries me. I warn him, "Do not do anything to hurt her."

He glares at me. "I will never do that." He doesn't see what I mean. "You don't understand. Her emotions are fragile right now. And I know she grows tired of her mother's antics." I continue. I need to know something. "I need to ask you; did you call a couple of weeks ago?"

He looks at me in shock. "No. I have had no contact with her in years. My warriors just reported that you were here, so I came to see who it was."

I nod. "The night Molly was nominated for high honors, she received a phone call. It really bothered Lucinda. She completely ignored us. She isolated herself in the restaurant bathroom."

His mouth drops open in shock, so I continue speaking

"It really hurt Molly's feelings. When Lucinda saw me comforting Molly, she abandoned us at the restaurant."

Rydon just stares at me with wide eyes. I hear Molly come out of the tent.

"Dad?"

Both Rydon and I look at her. I realize she's looking at me. Rydon tries to hide his pain. This tells me that Lucinda ignored the situation as usual.

I turn to her to find out. "Molly, when I left last night, did you and your mother talk?"

She shakes her head. We both growl. "I told her to talk to you."

Molly rolls her eyes. "You know Mom is not going to tell me anything important. Hell, I could sprout wings or turn into some werewolves like in the movies and she wouldn't tell me," she says trying to hide the tears.

Rydon and I both stare briefly in shock at her words. How dare Lucinda cause her this much pain. Rydon mouths to me as Molly looks away. I nod. I can see the anger in his eyes.

"Molly, what I wanted you both to talk about is your real father." She stares at me in shock. "Hunter? What do you know? You know I love you. But I have always wanted to know."

I hear Rydon choke on another growl. "Molly, this is your real father," I tell her as I point to Rydon.

Her hands fly to her mouth in shock.

"I apologize for us waking you last night. We were arguing." I still cannot believe Lucinda would be so cruel to those who love her.

Molly stares at him with us with a smile, and she looks at him with love shining in her eyes. "Could I have the chance to know you?" she asks Rydon. Her father smiles, teary-eyed, and nods.

I smile at her. I will not deny her. "Of course, you can. And Rydon is welcome as well so he can get to know you."

Rydon looks both in awe and content. "Molly, may I hug my daughter?" he asks as he embraces her.

She wraps her arms around him. And their embrace tightens like Molly doesn't want to let go. I smile at this sight, until I hear a scream from behind me.

"*No!*" I turn around to see Lucinda staring wide-eyed near the tent with a look of horror and rage. Before either of us can react, she throws out her hands. A powerful energy flows through the clearing, and Rydon is sent flying into the woods. Molly and I stand next to each other, stunned. Lucinda growls and runs into the woods. *Where would she go? At this hour in the morning, the woods are not safe for a human!* I instruct Molly to check on her father as I go in search of her mother,

I run in her direction. I look around. And I cannot find a trace of her. It is as if she vanished. How is this possible? Suddenly, I hear a shrilling scream and then dead silence. I notice that it is originating from higher up the mountain in the woods. I take off running again trying to search for her. I don't want to accept the growing dread I feel.

I search for hours without finding her. Her scent has mysteriously vanished, just like Garrett's did! God, please don't let anything happen to her. I continue to call out to her, hoping to find her.

CHAPTER 16

We have been searching for hours. Night falls. I still cannot find her. I'm feeling a pain in my heart. I pass through some bushes and find her strawberry-and-honey scent that is so captivating. I follow the trail her scent leaves behind. It's nearly faded. As I catch her scent, I have to work hard to keep my monster at bay. He writhes near the surface, yearning to be released. Her scent sends it into a frenzy of lust and blood. It stirs my loins. It makes venom flow to my mouth. And my fangs immediately spring into appearance. I use all my strength to control my body.

The monster whispers in my mind. *If anyone hurt our plaything, tear them apart,* it growls. This, I can agree on. I love her and don't agree with its twisted desire toward her. But I will kill anyone who dares to hurt her. Oddly, I don't catch any other scents except for the normal smells of the forest and animals.

I have been searching for hours. As I pass a patch of woods, I pick up Molly's scent somewhere. Damn it! This means she didn't listen and is wandering around here searching for her mother. I hope that I'm wrong. I don't need both of them harmed.

I searched all night long. And now dawn is beginning to break. I can see the sun behind the clouds trying to cast its rays over the horizon. Humans believe that vampires burn in the sun—this is myth. We do lose some strength in full, direct sunlight. Our physical strength is weakened briefly unless we feed. It feels like the sun rays steal a bit of our energy without leaving us destitute. So, right now, I'm running. But I feel my energy slack, almost as if I were turning human. Regardless, I continue to push myself faster as best as I can.

The sun climbs up the mountain. My theory is it could be around eight in the morning.

I look toward the sky, and I notice birds circling overhead as if there is carrion lying on the ground somewhere. I get a sick feeling in my gut as I breathe in the stench of death and the scent of stale human blood that has, no doubt, soaked the ground. I race toward it with the sickest sinister feeling in my gut.

I snarl at the birds that cover the carcass that's been thrown into a hole. I look inside and let out a gut-wrenching wail. If I were a human, I would have thrown up at the sight. I jump inside the hole, which appears to be an ancient spring well. I see Lucinda's grotesque body. Something or someone threw her into the hole but not before ripping her throat out and clawing her chest apart. I pull her out of the well and hold her to me as I scream in agony.

Someone is going to fucking die. The vampiric beast inside me wants to burn the world down. Someone killed the woman I love—yet again! This time, it is almost impossible to know. As I walk into the camp, I see Molly coming out of the tent. She looks at me and starts screaming as I lay the ravaged body of her mother on the ground. She runs toward her, picks her up. She starts rocking back and forth as the tears begin to flow. I let her scream her lungs out in grief. I hold her as she holds Lucinda. And we both cry in pain at the loss of Molly's mother, I hear someone approaching and a shocked gasp. I look to see Rydon staring at us.

His face twists in shock and agony, staring at Lucinda's shredded body as he falls to his knees. I growl at him and ask, "Did you have anything to do with this?"

He looks at me incredulously. Molly stares at him, hoping it is not true. "What! How dare you! I would never do this to her or to Molly. We wolves protect human life."

I don't buy it. He tried to attack her out of anger. How do I know he didn't plan it and send one of his warriors? "Bullshit! The night before she disappeared during our argument, you became enraged and nearly attacked her. You could have ordered it done."

Rydon glowers at me. "Fuck you, Hunter!" he spits at me as I growl at him. "I admit I lost my head. But that doesn't mean that I would kill the mother of my child," he says in disgust.

I continue to growl. I don't buy it. He has a hot temper. I don't believe that he didn't want to terminate her to satisfy revenge. He tries to move closer.

"Do not touch her!" I snarl at him.

"Or what!" he snarls as he shoves me.

I shove him back. Before we know what's happening, we are exchanging blows. He shifts into his wolf, and I bounce back. I stand in front of Molly and Lucinda's bodies right before he barrels into them.

I knock him into a rock, and he realizes what almost happened and starts to whimper. I turn to Rydon. "This is over. Until I find out who killed Lucinda, stay the fuck away from us."

The alpha wolf runs into the woods and comes back in human form, viciously glaring at me. "You're not keeping me from my daughter, your filthy parasite. I'm her real father. I make the calls here, not you, bloodsucker!" he screams at me.

I smirk then launch an uppercut at him at full force. This knocks him into a tree. He lands face first on the ground unconscious. "Filthy mutt!" I snarl. I quickly pick up Molly, who is shaking like a leaf, sobbing, and pulling at her hair, muttering words I can't understand. I place her in the back seat of my car.

I race back to the campsite and pack everything up. I cannot wait to get away from here. I wrap Lucinda's body in a sleeping bag and place her in the trunk. I jump in the car. As I take off, I hear howls and see wolves barreling toward my car. I push my car to full speed as I drive away, leaving the north woods, which will be my new mental nightmare.

This was supposed to be a happy family camping trip before Molly left for college. How in the fuck did everything go so wrong? How am driving away with only one half of my heart still breathing in the car while the other half lies cold and lifeless in the trunk of my car? I let the sobs rip through my chest as I drive Molly and me back to Liverpool.

This pain is not as intense as the first time I lost love. But agony still shreds through me. I peer through the mirror and observe my daughter in the back asleep. Tears pour down her face even during her dreams, and soft whimpers echo in the car. Having Molly here with me is a big comfort. Lucinda may be gone, but she left a child behind for me to love and protect. This knowledge is what will keep me going. I'm now all she has left. And I need to protect her.

CHAPTER 17

The next week is the longest of my existence. Molly and I endure the long drive back to Liverpool in grief-stricken silence. Neither of us talks about what happened. The tension and bitter emotions in the car are suffocating. Somehow, what started as a family camping trip turned into tragedy. I rack my brain trying to understand what happened and who is responsible. We stop at a service station to fill up on gas. I make my way inside to buy some chocolate for Molly. She cried her eyes dry and she slept during the drive.

I know how it is to lose a parent. Nothing except time dulls the pain. I'm grateful to be here with her. No one should suffer it alone. Over the next few weeks, we contact more family. I inform the bakery of her passing. Surprisingly, no one in the business wants to attend. I never realized that none of them liked her. I talk to her assistant manager. She informs me that Lucinda's behavior was at times erratic. She would switch from sweet to sadistic. She terrified the employees.

"I swear. It was like she was possessed," she tells me. Understanding her feelings, I don't blame her.

I arrange Lucinda's funeral and make all the necessary reservations. I'm happy when her entire family decides to attend. I know that Molly is comforted. Shortly after the burial, I close Lucinda's house. I decide to move Molly into my house so she's not alone. Since I became co-owner of the bakery shop, I sold it. I'm not planning to come back. I inform them all that, once all the services are taken care of, I will be selling the business. It was something that I did for her. I have no interest in a bakery. To ease their minds, I say that I will pass it to someone who keeps the staff.

The following month, she moves into Cambridge University and starts her academic career. I believed that she would become a nurse. However, she surprises me by choosing journalism. I decide later, after her birthday, that I will return to Chicago, Illinois, in America.

As Molly is officially an adult and living on her own, starting to live with her mate, she doesn't need a parental figure hovering. I use a bit of the funds from her mother's house to buy her a condo near campus if she chooses to use it. The rest of the money pays for her tuition. I use some of my wealth to donate some funds and I build a bookstore on campus in her name. She's not thrilled about that; she doesn't like to appear as a spoiled rich kid.

I'm not taking it back, even if I could. One month later, it's her birthday celebration. I throw her a lavish coming-of-age party, surprising her by inviting her favorite band, the Beatles, to play a small concert. She's over-the-moon happy. I invite all her college friends. I can't locate her college sweetheart much to her disappointment. The party is rocking, and it is sure to be talked about for years to come.

As the night grows later, the night turns into a fiasco on its own. It's the moment as a father I didn't want to face. Molly's body starts to pass from the realm of humanity into the supernatural. She's having the time of her life during the concert until she tells me she feels scalding hot and lets out a guttural scream.

I immediately send everyone home and drive her as fast as possible to her grandfather's house in the Scotland Mountains near Glasgow. I learned that her grandfather lives on the outskirts of a werewolf community and is friends with the pack. He informs the alpha of his granddaughter. She's shifting with no one to help her. The pack comes out and welcomes her. The son, whose name is Calen, stares at her like he cannot stay away from her. Interesting.

Before her shift, her grandfather comes to talk to me. "I know how you feel, Hunter. But this night is important. We have to contact Rydon."

I look at him incredulously.

"Hunter, I'm aware of Rydon. I didn't realize he was her father until you mentioned it. I know that he's a conceited asshole. Alpha Bryson cannot stand him either. However, he's her father."

I speak quietly. "I know it is. I just don't want her harmed; we have not found Lucinda's killer."

He sighs. "I know. But I feel it in my gut. It is not him. He used to love her. He claimed her as his chosen mate. He wouldn't kill her."

I stand there and gasp. "I thought they just had a fling."

Molly's grandfather shakes his head. "No. I learned that because he was rogue, he thought he wouldn't find a destined mate, so he claimed her. That is what makes their breakup so much harder."

I want to believe him. But I still don't trust Rydon. Either way, I'm left with no choice but to call him or find her mate to be with her. No matter what, I know I will have to call him. He's her natural father. He deserves to be there. My anger rises through the roof, needing to connect with that fucker.

Most of the night, she's shaking and hot with fever. Her skin is luminous in the moonlight, and her eyes glow like the moon. Alpha Bryson lays her in a clearing in the woods. Calen comes over to make sure she is comfortable; he's whispering encouragement into her ear. I get concerned when I hear him growl and hover over her. But that moment is not the time to start anything.

I walk into the house and call her dad. "Richard, I never thought I would hear from you," I hear Rydon say.

I bite back a growl. "Rydon." There is silence on the phone.

"What the fuck do you want parasite?"

I chuckle. "In case you don't know what day it is, come to Richard's house. Molly will be waiting."

I'm just about to hang up when I hear him speak. "Where is she?"

I respond, "She's in the woods under the moonlight. Alpha Bryson and his son Callan are with her."

He growls at me. "What the fuck is going on?"

I shake my head and scoff. "If I knew where her mate was, I would call him to come instead, but unless you want to miss this night when she passes into the supernatural world, I mean, as of today, she's eighteen," I taunt him.

"Fuck!" is all I hear then the line goes dead.

I walk into the woods to be there with her this night. Within about a half an hour, Rydon is walking into the woods. Bryson and his son bare their teeth at Rydon. He rolls his eyes and ignores them. He walks over to her. Molly whimpers and cries quietly in pain. Her back is arching in a sick manner. It looks twisted as if something is bending it and sawing it in half.

I hear him tell her, "Molly, I know it hurts but don't fight it. The pain will only increase. Once you are through this, it will never hurt again."

She lets out a painful moan and a scream.

The moon shines bright in the sky. Her eyes snap open. And something incredible happens. Molly starts to nearly float; she's being surrounded by a strong aura, and her skin is illuminating with a purple glow. Her eyes shine with a purple fire. I'm not fully familiar with werewolf shifting. But judging by the shocked looks on everyone's faces, this is not normal.

Her mouth opens in silent scream. Suddenly, we watch her body being covered in a glowing purple ball of energy. It is like watching her being wrapped in a purple energetic bubble. Her eyes, her body, and her hair all glow with this blinding light. Then her body starts to shift and bend in disturbing ways. Fur starts to sprout from her skin. The light shines brighter, causing us to shield our eyes. Once it is gone, she's lowered back to the earth. Where once Molly stood, a beautiful white wolf with lavender eyes now stands.

We stand here in the forest in awe at the spectacular sight of my stepdaughter. We carefully approach her; she stares at us as if she's unsure of what to do. She looks at me. She lowers her head. Molly starts walking toward me with a whine. And I wrap my arms around her.

"You're so beautiful, darling! I'm so proud of you. Welcome to our world," I whisper to her with love. I step back and let everyone have their moment to welcome her.

About thirty minutes pass. Both Alphas present help her to shift back. This time, Molly's transition seems to be normal. When she's human again, she lies on the forest floor, screaming, naked, and embarrassed. Her grandfather runs to his house to retrieve a blanket to cover her. He lays the blanket on her; he informs us that she has fallen asleep.

I pick her up and carry her inside the house. I inform him that I'm going to leave her with him to rest. We all agree she should stay in this area now that she has shifted. She needs to learn more about herself, her new identity, and discover pack life. I call the university and cover her tuition for the next four years. I inform that that there has been a death in the family and she will start school the following year when she's ready. They agree and give their condolences.

I head back to my house. The following day, Alpha Bryson calls me and informs me that she's doing well. She was upset I was not there. However, her grandfather talked to about what we discussed. She's sad not to see me anymore. But she accepts our advice. I'm happy about that. While I'm in America, she will be safe. It's her time to lead her own life.

Alpha also informs me that he was able to locate her mate, David. He was informed about her transition and immediately arrived at the house to be with her. I'm pleased by this; she will always have someone with her and somewhere to call home. He thanks me for being in her life and everything that I have done to help her to this day. We both wish that she could have been more prepared. And silently, I curse Lucinda for the damage she nearly did. That is now in the past, and Molly has an amazing future ahead of her.

I make the call to Chicago that I have not done in years. "Charlie?"

I hear a gasp on the other side. "Holy shit! Hunter!"

I laugh and greet my old friend. We talk for several hours; I inform him that I'm finally coming back. He is ecstatic to hear my announcement. I'm very grateful for all his hard work. He has been updating me over the years about the company's progress. I cannot wait to return to Chicago and resume working at my company.

I walk out of the door and close the house, knowing that I will never return here again. I will ask Charles to put it on the market for me. I have a condo I bought near Cambridge when I visit Molly. My time in Liverpool has been amazing. But I feel it is done. I walk out the door. I start to feel that tingling sensation again of being watched. I ignore the feeling; I cannot let myself become paranoid. It is a beautiful September day, and many humans are out being active. I arrive at the airport, entering the plane to endure the flight back to Chicago.

Once I arrive, I smile at the sight before me, as my old friend Charles greets me. It is amazing to consider how much time has flown by. I left Chicago for England in 1940. Here I am, arriving back during the 1970s. Everything has changed. There is a new feel to this city. It feels liberated; everything seems different. A new energy is in the air. We are driving toward my house; Charles is showing me around.

As we move along, I decide to eventually buy a condo or penthouse somewhere in the city close to the office. I have missed this city; I have missed watching the Cubs play ball. I hear the music from the amphitheater playing. Liberace is very talented. And I have missed hearing his music. Navy Pier is roaring with life. People are on the shores of Lake Michigan enjoying different human activities. I rest my head back. Content to finally be home.

Charles is chatting nonstop, catching me up on everything that has happened in the human world in America. I look at the movie house, and a new movie called *Star Wars* is playing. There's a line of people in front of the theater all the way down the street. We turn on to my old street and arrive at my riverside mansion. I exit the car and walk into my house that I have not seen in so long. Everything has remained exactly how I left it. Damn, it feels good to be back.

CHAPTER 18

Thirty Years Later

It is incredible to think that today is the thirtieth anniversary of Lucinda's death. The year is 2008. I sit in my in-home office with a glass of cognac, reflecting on the memories of my life, the twists, turns, and dark roads that life has taken me on. My biggest pride is Molly's success in life. I'm so proud of her accomplishments and the career that she worked hard for. I recently offered her the opportunity to work in my publishing agency as an executive if she decides to step away from the *Sun* newspaper in London.

She used to come to stay with me during the summers. Unfortunately, her mates are prejudiced. They have never accepted me and didn't like her being overseas by herself. They would come when they were available. The idea of having a vampire stepfather didn't thrill them. I don't give a fuck; I'm not giving up my daughter.

I get up from my desk. I cannot continue reflecting on the past. I read over the letter from the coven again.

Dear Master Eldridge,

We are pleased to offer an invitation to the North American Coven. We have hear about numerous things you have done in the past century. Your decimation in Canada of the tyrannical witches' kingdom has not gone unnoticed by our body of representatives.

Rather we have seen such heroic efforts as a liberation of vampiric kind against the evils of our adversaries. You are hereby invited to the coven. We need someone with ruthless aggression at our leadership table. We feel you are the best candidate.

We await your response.

Sincerely,
Coven Ambassador
Theodore Cumberland

Yeah, that was a fun moment when I visited those pansies with Victor. I enjoyed introducing him. And I enjoyed watching them squirm. I don't give a shit if they hate me because I continue to grow in power. After I absorbed Minerva's magic, I noticed that it never quite left me. Instead, it increased what power I already had. I have tried my best to adjust to it over the years and also not use it unless I have to.

I pore over the letter. I realize I need to see them; I have put off this letter for years. I have never been interested in them or their council. I have never been interested in becoming the vampire king. However, in the last three decades, I have seen a rise in devastation. I have been an abiding citizen. I have made reports and watched them do nothing concerning them. Long ago after Lucinda died, a year after I returned to America, I started to investigate her death. I discovered it was vampires at fault. I learned the council was made aware of their actions. Someone had informed them as a threat against me. And they did nothing. The council told the anonymous caller, "Do what you want. Do not waste our time."

I remember I broke my desk when I learned that. I was so furious. They were warned about a threat aimed at me and brushed it off. They continue to brush it off. Death tolls are on the rise. Brazen vampire killings are all over the human papers. Thankfully, the humans are labeling them animal attacks. However, this rising storm risks exposure of the supernatural world. The council just sits by and lets it happen. I cannot understand why unless they are in league with the individuals who are creating the havoc. This council needs to be purged. These lazy schmucks need to end.

I need to claim the title that is rightfully mine and clear out the trash that is the council. I walk out the door of my penthouse and step into the elevator. If I leave now, I will be thirty minutes early to the office before the associates arrive. I love getting there early and keeping them on their toes. I step outside of my building and glance at someone who I never thought I would see again after he mated with a good female vampire years ago. I stare in shock.

"Victor!"

He smiles. "Long time, sir."

I shake his hand and give him a quick embrace.

"Do you still have any service for me, Master Eldridge?"

I smile with a gleam. God, I have missed my friend. "Welcome back, Mr. Nelson," I say to him as we walk down the street.

It feels like it has been forever since I have seen my old friend Victor Nelson. Seeing him show up in front of the building where my penthouse is located was a true delight. We embrace each other and took a stroll along the beachfront of Lake Michigan in Chicago by Navy Pier. It's amazing to catch up with him since he has been absent from my life for so many years. I inquire how his mate is doing, where he is in life now.

I am pleased to learn that he and his mate are very happy together. She helped him redirect his life, and he became a lawyer. I invite him to join my legal team and be my official legal adviser, if he'll accept it.

Later that night, we enjoy ourselves like old times. We travel out of the city and paint red each town we happened across while satiating our thirsts. After hours of hunting, I don't even realize that I'm once again in the clearing of anguish from so many years ago. Garrett's cabin is still there, a bit weathered by nature but still capable of being used. We decide to rest there while we clean up. During the night, I regale him with the tale of my years after our parting—the love I found in Lucinda, her daughter, my joy at being a stepfather and raising her, Lucinda's heartbreaking demise.

The following year, Molly went on to college at Cambridge University to study journalism. Her life after her eighteenth birthday was never the same again. Transitioning into the supernatural world is a daunting task. However, I'm proud that she handled it gracefully. She excelled in life, fell in love, proved to be an amazing woman, far better than her mother.

Honestly, reliving that, I realize that I didn't truly have Lucinda's heart. It hurt when I realized it. But I don't think any man would have truly held her heart. She was more self-centered and treacherous than she ever showed herself to be. In the end, her true colors came out to me and her daughter. She truly hated supernatural beings and had hoped that, by isolating Molly from the magical world, her magical blood would stay dormant. It was my presence that turned the tide and started to awaken everything.

I honestly have no regrets. I set Molly free. I share everything with Victor, and he silently listens.

"Wow, Hunter, life surely has been a roller-coaster for you! Honestly, how did you fall for a human in the first place! Wasn't that difficult?" Victor asks me.

I sit on the sofa as I tell him everything. "It was. She was beautiful and so different from Eliza. I thought in the beginning that she was my true soulmate. Everything seemed to click with us. When I realized that she had a half-blood daughter. I was shocked and interested more. If I had known in the beginning her true colors. I don't know."

I reflect on his question and tell him everything about Molly. Victor nods.

"I love being Molly's stepfather." I think that is the part I would never change.

Victor smiles at me. "That's awesome, man. I know it is something you craved. Even as a human." I'm so encouraged by a friend like him.

We sit there for a while before we return to the city. During the drive, he tells me more about his beloved and everything that has happened in their lives over the years. He then gives me an invite to his wedding, which I'm honored to attend. Once we are back in Chicago, we exchange cell phone numbers to stay connected, then part ways. I return to my penthouse and change into my usual attire for the office.

I drive my Aston Martin to the office building, and I'm not surprised by the looks that I receive. Every human girl who works for me has her imaginary version of me in her head. I have blocked out the erotic images from my mind over the years so I don't slaughter my employees. As I head to the VIP elevators, I hear some of them discuss me. They think they are out of range of my hearing.

I turn around and gaze at them sternly. "Unless you want to find yourself unemployed. I suggest you stop dilly dallying, gossiping, and foolish daydreaming about your superiors. Do your jobs. I don't tolerate laziness."

They stare shocked for a fraction of a second before scurrying off to their assigned tasks.

Once inside my office, my personal assistant, Allison Tomes, meets me and goes over the weekly schedule and the daily tasks on the agenda—a meeting in two hours, plus three more afterward, and a needed visit to an Eldridge Books store that is falling behind in business before the end of the day. My stores and businesses have always thrived, so I need to see what the issue is. I'm worried about what I will learn. They better not be doing anything shady.

The first meeting takes hours to finish. A new upcoming author is looking to join our publishing house. I'm more than excited to work with him. His manager is a pain in my ass. During the entire meeting, I imagine throwing him through the brick walls of this office. It wouldn't hurt him much. After thirty minutes, or what felt like hours of reasoning with him about the contract, he finally accepts our policies. Thank God, he doesn't know I'm a vampire. If he knew I compelled him, that wouldn't bode well.

After hours of meetings and dealing with irritating humans who don't want to cooperate, I finally am out the door and heading to the bookstore that's falling behind on sales. I start to drive there. I flip on my radio and listen to my rock music. This music soothes my long-lost soul. I arrive at the place and intend to speak to the manager. As I walk through the doors, certain things are evident. The staff are lazy and untidy. I see two people in company uniforms, lounging and not working. I see books behind the counter that need attending to.

I'm about to go inside when I hear the door ping. A customer walks in. The girl on the sofa gets up rolls her eyes and goes to greet the customer. I'm beyond pissed. The staff doesn't even greet me or know their boss is here. I walk into the office and look at the man. I'm so pissed off that I could slaughter him where he stands.

He notices my presence, and he pales. "Mr. Eldridge!"

I stare at him. "Mr. Murphy, you were informed of my arrival, were you not?"

He shakes. "Yes, sir. Just with the late hour, I didn't think you would arrive until tomorrow."

I place my hands on his desk. "So, you thought that you could slack off?"

He stammers, "S-s-sir? Wh-what do you mean?"

I look around. "When I arrived, the front-end employees were not only sitting around. But were rude to customers who came into the business. No one is doing anything. there is a girl in the breakroom who might be on break. If she's the only one doing actual work here in this store. I may as well put her in charge with how much you are slacking off."

He pales again and starts to shake more. "Mr. Eldridge, Amanda doesn't have the qualifications for my position!"

I glare at him. "Regardless of whether I promote her, I have seen enough. As of today, you are released from my company." I hear him start to start to sob, and I leave the room.

As I walk out the door, I text Allison to get me all the information she has on Amanda Williams. I see the customer leave, looking irritated, saying, "Can't get any fucking helping in this fucking store, lazy assholes."

I turn to the two loafers on the sofa. They stare at me with confused looks. "You're fired!"

They pale, realizing who I am. I hear them say in unison, "Shit!"

If you had done your job, you wouldn't be fired, I think. I'm so irritated at their behavior. I quickly drive away before I turn everything in the store red with blood.

While on my drive. I stop at a Starbucks coffee shop. I order a cold-brew coffee with cream and sugar. I'm just passing the train terminal when I notice I have a voicemail. It is the dean of a university in Portland. They want me to be a guest lecturer in the English literature department. As I listen, I'm assaulted with that intoxicating scent again! It's the same scent I smelled a week ago as I was driving out of my underground parking garage. It stirs my loins and drives my blood lust wild.

I look around, desperate to find this person. This is the second time. I have smelled her previously and not found her. I continue to search for this mysterious lady. I'm desperate to find her, so I can put a face with the smell and all the emotions she's triggering in me, emotions that I that were long lost. This person triggers feelings I have not felt since my wife.

I just walk into the center square in Evanston where the train terminal is. There, I notice a beautiful woman with long, blond, curly hair. God, she looks like Eliza. She's just boarding the train. As I start to move forward at ridiculous human speed, the scent gets stronger. I'm on the platform when the train just leaves. I stare at her, and she stares back in shock. Something flickers in her eyes like she recognizes me. But it's only for a second. I notice she's wearing a Linfield University hoodie. How ironic. I was just listening to a voicemail from Linfield University's dean.

My dear, you don't realize it yet, but you can no longer hide your delicious self. I'm coming for you, I think and smile, watching her figure disappear as the train continues to move out of sight. *Portland just got a whole lot more interesting*, I think as I make my way back toward my car. I drive myself home to riverside. After arriving, I check my mail from the postman. I notice a letter with a rich insignia on it. I know this didn't arrive by human mail.

I retrieve my letters from the mailbox and close myself inside the house. I pull the shades so no one can snoop. I rip open the letter. It is just as I feared—another letter from the coven council, which is in New York State. I groan. I have been giving them to silent treatment. I really am not interested in them. However, I feel they are forcing my hand.

I cannot just sit by anymore and watch the desolation of thousands of human lives, not just in America but throughout the world. Charles, Marcus, and I have reported it on several occasions, yet we've been told to wait for assistance. If things don't stop, the supreme vampire council, the ones who have been functioning for close to a thousand years in Europe, will step in.

I know what I must do. I have put this off for far too long. I cannot delay meeting them any longer. I dread meeting with them, but their lack of effort to eradicate the situation is becoming a constant strain. They continue to send letters to me about arranging a meeting. I know that they hate me; the feelings are mutual. I know one thing, though. If I'm going live my life how I want to, if I'm going to find that sexy minx and eventually be with her, I need to take the mantle of vampire king that is rightfully mine.

CHAPTER 19

I sit with Charles in my private jet. I'm filled with boiling rage as he tells me shocking news. He learned that some of the delegates went overseas a few hundred years ago and confiscated my family's ancestral throne. It belonged to that twisted ancestor of mine. I have no interest in Abner. However, I cannot help but feel robbed on behalf of my family. Charles and Markus, my other companion, both feel I should take up the mantle as king. Markus is a good friend I met a in 1933.

I was in California. I had followed a false lead in my search for Bathilda. I was thirsty and went hunting. I found a place called Thirsty Souls. It was a night club in San Francisco. I was enjoying a drink at the bar. I met him and we immediately clicked like lost brothers. He had a stunning redhead on his arm. After talking for several minutes, he took her upstairs. And a couple hours later, he came back alone. We bonded, talking the rest of the night. In 1990, I reconnected with him when I opened an Eldridge Books store in Los Angeles. He is my store manager. Now, he will be my right-hand man when I reestablish new order on the council.

I'm considering their advice. Claiming the throne is no small feat. I will not be a sadistic king. I will work to unite all species and coexist with humanity. There are ways we can quietly coexist together. However, before I figure out anything involving politics, I need to handle the council first.

The flight feels like it lasts for hours before the plane finally lands. I am relieved to be exiting the plane. As soon as I am outside, I locate my car. I'm very thankful to Mrs. Tomes for arranging for my driver, William, to meet me at my location.

"Hello, Mr. Eldridge," he greets me with a professional smile.

"Hello, Will, how is the family?" I ask him as I place myself in the back seat. He informs me during the drive of their well-being. He tells me that his son just graduated from Yale with honors. I wish his son well and pray he finds a successful career.

As I exit the car, I give him five hundred in cash as congratulations for his son after I remove my luggage. Shocked, with a smile, he thanks me and drives away. I head to the concierge desk. The woman behind the desk is blatantly ignoring me while talking on the phone in what appears to be a personal call. I think right there if I should invest in buying this whole to hire acceptable people.

I clear my throat. "Ahem. Excuse me, Miss." I speak loudly even when I shouldn't.

She rolls her eyes, puts the phone down, and turns toward me. Now, that she has seen me, she's eyeing me like candy, ugh! Despicable human!

"Miss, you should be tending to your job, not on the phone and eyeing me like a piece of candy! Where is your employer?"

She scoffs. "Yeah. And who are you?" she sneers.

I'm done with her attitude. "I'm not tolerating your attitude. Direct me to a manager before I buy this hotel and fire you!" She pales and calls for a manager. I have been booking at this hotel for years. I will not tolerate such disrespect.

The manager walks in, recognizing me as an esteemed patron, with stock in the company. Immediately greets me with respect. "Good evening, Mr. Eldridge," he addresses me while shaking my hand.

"Good evening Mr. Richter," I greet him in return.

The manager studies the situation. "What seems to be the distress?" he asks. Mr. Richter is originally from the fae realm. His mythical name is Fenrilol and has been working here with this company for decades.

He understands what I am and why I come to this specific hotel. Honestly, if humans knew how many mythical creatures interacted with them every day in disguise, they would freak out.

"I will inform you that this woman right here was extremely rude to me. I have been coming to this hotel for quite some time as you know, yet I will not abide such insolence. She purposely ignored me while I came to check in to take a personal call. Then when I attracted her attention, she began undressing me with her eyes. Is this the type of person you are employing now?"

He stiffens and sends her a cold glare. "Brittany! What do you have to say for yourself?"

She glares at me, flips her hair, and insists that I'm lying.

I insist she's fired. And I do arrange to buy the hotel on a whim to make sure that employees like her are not employed in the company. Fenrilol begins to object. He speak to me telepathically. He reminds me that the fae Countess Merilia owns the hotel in this region. He tells me that most humans don't realize that there is a tree in the woods on the border of the hotel that is a portal to Pendaria, which is the fae realm.

I decide to rescind my offer. I didn't realize how valuable to his species this was. I don't want to damage our friendship or start a war with the fae. I wouldn't survive that one. The fae are the oldest supernatural creatures in the world, second oldest to elves. Fae and elves are the original keepers of magic.

We resolve the dispute by terminating her job. Apparently, this is not her first warning. We shake hands, and I head to my room to freshen up. As I'm passing the reception desk, I ignore the glare from the rude woman. I feel her anger burning a gaze into my back. I stop at the elevators to wait. I turn my head as I see her step away from the podium, dialing a number with a devious look on her face. I step into the elevator. However, I let the doors close without moving an inch. I listen to her. She seems suspicious.

"Hello Lord Dennilworth?" I hear her say. There is a short pause. "It is him, Hunter Eldridge. He is in the hotel." I hear a growl and retort on the phone from a council leader. "Yes sir. I will, sir," she says as the phone call ends.

I click the fifth floor for my suite. I need to be on my guard now. She's a human working for the council. I have no idea what is going to happen next.

It has been an hour. I'm waiting. Inside my room, I'm taking a shower when I hear my door creak open. I know this is not my colleagues. One of them would have called. I shut off the water and hide in the room. I inhale deeply and notice the scent of chamomile with vanilla. I peek in the room. There is an attractive woman lying on my bed. She has hazel eyes with dark brunette hair that has a red hue to it. She's wearing a silver sequined dress that stops two inches above her knees. It is clearly designed to show off her long stunning legs. I examine her, and I can tell that she's a vampire.

Great, the council sent me one of their succubi to deter my visit, I think.

I walk into the room; she smiles and slightly spreads her legs on the bed. Bloody hell, she's also not wearing any panties. That is just gross!

"Master Eldridge?" she purrs. I nod as she crawls over toward me. "I heard you were in the area. Let me take care of you," she says.

I play along as she starts to kiss down my neck. I growl. She thinks it is in approval so her hands start to explore more of me. I shove her on the floor hard. She climbs back on to the bed and spreads her legs wider, toying with herself. *God, what do they give these females to make them this crazy?*

She tries to grab me. But I block her hands. "Listen here, Miss. I'm not reciprocating! I have no interest in sleeping with you!" I tell her.

She gets this crazed smile and look in her eye. Quicker than I expected, she swings a dagger.

Where the hell was she keeping that? I think briefly. I dodge her attacks as she tries to swing at me again. I punch her in the gut, and she falls to the floor, laughing.

"Lord Timbrel said you were strong and hard to kill," she chuckles.

I see red and grab her by her throat.

"Leave now, Hunter. You are not welcome here, or face their wrath," she says as she kicks me in the tenders. I double over in pain. Doesn't matter if I'm immortal. It still hurts like hell. She goes to walk away.

I suck in the pain and grab her ankle, pulling her down on the floor. She hisses at me and punches me in the face. I headbutt her, knocking her back. I stand to my feet and retrieve the dagger as she lunges toward me. The dagger immediately plunges into her heart. I shove it in farther, then twist the dagger to cause further damage. She looks me and snarls as she drops to the floor. I stumble backward still hurting from her assault.

I find her clutch on the nightstand with her phone in it. I dial the council. One of the Elders answers the phone.

"Edith?" I wait and say nothing. "Edith? Is it done? Is Hunter dead?" the man asks.

I chuckle darkly. "No, thank you for asking. But Edith sends her regards," I say with a smirk. I hear a growl through her BlackBerry.

"Eldridge! What is the mean of this! Where is Edith?"

I scoff. "She's no doubt in the great beyond right now, probably facing the Almighty Creator's judgment."

He growls. "How dare you!"

"I should say the same. I receive a letter inviting me to visit the council, and this is how you treat me?" Really, the nerve of them all.

"I have no idea what you are referring to Hunter. We never sent you a letter! Now, leave before we rip you to shreds!" I cannot contain my laughter at his comment as I hang up the phone.

I pick up her body. I search around the room and area outside the window for what to do. I decide to call the manager. I explain to him what happened. He is livid. I know that human girl is behind this. It makes me wonder who else she has set up to be assassinated. If I ever find her again, I will kill her.

Fenrilol arrives a few minutes later and takes her body. He informs me that he contacted his homeland—there are dragons there—and offers to help burn her remains. We decide to act fast as I see her slightly moving. I decide to quickly rip out her heart. Her body goes limp and turns a putrid green color. I throw the heart in the fireplace that is in the sitting room of my suite. I chance a look out the window. I see him outside walking into the woods, no doubt heading toward the portal. I see a blazing pink light. Then it disappears.

This entire assault fuels my rage. They dare to try and assassinate me? I FaceTime Victor and Marcus to make sure that they are arriving on time tonight for my showdown with the coven council.

"Hello, Hunter!" Markus greets me.

"Hello, Master Eldridge," Victor says.

"Hello, gentleman, have you arrived in my area or location?" I'm waiting for them to arrive before I confront the council on their actions. I want my wingmen as back up to help me fight. "The sooner you can arrive, the better. I already assume this is going to be a battle."

Markus nods.

"They just tried sending someone to assassinate me in my hotel room," I inform them. I'm met with angry hisses.

Victor shouts, "What!"

Markus shrugs. "I'm not surprised. Most of the elders hate you. They think since you are Abner's descendant, that you are going to bring back his days of carnage."

I shake my head. "You know that is never going to happen." I sigh.

"We both know that. But they refuse to see that. They see who you are, you are resilient fight. And a fierce leader. I heard them say you are like Abner in the flesh. They are afraid of you."

I look at him. "Are you?" I need to be sure. He is my friend. But I want him as my right hand.

He snickers at my insecurity. "I will follow you anywhere. Anyone else who doesn't agree is not worthy of your loyalty or service."

Victor raises his voice in agreement with Marcus.

Victor's bride is in the background, listening to our conversation. I'm not fully familiar with her or what side she would be on. But he assures me that she will support us. I'm thankful for their allegiance and friendship. I know Marcus is a skilled fighter. I hope Victor is up to the task. It has been decades since we shared company.

I don't know if he has had any training other than what I gave him in the beginning.

"We should be there within an hour. We will phone you once we arrive at your hotel, we're arriving together. And Victor's wife has come along as well," Marcus tells me.

"Is she up to this?"

She snarls from the phone. "Mr. Eldridge, you don't know how long I have been waiting for this moment." She begins to tell me her story. I can see and hear the rage and revulsion clearly in her tone and eyes. She truly hates him with a deadly passion. She requests the ability to kill him in retribution for her entire life that he destroyed.

I am sure she will be an asset and tell her I'll never stand in her way, for I too know how she feels. This, though, makes me worry for Victor, if she truly is his mate, and he does lay claim to her. He will see Victor's relationship with her as a threat. He will see Victor as a thief stealing what is his. I advise them to keep their relationship hidden for Victor's sake, which they agree to. I know this is going to turn into a bloodbath.

The coven council hates me; they always have. They are overrated relics who have been seated on their ivory thrones for too long. The last king was their friend; that is how they got their seats to begin with. That is an unfair advantage to people who truly deserve the titles. I intend to be sure that people who have earned the opportunity will sit in those places. I intend to shake everything up and change the vampire world. These old men sit there like they are gods, lording over everyone. They wrote most of the vampire laws almost a thousand years ago. They have not progressed with time. They still act as if the year is 1307, old fossils. They deserve to be sent back to that time and never come back.

I intend to help our world be reborn. A humorous thought comes to my mind. If Lord Byron knew that his so-called mate Elizabeth was an ambitious and successful female attorney in a man's world, he would have a coronary, for sure. An hour passes, and Marcus's party arrives. I greet them. I welcome Victor's bride; she's as beautiful as he has told me. We arrive at my suite. I pour them a drink and discuss how to handle the upcoming event that is going to happen. After some time discussing everything, we agree that it is best to keep a united front.

I caution Marcus. He is a member of the council. He is Lord Dinothere's second-in-command. He needs to be cautious. They could view him as a traitor. And I would hate for him to be killed. He is aware of this and still wants to fight. I value his loyalty. We agree to everything, make our way out of the hotel toward the situation to come. We open the doors, walk to the valet, and settle ourselves in the car. It takes three hours to arrive at the seventeenth-century estate outside of Rochester, New York. The extravagant mansion houses the coven council.

We walk through the doors and are greeted by the receptionist, Ingrid. She greets us, and her eyes light up in carnal appraisal as I walk into the manor.

"Greetings, Master Eldridge, may I help you with anything?" she purrs suggestively. She takes my coat. I feel her hands caress my back seductively. Filthy whore!

"No, thank you," I say tartly. She huffs with an annoyed tone and returns to her desk. I turn to her and reply, "Edith sends her regards. Try anything like that with me again and you may join her charred remains beyond the grave," I say in a cold voice.

She hisses and throws her lamp at me. I bat the item away with my hand. She bares her teeth and disappears somewhere in the house.

Markus and Victor try to contain their laughter, grinning as they watch the situation.

"Damn, Hunter, you have a death wish," Markus says.

I just shrug and continue walking.

Esmerelda greets us with a purr. "Greetings, gentlemen, so pleasing to see you again. May I be of any service?"

I ignore her sexual suggestion and continue. Her mate is Lord Bentley. But her sexual appetite is insatiable, and he doesn't stop her from seeking other men when she's here as he sits in meetings. She can willing take men upstairs for her desires. Ugh! Why are female vampires succubus sluts?

I ignore her as I continue to walk. I hear her whisper as I walk past her, "I will see you burned by dragon fire, you murderous snake!"

I growl and turn to glare at her. At that moment, three of the women come up from behind us and attempt to pin us down. The women start to kick, bite, and scratch us. I slap Esmerelda hard in an attempt to push her away from me. She falls to the floor. I take a defensive stance.

All three women join her and begin to attack. One pulls out a pistol, screaming, "Traitor!" at Markus, and shoots him. The pistol fires a wooden stake at him. He drops, screaming in pain with a stake lodged in his gut. We struggle to fight them off.

Elizabeth enters the house and gives out a shrilling scream at the sight of her chosen mate being kicked and scratched. She lunges and attacks Ingrid, ripping her head clear from her body. The other women stare at her in shock.

"Did you think she was here for you?" Victor says with a smirk and bloodied grin.

The other women begin to attack her. I'm amazed how skilled she is. She rips the hearts out of two women as more women come in and start an assault.

I'm over this catty squabbling. "Enough!" I shout, and for the first time in decades, I pull forward my absorbed powers. As I shout, I throw all the council women into the walls of the room. Some fly out a window. My companions stare at me in shock. No one but Charles has seen my abilities. It feels good to use that power again.

"Holy fuck, Hunter!" both my best men say.

I tell them to not dwell on this. We have more important matters. They nod. Markus is still gravely injured. I inquire about his wound. He is bleeding. He excuses himself and leaves the room. I hear him going upstairs. We decide to wait for him. I have never been up to those floors, never asked what is up there. I hear a terrifying scream from a woman and now silence. I can now imagine what is up there. The thought of drinking makes my mouth water. I try to distract my mind on the confrontation in the council chambers.

Markus descends the stairs, looking clean, refreshed, and healed. I notice that he looks well. He confirms my question as we walk into the congregation room. Upon our entry, all the men in the room turn to our entourage. They pale as they take notice of me covered in blood with what they can tell is the beginning of my council. Their looks turn from terrified to murderous as they examine us.

"Master Eldridge, what is the meaning of this?"

I take a stroll around the room. Their eyes continue to burn into my body. "You ask this question. However, I believe you know the answer." I stop and stare at all of them.

Victor guards the door with Elizabeth.

I address the crowd. "You dare to even ask! Did you not twice now try to exterminate me? You send me a letter requesting my presence then you attack us?" I growl.

They look incredulous. "What letter? We send no such thing to the likes of you!"

I hold it in my hand and open it for all to see, reading it to them. Many of them shrink into their seats with true faces of fear. "You all look as if you could die for gazing on it?" I taunt them.

Sir Gedell stands to his feet. "We never sent that. I don't recognize that writing from anyone here! How do we know you didn't fake it?"

I laugh. As if I would want to associate myself with them? The elder Lord Collins from Seattle throws a wooden stake right toward my heart. I catch it as it flies toward me. I growl. However, another throw that I miss hits my shoulder. I pull it out and throw it back at Lord Collins, hitting him right in the head. He drops to the floor in front of Elizabeth. She quickly rips his heart out and tosses it through a window.

Damn, that little wanker! I'm lucky it missed my heart. It is not too deep. But it still hurts. At this moment, all the council members jump to their feet into attack mode. I can see that this is going to be.

"Aggressive negotiations? I didn't want this to come to a fight, yet you leave me no choice! You continually attack me!"

Everyone in the room is crouched, poised to strike.

"Regardless which of you lying miscreants wrote this letter. I delayed meeting you because, none of you are worth my time." I hear someone scoff. "Your greatest mistake is stealing with is rightfully mine! You have long held something that belongs to me, something that I'm here to claim. Give it to me. And you all may live."

The men stiffen. And if looks could kill, I would be a cinder pile.

Lord Byron stands at attention. "One, I wish to say that we would see you burned to ash before we hand you that throne!" he growls at me.

I tsk in disappointment. "Your time is over; you are not serving the vampire nation! You sit in this room, drinking your blood wines and having raunchy parties with these whores while a sadistic coven of vampires is purging the earth, attacking anywhere and everywhere they show up. Yet you do nothing about it!"

They are growling at me at this rate for pointing out their flaws.

"How long before the European court decides to visit?" I ask them, and they immediately pale. Apparently, they never considered this.

"Who is going to call them? You? You are nothing but an insignificant worm! You have no claim here, you worthless rat!" Lord Byron taunts. All the other elders laugh, mocking me.

Lord Byron addresses me. "I have a proposition. Despite your insolence, I'm willing to negotiate since you were kind enough to locate and turn over my mate to me." His smile is vicious like an evil serpent. Elizabeth hisses. Upon hearing this from Byron, several guards block the doors, cutting her off so she can't escape. Two guards stand in front of her. She does her best to fight them, yet they take hold of her to be certain she's secured.

I look at him. "What makes you think I brought her for you? And who says she's your mate? You have never mentioned this news? Doesn't the law state the mate should be forever by your side. Bear your mark?"

At this moment, Lord Byron lets out an evil growl. "Don't you dare impugn me, boy! I changed her with that intent. But she somehow managed to run away from my grasps. And disappear! I have looked for her for centuries!"

I chuckle. "You did a poor job considering I met her decades ago and you have never mentioned her."

He growls again and throws his chair at me while looking at her. She snarls at him.

"Who is this parasite next to you?" he says, looking at Victor. "Say he's your lover, and I will slaughter him where he stands and remind you who you belong to again!"

"He is my friend and colleague," she tells him with disdain.

He smiles sinisterly. "Let it be only that, my pet!"

I read her mind. *Can I kill him now?* I quietly shake my head. This is getting me nowhere. As I talked, I noticed Marcus get into the private position I'd instructed him to. This will shake things up. May the torture commence.

I stop at the head of the room. I look at the majestic throne of Abner, my ancestor. It is not only a marvel to behold, but also I sense a presence around it. After five hundred years, it still reeks of evil, as if it is bewitched. This throne symbolizes the darkest history of my family's lineage. It also is a symbol of the strength and power in my bloodline, a title and heritage that has always been mine. It has an aura of the darkest powers like it whispers Abner's name. I sit down to their outrage and protests. Their screams of outrage fade from my mind as I suddenly feel a presence with me, telling me to claim the throne, to claim my powerful blood. This feeling is ancient, dark, and deadly.

I shake off the unholy feeling of hands wrapping around me just in time as one of them launches himself at me. I quickly catch him by the throat. His teeth bite into my wounded shoulder. I scream in pain. I knock him back a bit.

He snarls, "You will never be king. Burn in hell!"

I snarl back at him as I rip his head from his body. "You first." I groan. My shoulder is stinging in pain. I do my best to ignore the burning feeling and I look around as they all stare and quake in rage. Blood coats the throne, as it should. It has rivets that were designed to hold blood centuries ago.

"You all know who I am. You all know my lineage!" I feel like an unknown power is speaking through me. This power demands their obedience, demands their blood. I don't know what is coming over me.

"You are worthless maggots trying to be what you are not! You purposely hold back what is *mine!*" I shout at them as dark power radiates through me.

I motion for Marcus to join the room. The elders are glaring at him for doing my bidding. His elder is pissed and sending him murderous glares.

"Marcus! How dare you betray us!" he growls.

Marcus walks past them and chuckles darkly. "I know whom I serve, who is worthy of my loyalty." He dodges a knife aimed at his heart, catches it, and throws it into the wall next to his elder's head. He walks to the back of the room, silently waiting for my cue to return and purge the room.

As they are distracted by Marcus's exit, I give a small nod to Victor and Elizabeth. She springs into action. She tackles Byron. They wrestle on the floor. He throws her against the wall, gets her in a choke hold, pins her down to bite her. She panics and donkey kicks him. He releases her. She drops down below him, delivers more kicks as she rips his heart from his body while taking an ancient sword from the wall and dismembering him like he no doubt did to her family. She bathes herself in blood.

As she's fighting with Byron, everything erupts into chaos as some of the men try to escape. Marcus, Victor, and I are fighting for our lives against the entire council members.

Sir Stefan Gedell lunges toward me, knocking backward toward the throne. I see him pull out his saber, as if the year is 1750. I stand, picking up the sword Elizabeth used and position myself to engage in combat with him. I have not held a sword in decades. But I still feel all of my training and experience come to life in me. We pair off and duel. The sounds of our swords clashing echo through the room. I notice in my peripheral vision Victor and Elizabeth fighting together as some of the guards attempt to destroy them. I try to concentrate on my fight, looking for an opening. After several minutes, he makes a fatal flaw in his block, and I take the chance to slice his head off.

I rush over to aid Markus as he fights off his elder and other members. The odds of our victory are slim. There are still six other coven elders, plus nine guards, against us four. I hear a loud sound by my ear. I turn in time to block Lord Wilfred as he attempts to attack me. I'm shoved away from Markus. I skid across the floor and collide with a wall. Wilfred jumps onto me, trying to dig further into my wounds. I grit my teeth. I wrap my hands around his throat. I snap his neck and tear his head off his shoulders. After this fight, I need to hunt to restore my strength. The council members are lethal and ancient. I'm standing where I am right now and not as a corpse thanks to pain endurance, my military training, and my friends with me.

I turn around, and Lady Mildred is hissing at me. I mentally command her, *Bring it, bitch!*

She snarls at me. "*Die!*" she screeches.

I block her attack. "The Sloyan line is dead, never again!"

She screams as she punches me hard in the gut, sending me through a window of the house. I fly into the forest, hitting a tree. I groan in pain. I feel as if my back broke. She smirks, which gives me the gusto to straighten up. I ram myself into another tree in an attempt to correct my back. By a miracle, it works. But it is agonizing. I use some of my powers to jump back into the room, while also hovering over her. I tear her head from her body.

With pain and scars from battle, we tear through the remaining men in attendance and rip apart their bodies. This is a bold statement, letting everyone know that we will not show mercy. Throughout this whole scene, only half of the guards who are stationed in the room attack us. After the battle is won, those guards who are not killed are given a chance to return to their posts. They bow to us and return to their duties.

It is clear where their loyalties lie. They knew that I was the rightful person for the throne, which it was mine long ago but was kept from me. After we lay waste to the room, the guards kneel to me. Amidst the blood-covered room, I sit on the throne, Marcus on my right and Victor on my left, with his fiancée beside him. We display the new image of power.

The guards shout, "All, hail King Hunter!" The doors burst open, and everyone stares in horror at the room's gruesome scene. The women scream and cry. The men who were not in the meeting stare, frozen. However, one by one, they bow to us.

Except for Esmerelda. She screams in horror and outrage at the sight of her husband's body. "Esmerelda, if you cannot accept Hunter, meet the same fate as your husband," Marcus tells her with a hard look.

Teary-eyed, she bows her head and kneels before me, choosing self-preservation. However, I will have to be wary of her. When a vampire's mate dies, the other half can become overcome with grief and revenge. Everyone at the manor bends their knee in subordination to the new vampiric era.

Tonight marks a historical change in the vampiric world. Here tonight in this grand manor isolated in the upper New York State countryside. I, Hunter Eldridge, have brought about a reckoning. All these council members who sat in their lofty thrones learned how it would feel to meet their creators in death. This change has been needed for centuries. And I happily paved the way with my associates. Broken, injured, and bloody, we stand tall for the world to see a new era on the horizon, a new council that will fight for the good of all people.

I turn to Victor and everyone who was with me, suggesting, after everything that has happened, we need to hunt. The council really gave us hell. I have been stabbed a few times, bitten, and bones broken. Victor would have been killed if not for Elizabeth being at his side. Markus showed his warrior spirit and fought nearly to his death but emerged victorious.

We all run into the night. We are not at top speed because of our injuries. However, the vampiric beasts inside are guiding us to devour the sweet red pulse we crave.

We slow to a stop outside of a camping area. I inhale deeply. The rich pulsing warmth of the humans is inviting us in to quench our thirsts and heal. I observe the train of campers. I have one rule they all know: *Never kill a child; we are not savages.* I scout a large group of campers that look like college kids, perfect! I signal them to move forward, and we stalk through the night. Once we are in hunt mode, our senses and instincts take over, leading us to what our monstrous inside is craving, the need to feed and gorge ourselves in blood.

I sneak up behind a young woman and sink my teeth into her, absorbing her warmth. The minute I do, I feel my body healing. The monster in me is not done. I find a man and drag him into the darkness of the forest, making sure he doesn't scream as I drink my fill. I return to the campsite where the rest my coven are indulging their thirsts. I'm glad they are being discreet and preventing the humans from screaming. Exposure is forbidden unless the human is going to turn.

After we drink our fill, we walk away deeper into the woods. I notice we are near Niagara Falls. This is about twenty miles away from that witches' kingdom I razed to the ground. It feels weird to think that was so long ago. I miss my friend Charles. I should have invited him along with us. It would be nice to have him here. I lie down and gaze at the stars like I used to do so long ago. I hope Eliza is gazing at them with me like we used to.

I stare at the heavens, thinking. Markus lies down next to me.

"Hunter, let me ask you something?" I turn toward him and he continues. "Why are you doing this?"

"What, the stars?" I ask him sarcastically.

He laughs. "You know what I mean. Why now did you decide to claim the role of king? You used to hate the idea?"

I sigh. I do have my reasons for my change of mind. "You are right. I do have a hidden motive." I take a deep inhale before I continue. "Once I'm king, I can put an end to the calamity that is happening around us. I can end the needless torture of the humans who are dying brutally. I understand we prey on humans, but there is a difference between feeding and leaving them alive as I do, or giving them a silent death, and ripping them apart."

He thinks about what I'm saying. "I understand what you mean. But is there more behind it?" He knows me so well.

"All right, yes. I also intend to use my kingship to weed out that red bitch."

He laughs. "I knew some of this has to be about her. After all the years, you still have not let it go as much as you pretend to. Damn you are stubborn!"

I roll my eyes at him.

"You think there is a connection?" he asks me as he thinks about it.

"There has to be one, and she has to be behind it. This is her style of attack. Always in the middle of the night or in secret. And always brutal. She only left me alive cause she wanted to turn me."

He ponders what I'm saying. "All right, we reform things. And finally bring her in for justice, rather than chasing her throughout eternity. It is honestly brilliant."

I smile. I'm glad to have confessed this. And I'm glad he's on board.

Victor and Elizabeth join us. We lie there for a little while longer. As I lie there, I turn toward the witches' kingdom. I was so filled with craving for revenge. I was not smart about it. I should have claimed this title long ago rather than chasing Bathilda all over the world. At least now, I will have resources to find her. I realized a while ago that you cannot easily find someone who wishes to stay hidden unless are smart about it. Following hearsay never works and is a huge waste of time. If I can find her and pin these attacks to her, I will bring justice for everyone.

We walk away from the hillside. The falls during the night are a beautiful sight. I say a silent prayer that Eliza will be with me. I have not felt her in a while. She pulled me back from the darkness that was trying to consume my heart. And I can only hope I have redeemed myself enough to earn her forgiveness.

CHAPTER 20

We arrive back at the estate, and I can feel the anger toward us as we walk into the house. One of the women hisses at me yet doesn't attempt anything. This is going to take a lot of work. The corruption has been thick in these walls for centuries.

I hear Markus. "If you don't stop with your childish act. I will take you upstairs and teach you some manners, or this will be the last day you will ever see!"

She stares wide-eyed in front of him with a look of fright. She bows and runs away.

"This is not going to be easy. A lot of these women here, you killed off their mates or benefactors as of last night."

I claimed my title as vampire king and eliminated all who would oppose me. I know last night was the thunder before the storm.

Markus continues to talk with me. "Some of them were turned by the previously elders for sexual desires." I nod. "Like Gretchen. In 1840, she was a human working in Texas as a cancan girl and whore. Lord Gedell found her pleasing. He turned her to be his bedfellow. She has been stuck since."

I gaze upon her in pity.

She sneers at me. "I don't need your pity. Thanks to you, I have nothing and no one now!" She walks out.

I understand that with change comes opposition. It is not going to be easy. But I hope they realize that now they can redefine themselves and not be puppets to the former council.

I slaughtered the council members that were present. I know more members were away on assignments. I will need to face their wrath at some point when they return. But today is not the day. I leave Markus to tour the house. I'm greeted respectfully by various some servants. I'm thankful I'm gaining a little appreciation.

I walk through the halls; I stop in front of the council chamber room. I open the doors and walk inside the room. I take in the awe-inspiring features of the room. I notice with relief that the room has been thoroughly cleaned. The walls are burgundy-colored, with wood baseboard along the bottom. There is one massive portrait that is mounted on the center wall. The man shines with arrogance and royalty. It is no doubt their version of a vampire king. I cannot help but contemplate how the true vampire king in England feels about their America copycat?

I continue to pace the room and observe the surroundings. The floor is black-and-white marble leading to the dark-oak platform where the glamorous throne sits, a throne that I know once belonged to my ancestor centuries ago. Looking at this throne, I feel a cold chill crawl up my spine. When a vampire feels something so evil and it makes them shake like a human, which is terrifying.

I sit on the seat and marvel at its beauty. It is a majestic sight to behold. Completely gold. It is easy to tell how ancient it is. The throne looks like it was stolen from Solomon's court. It has a velvet red fabric seating area that rides up the backside. There is a crest with the image of a dragon with vampiric fangs that look like a mouth dripping blood. On either side of the crest are precious gems such as garnet stone and ruby stone. There were three of each on either side in a V shape. It's impressive and royal.

For some reason, it calls to me, and I cannot understand why. I hear a voice, eerily quiet, like a hushed whisper calling my name. As

I study it, entranced, I cannot look away. I look at the fearsome beast. At that moment, the eyes of the dragon begin to glow. Shocked and freaked out, I stumble away from it. I look away, trying to unsee what I thought I saw.

When I observe it, the dragon looks like a crest again. On either side of the armrests are holes like cupholders. I know that this is not something in existence at this time, so I have to believe, considering it is a vampiric throne, they are to hold blood for a reason. I remember something from last night. Blood. The throne was bathed in it, yet now there is no blood in sight. There are no stains. It's as if the throne is brand new. What can that mean? Did the throne absorb it? It's very unsettling. What exactly is this throne?

As I marvel at the throne, Markus approaches me, "Hunter, I was wanting to ask you something."

I encourage him to ask about anything going through his mind.

"How soon do you want to start with the council reformation? I'm not saying that we start today. We all need rest after the chaos last night."

I know what he's talking about. "I know. I need a holiday." I laugh. "This is going to take time. Nothing can be rebuilt in a day. We first need to gather new delegates, new people who would want to serve with us on a new council. So for right now, I'm calling a shutdown of this house until we can appoint new members. The maids may stay and continue their work. But I don't trust anyone else here."

He nods and walks away. I decide to visit the upstairs where I have never been.

As I ascend the stairs, I hear soft moans but not of pleasure. It sounds as if someone is faintly saying, "Help me." I follow the sounds into a large room. I abhor what I see—various humans strapped to beds and connected to IVs. Most of them are women. Many are missing clothes. Some have their clothes ripped. All of them look deathly pale. This makes my mind drift back to Margaret, and I snarl in fury.

A woman turns to me and whispers, "Please." Another whispers, "No more, please." One is shuddering at the sight of me. "Another one," she says.

I walk toward them. "Today is your freedom and day of reckoning! This slaughter is going to end," I tell them as I remove their IVs and free them.

I holler down the stairs for Victor and Elizabeth. They run into the room. Her eyes go wide with shock. Her hand flies to her mouth, and she whispers, "Oh dear God!"

I think, if she could cry, she would be in tears. I instruct Victor to find a way to move the victims out of the house, compel them to forget, feed their minds a new story, and call the authorities. He nods. They both start carrying the women somewhere else. After they are free, I tear the room apart. This will never happen again!

I descend the stairs. The council women and some men who are there all try to attack me because of what I have done.

"I don't give a shit if I took away your snack room. This is not how we can go about feeding. There are blood banks for a reason. You should have set up willing volunteers under a false pretense if need be! As your king, I will not abide by kidnapping innocent humans and torture. Never again. From today onward, this place is shut down until I can appoint worthy people!" I shout at them. They all start panicking and yelling at me.

I walk away, not intending to hear any of it. I tell them while walking away I have made up my mind. "Now leave this house and do something useful!" I say in a cold voice.

One by one, they depart from my presence. If I were still human, I would have a headache. Once Victor returns, Markus joins us with the mansion keys in hand. We lock up the house. But leave the maid doors open for their use. We then leave the estate.

I call my assistant and request transportation arrangements to be made for my journey back to Chicago. She also informs me that everything is set for my Portland departure.

I decide, *Fuck it! I will leave from here*, and I request airline passenger to the West Coast. Mrs. Tomes also informs me that my wishes are being fulfilled and we will have a new publishing house catering to the West Coast open by next year. I smile and thank her for all the hard work.

I head toward the hotel, say goodbye to my friend, and sign out of my room. Within an hour, I receive a text from Allison that my private jet is waiting at Niagara Falls Heliport. She sends me directions. I call an Uber and head for my destination. I greet my pilot and take my seat to enjoy the flight.

Soon, my little vixen, I will have you in my arms soon, I think as the hours pass.

I have yet to meet her. But I know there is something special about her. Her scent of vanilla and cinnamon, so sweet, so addicting. It not only stirs my bloodlust but also drives my manhood to oblivion. I have not been affected so strongly since my wife. Could it be her? Could she have been transformed as I? I don't know the answer. I just know that I must meet her. I feel myself grow hard as I let thoughts of her consume me.

I focus on her so I don't ponder everything that happened in the council chambers and what has transpired over the last several months. These next several weeks should be very entertaining. I know I need to reform the council right now. I need to clear my head and work on making that whole scenario brand new. That means new laws, new people in charge. If I start to think about everything that it entails, I will go mad. I decide to concentrate on the college opportunity I'm being honored with.

The stewardess passes me with carnal approval. The last time I flew on this plane, I relieved myself sexually. As appealing as that is at this moment, I try hard to refrain. Thankfully, the stewardess crew is new, and none of them smell appealing. I concentrate on the situation to come to distract myself. I think about that blond doppelganger of my wife. I know the risks that will befall her if she feels the same and chooses to be with me. It is dangerous for a human to associate with a vampire—the death of Lucinda proved that. If this girl is the keeper of Eliza's soul, I will be there this time. I will not let her be harmed.

Eliza. I was not able to prevent our lives from falling into death and darkness. I'm so sorry.

If this girl holds a piece of your soul, I will love her as I did you. I will be there for her when I failed you, I say in prayer while speaking to Eliza. The plane descends to Portland. After the plane stills, I receive a text from Mrs. Tomes. She has called ahead to a car rental company, securing me a car and driver. That woman is such a blessing. I'm going to have to give her a raise after my return.

The driver informs me that his name is Hector, and I cannot believe it. The driver she secured is a vampire! I want to laugh my ass off at this turn of events. I step into the car and enjoy the ride. I talk with Hector about various things. He informs me that he's originally from Spain. He was a member of the Spanish Armada some four hundred years ago when he was turned. He was a simple foot soldier during the Ottoman War. He had no idea that there were any vampires mixed in with the war on the side of the Ottoman Empire.

I sit back and listened to the story of his life and how everything transpired. He said that, from what he remembers, the vampire who turned him was from Romania and was later assassinated. Little does he know, his description fits my ancestor Abner the Ruthless. He, with his wicked wife, were both executed by the Romanian people who had discovered the monsters their leader was. I quietly listen to his story.

"Rumor has it, somehow, she bore him children, and she trabea'd them out of the country. I pray that is a lie. Rather than disappearing from justice, I pray they were captured eventually. What a walking nightmare that child would be," Hector says.

I, however, already know that it is true. I had the misfortune to meet remnants who were the immortal witches that I destroyed.

Somehow the children must have been captured after they appeared in Canada. Hopefully, they were brough to justice.

We carry on until we get to the hotel, and I say farewell to him. I hand him my card, and I inform him that if he ever wishes to reconnect with me, he can reach me through my contact information. It's good speaking with him. It is now seven in the evening, nighttime in the city. The humans are busy hustling everywhere, and I'm feeling a stirring sensation—the monster kept at bay is craving. I guess it is time to find someone to indulge in. Hello, Portland, here I come!

I take off from the hotel and disappear into the night to search for someone to sustain me. I stay out all night long, enjoying the various tastes of Portland. By the time I arrive back at the hotel, it is late. Thank goodness, I don't sleep. I just go lie down on the comfortable bed. I arose early this morning in Portland. I could honestly get really accustomed to this area. One drawback to living in Chicago is the sunny days.

Portland's cloud cover is incredible. Washington State would be even more ideal. However, I don't want to venture there. I could not tolerate the constant rain. It is also the land of the dark fae. These creatures are said to be spirits who are pure evil and dwell on negative emotions and sadness. They live in the mountain areas of Seattle; such emotions are very highly circulated in the Seattle area. With the high rate of depression and suicides, it is a dark fae hub.

Humans don't know. Only supernaturals know that Algea and dark fae are what induce the seductive temptation of suicide. Once the Algea collect a soul, they never give it back. And their favorites are immortals. A vampire is not truly soulless. Their souls are lost but not truly gone. An Algea can find it and claim it for eternity. I pray they never migrate this way. I would take my little minx and bolt back to Chicago.

Speaking of which, I check my watch. It is already seven in the morning, time to greet the new day and hopefully find a certain little temptress. I receive an email on my iPhone that Mrs. Tomes used my money and bought me a penthouse suite inside Harrison Tower. It is a bit of a drive from Linfield University. But I will make it work. I would rather not live near the noisy halls of a college, too great a temptation regarding "savory morsels," as Marcus phrased it.

I just need to keep everything together as I'm going to be teaching over the next few months. Here's hoping I also get to enjoy some time with a certain lady. I don't want to struggle with my desires more than I know I already will. I cannot run to Scotland from Oregon to hide and hunt. I could spend time in Canada like last night. But I would have to pass through the dark fae. Even running top speed, I had a few of them trying to follow me. I would rather not risk my life again. I need to have my wits about me and my inner demon caged.

The last thing we need is for there to be any further human murder cases caused by vampires while I'm here. I have never been that sloppy. However, I was always able to hunt in northern Wisconsin. I try to shake these thoughts as I exit the penthouse building. Mrs. Tomes even arranged for a car be to at my disposal during my stay here. God, that woman clicks with me so well—she's the best executive assistant I could ask for.

I pull away from the building and head to find a Panera Bread for a bacon, egg, and cheese croissant with a cup of coffee. Honestly, it doesn't taste the same, being a vampire. But it is still edible. As a vampire, human food tastes bland. This is preferable to some other human food I have had that tastes like swill. After draining the coffee cup and eating the croissant, I decide to take a drive around the city. I have never been in this place before. And if I'm going to live here for a while, I need to familiarize myself with my surroundings.

As I'm driving around and finding my way toward the college, I'm hit with that intoxicating scent as I drive around a corner. I press on the brakes and find a parking spot. The need to find her becomes strong. I exit the car and start to walk; she's there across the street. At a café, it looks as though she works there. Perfect! I could go with another cup of coffee. I walk across the street; she's outside serving in the garden patio. I casually stroll inside; I order a scone with a coffee and mention that I will be eating outside.

It is early spring, but I never get cold. I sit down and wait for her to approach me. I'm scrolling through my iPhone when I hear a hitch in her breath.

"Hello, my name is Camille, and I'm your server, Mr. Eldridge," a soft voice addresses me. She knows of me, wonderful.

"Yes, thank you." I smile at her.

She gives me an appraising look. Time to turn on the charm.

"So, you know of me?" I say smoothly.

She clears her throat, and I hear her heart skip a beat. I also didn't miss a slight hint of longing in her voice.

I decide to reach out in my mind. *Eliza, if you're here, hear my voice, my love.* I look at her for the first time. She's beautiful, just as stunning as Eliza and just as short. I would guess five five, pure blond hair, eyes as blue as the sea. Eliza's eyes! I see a brief flash in her eyes.

Yes! My love heard my voice somewhere deep in this girl's soul. I'm pulled from my thoughts as she answers my question.

"Yes, my sister Allison works for you."

I stare at her. "Allison Tomes? My executive assistant?"

"Yes, sir. She's my eldest sister. My other sister, Amanda, works at your bookstore in Evanston. It's an honor to meet you." I hear her purr in a soft and sweet voice as her hand lingers in mine for a little longer and her eyes roam my frame.

I notice what she's trying to do. Is she really trying to flirt with me? Girl, you don't know who you are playing with. A vampire is a master at being seductive.

I will admit she has great skills. This shows she has great sexual prowess and can get a man in bed. Luckily for me, she has met her match.

So, Eliza, your incarnate is a little sexual seductress. How did you manage this when you in life were so shy and reserved? I think, trying to call out to her soul for answers cause. It is so hilarious. I'm excited to see how things develop now. I talk with her for a few more minutes before she returns to work.

I finish my order, leaving a generous tip of one hundred dollars on the table. I stroll away from the place while discreetly observing the area. I can see her in my corner eye. She's watching me leave and talking to her friend. Curious, I listen in.

"So, Cami, who was that? He is so sexy! And, fuck, he left you a hundred-dollar tip!" She giggles.

"That is the famous and scrumptious Hunter Eldridge, world-famous billionaire and my Miss Perfect Older Sister's boss."

They stare at me like they want to devour me. Girls, I'm only planning to devour one of you. As if a part of her can hear me, she blushes crimson. I know she can't. But I can see her thoughts are very salacious. And, fuck, I can smell her arousal! I hide my grin. Now I know: she wants me just the same.

I am lost in my thoughts until I hear her speak again.

"I'm definitely getting that piece of ass," she says while wiggling her eyebrows.

"Girl! No. I know you. I don't think you should pull a one-nighter with Allison's boss!"

So, she only does one-night stands? This displeases me. Yeah, not going to happen, sweetheart!

"Deby. I'm not going down that way again. Chase was enough! I'm not going through that heartbreak again!"

Aw, sweetheart. I realize now that she has been hurt by some asshole somewhere.

I whisper into her mind, *He will never do that to you. You are safe with him.* I conjure an image with my arms wrapped around her in a sense of security. She turns facing where I'm hiding, blushing, with a smile on her face as she walks back into the café. I head back to my car to continue my tour of Portland.

I know now. I need to thaw the ice around her heart before she will commit to staying with me. As I drive, I think of what to do. I decide to just wait, let the opportunity to meet her present itself. I do admit that the time is nagging at me. I remind myself that we will have plenty of time to get to know each other. And I will take it slow.

Over the next few weeks, I continue to meet her at the café. I have a coffee and something edible for a human style breakfast. As I meet her there, we talk a bit and get acquainted. My desire for her grows, and she continues to flirt with me. She's making it clear that she wants me in bed with her. I admire her determination. I just don't roll that way. If she does decide be with me. It will be forever.

Would she, though? Would she want eternity with me? Or would she want forever as a vampire? Would she hate me for stealing her soul from her? I know I'm getting ahead of myself, we only just met. I will not deny, though the fact is, I have felt Eliza's spirit fighting to come to the surface. It's her. She recognized me. I hear her. I felt the longing. When I called out to her, I felt the touch of her spirit, something I have not felt in decades. I long for that again, for my wife to return to me.

I know that Camille is not officially Eliza. She's more daring than Eliza ever was.

Honestly, I think I like it. It is refreshing. It is very similar to myself, showing that the universe paired us completely. What am I going to do about her broken heart? The only thought that comes to mind is going along with her fling ideals and warming up to her. Yes, that will work. And meanwhile. I can continue to call out to Eliza.

I'm driving around the city. We exchanged phone numbers. I was about to call her when I notice a multipurpose building that looks close to opening. I see the E. H. Publishing banner in front. Suddenly, a brilliant idea comes to mind. If it can even work, I will offer the good students of Linfield internship positions in my company at this location or the Chicago location. With any luck, Camille will be one of the recruits.

Today is Monday, first start of class. I learn that the students were on a spring break. Camille had gone to Chicago for a few days to visit her family ahead of time. That explains my seeing her on the train platform. I just could not reach her then. Now is a second chance and a new day.

I make my way to the school, and I arrive at the school way ahead of schedule. I park in the faculty space closest to the building. I step inside the school. Not many of the students have arrived for classes yet. I pull out my email that was sent to me, and I go in search of the lecture hall where I will be instructing. Once I find it, I instantly memorize the room number and pathway I walk to arrive. After this, I make my way back down the stairs to greet the staff inside the front office.

The secretary immediately notices me. "Hello, sir, welcome to Linfield University. How may I assist you?" she says in a polite yet professional tone. I really appreciate that; it becomes tiresome having women who are supposed to be doing their jobs fawn over me.

I straighten my posture. "Hello. I'm Hunter Eldridge. I'm invited here to be a guest lecturer."

Immediately recognition dawns on her face. She arises from her seat and runs into one of the back offices, presumably to locate the dean or the chancellor of this university. I pace around the front room, while I observe the students hastily entering the university. So many young humans in such a hurry, to get somewhere, unaware of the dangers lurking around them, blinded and unaware of how easily fate can change their life, whether by weather, accident, or my hand. Yet such was I.

Consumed with my fears and ambitions of success, I never saw the truth. From the corner of my eye, I catch a glimpse of Camile running down the hallway. She has a drink carrier filled with four cups of coffee in hand as well as papers, folders, rolled paper tubes, and an assortment of other stuff. I see her doing her best to manage everything in hand while she heads toward an elevator to transition upstairs. There is a part of me that wants to go assist her. She looks like she's having a difficult time, yet I need to stay here and wait for the dean.

The other receptionist sees me watching and looks at me. I make an excuse. "I was just watching to be sure she doesn't need help; her hands are quite full."

"Oh, that is Camille Williams. She's attending here with a major in journalism and English literature. From what I understand, she transferred here from Chicago a couple of years ago."

I'm interested in this story. "Really? Do you know why?" I say to her in a charming yet compelling voice.

She blinks then answers. "She apparently was involved with a student there whose father is a highly regarded faculty member. The asshole completely cheated on her apparently, with every girl on campus, then embarrassed her in front of everyone by making her look like a liar and stalker when she confronted him."

She shakes her head in disgust. "She quit school for a year, then transferred here. She said in her own words, 'Fuck Chicago!' She has not trusted a man since, just to let you know," she says then turns back to her computer.

I must say that was a lot of information to give me. I was not expecting that. This woman is a chatterbox. I listen to her story while trying to contain my rage. What a fucking douche bag! I wish I would have met her soon before she left. I would have ripped that man's head from his body.

I turn back to the receptionist. "So is she just a student? I saw how much she was carrying. Usually, my interns would have such tasks."

She responds, "No, she also has a couple of other jobs here in different departments assisting them similar to what we do here in the office." Then I hear her mutter, "Girl needs to get paid; she works her fingers to the bone for some reason. She's weird too."

I chuckle. "Why do you say that?"

She looks surprised that I heard her. "Just the running joke people have said that she's a vampire." She laughs. I just stare at her. She cocks her head at me. "What I mean is people joke about how she doesn't like the sun, and she's rather grumpy in the morning from what I understand."

I cover my face with my hand, trying not to laugh. These people wouldn't know a vampire if it was in front of them. Movies don't portray my species accurately. I swear I did hear Allison say that once. I had become concerned she had learned my identity. I'm relieved hearing this.

I hear the door open and a voice growl, "No. I have said before. I don't hate the sun just getting up in the morning, the sun shines directly in my eyes blinding me! Stop spreading shit!" Camille curses. So, she's not a morning person and has a temper. This will be fun!

"Oh! Mr. Eldridge! I apologize for my outburst! I didn't know it was you."

I smile and smoothly take her hand while kissing it. "It is all right, love. I'm not upset. I don't like the sun either for the same reasons," I calmly tell her. I watch her as she blushes. It is so cute.

"What are you doing here sir?" she asks me.

I tell her that I'm here to be a guest lecturer for some English literature classes. *Classes that you are also attending*, I think. She stares at me in wonder and looks like a deer caught in the headlights.

I notice that she also has not removed her hand yet. I feel the connection. She looks dazed. Her eyes shift. I hear a voice faintly in my mind. *Hunter*, it whispers. Eliza is trying to gain control and see me. It lasts for a second. Then she quickly shakes her head. It seems like she was possibly in a stupor, shaking my hand. She says farewell.

After she hands the receptionist some papers, she walks back down the hall. At this moment, I see the other secretary returning to the front, walking next to someone else. I see a slender yet very tall man in a three-piece navy suit with a power tie step into the hallway. I stare at the man in shock. It has been decades since I last saw this man. I don't know how this is possible. I heard that he was killed during the Civil War.

He had to have become a vampire as well. How could I have not known? He must know it's me. He's the head of this school; he must have known it was me. Perhaps this is another reason why I was invited here, other than to talk about the publishing field? He looks up from his paperwork, just as shocked as I am. I'm standing here baffled, trying to comprehend everything as I stare into the eyes of my brother.

CHAPTER 21

I stand here in the center of the main office frozen, so many questions are racing through my mind. He looks at me completely frozen as well. I don't know how long we stand there until the shock wears off and one of us breaks the ice. In a matter of seconds, he rushes me and gives me a huge embrace. I have not seen my brother in decades, ever since he relocated to America before our father passed away.

After several minutes of embracing each other, as long-lost brothers do, we both ask the same question. "My God how is the possible?" we say at the same time, which makes us laugh.

We used to be so close like this. It feels like nothing has changed, yet I know everything has. Everyone has passed away except us.

"How?" I ask him. "The last time I had knowledge of you, I had received word that you had been killed in action during the Civil War?"

He looks at me. "Let us go in my office for some privacy."

I nod and follow him. We walk into the back, and I take a seat on his sofa. "I could ask you the same. I remember a time when I attended your wedding. Then you were caring for our decrepit old man of a father with Eliza."

I stay silent at the mention of her; the pain is now a dull ache. "Yeah. A lot has changed. For starters, Eliza died a long time ago. The night I was changed."

He stares at me with a remorseful expression. He knew Eliza and genuinely liked her. He was the best man at our wedding.

He quickly embraced me again, saying how sorry he was. "Thank you. It was Bathilda, our neighbor. I suspected something about her. But a vampire was never something that crossed my mind. I discovered the same night that Garrett was a vampire. In the beginning, it seemed as though he rescued me from her now. I'm unsure what is truth about that night."

He nods. "You know, I always felt weird around him, like he was looking at you and me expectantly. I dare say he looked at you a lot more, though."

I understand what he meant. I start to feel that way later in life. Why did I not see it then?

"That is another reason why I moved. You were too goodhearted to see it. But I didn't trust him. I always believed he might harm us."

Truthfully, I knew he was right. I never noticed it during my youth.

I need to know his story, "So, what about you?" I ask him.

"A vampire female named Adelaide. I had previously met her while I was in service. She was a nurse. How, I don't know. I had the same feeling about her as Garrett. But different. She was nice and never showed me harm. We became friends."

I nod for him to continue.

"I was captured by the Confederate army and tortured. They were going to hang me up by my feet and let the pigs have me. She came in like an avenging angel."

I stare at him impressed. "I hope that I can meet her to say thank you."

He smiles. "I will talk to her about it," he says, which tells me they are still together. "Before she could get me out unscathed. A soldier threw a knife right into my neck. She ripped him apart, then felt compelled to turn me into a vampire to save me."

I clasp him on the shoulder. "She's your mate. She did what she needed to do, to save you and for that. I owe her everything."

We promise to talk further after the day is done and catch up some more. Right now, I have a class to attend. I walk down the hallway. With no one looking and no human in sight, I use my vampiric speed to reach the second floor. I walk down the corridor and enter the great lecture hall. Damn, seeing this takes me back.

After I moved to America, I wanted to expand my business into publishing. Firstly, I wanted to make sure that I did so authentically. I attended the University of Pennsylvania to obtain not only a bachelor's degree but also a master's degree in literature and creative writing, business, and marketing. I wanted to do everything I could to make sure my efforts were successful. I wanted to be sure that my business thrived and provided jobs to everyone that it could.

That is part of why I'm here today, to help guide these children into the field, to teach them, and help prepare them. I step up the podium and scan the crowd. I look over every student in the audience, making sure they are at attention. I'm also observing the crowd.

Where are you, little minx? I think at all sixty students. At that moment, I feel a connection as if a pair of eyes are on me. Sure enough, I spot her in the upper left-hand corner of the room, seated at a table. *There you are, sweetheart,* I think as I lift my eyes to briefly look at her.

That short moment is enough. I feel her heart quicken, her pulse race, and her cheeks flush. Her thoughts are confused as to why she's having such an intense reaction to me. *Oh sweetheart, I can feel it. And so can you. You were made to be mine!* I'm fully certain she's my mate. She's not fully Eliza. That doesn't matter. I can feel it in my essence.

Camille Williams is my true mate! Now that I know this, I'm never leaving her. I will find a way to be with her. "Good morning, everyone, thank you for coming today. I'm thrilled to be here. In case some of you are not aware, my name is Hunter Eldridge. I own a publishing business, plus a surplus of bookstores which started in London, England, and have spread across America."

I start the lecture. The first thing I discuss is the ethics of creative writing. I spend the next week working with them on comprehending writing fiction, the legal necessities of being an author, and so on. I don't want to overload the kids; I still have the rest of the semester to work with them. I end the class and collect my stuff.

I'm surprised to see Camille as one of the last students.

"Fucking shit!" I hear someone cuss. I look up and some asshole knocks into her, which knocks her laptop down to the floor.

"Fuck you, Todd!" she yells.

"Eat my dick, whore. Oh wait, you did that and bailed!"

She stands there with her mouth gaping.

I look at her. I see tears starting to come from her eyes. I hold myself back from strangling him.

"Wish I was a vampire. I would throw his ass through a wall. Douche bag, he said he was fine with one night," I hear her say quietly while choking back tears.

I walk over to her and make sure she's all right. Humans are so blind. She doesn't know what it is to be a vampire. They watch movies and think they know.

I invite her to go for a cup of coffee with me.

"Mr. Eldridge—"

I cut her off and correct her. "Hunter." I want her to know me and not be so formal.

"Okay. I don't know about that," she shyly says.

"Oh. Come on. It's just coffee. After hearing that douche bag, I thought you could do something comforting." I persuade her. She nods her head and walks out of the school with me heading toward my car.

"I guess this is the first date!" I joke. She freezes and stares at me, looking mortified. I smile at her. She relaxes, and I hear her mumble. *God. I thought he read my thoughts.*

I try not to laugh at this; she was thinking the same as me. This is easier than I expected—we're getting along really well. It's like breathing. I'm happy and amazed at just how comfortable she's with me. I'm being myself and really trying to be here for her after seeing that schmuck upset her.

I can hear her thoughts; she feels ashamed of what happened and nervous about how I would perceive her. Deep down, she wants to find love. She's just scared of history repeating itself with someone new. She's still trying not to cry so in a comforting motion. I wrap my arm around her shoulder. She surprises me by laying her head down.

"Sorry. I hope you don't mind," she says.

I smile. "Not at all. I'm fine with it."

She smiles. "For some reason, I feel very comfortable with you. It is like I have known you for eons."

I close my eyes. I decide to make a joke. "I've been told that I'm quite comfortable." I snicker.

She rolls her eyes and playfully smacks me. We spend the rest of the day talking and getting to know each other better. This feels so good, so right.

I drop her off at the school so she can drive her car. Suddenly, I start to feel a sense of dread growing in my core. My skin tingles with a creepy feeling. I have a strong sense that I'm being watched. I have not felt this way in a long time. I feel my anxiety start to peak. And my guts feel like they are being twisted in blender. Someone is stalking me. I feel the chill in my bones.

To shake my feeling, I decide to run around the city and search for the person who might be stalking me. After a few hours of looking, with the sky growing darker, I conclude that whoever it was is long gone and has covered their scent very well. There was no trace of any scent that I could distinguish.

I return to my penthouse. I undress from my suit. Attempting to relax, I lie in bed and concentrate on the sound of the nearby ocean shore. The sound of water and crashing waves has always lulled my mind into a state of peace. As I listen to the sound, I think of her. Within a few hours, I feel more relaxed than I have in a very long time—all these years without my soulmate, so many decades of grief and despair since she was taken from me.

It's the first night in so long that I nearly come close to sleeping again. Not humanistic sleeping but a sense of rest that some vampires are able to obtain. Once this happens, they look asleep. But their minds are in a coma-like state of contentment until they are awakened by their love.

I have heard it happening once some vampires meet their destined soulmate. I have longed for such an experience. I need to keep a sharp eye now that I have Camille. I'm aware that I have not caught that fiend who destroyed us in the beginning. Now, it is only a matter of time before she strikes again. I need to get closer to Camille. Perhaps she should eventually move in. I know Allison will object. However, Camille is a grown woman. She can choose for herself. I feel it is the only way that I can protect her. I don't know where she lives here. And anyone sadistic could locate her by following her home. I need to be able to protect her.

I'm overwhelmed by my thoughts as I arrive at the school. I have arranged to meet with my brother over the weekend to do more bonding and perhaps share a hunt. I just cannot believe that I found him and he has been here this entire time. I'm excited to reunite with my little brother, just like in old times.

As I'm exiting my car, I notice something in the back seat. Something I must have missed. But it was not there yesterday when I drove home. It is a note, addressed to me. The envelope is written in an elegant script that looks vaguely familiar. I grasp it tightly; I have no doubt this is going to address my Camille. I open it up, and the writing causes me to growl. It plainly says:

Stay away from the human, or history will repeat itself. Claim your true birthright and heritage. Accept who you are meant to be. Leave the blood bag alone, and no one gets hurt.

I read the note. And I seethe. Whoever this fucker is, he or she is not going to dictate my life!

Fuck them! It also makes me weary. I just found Camille. I don't want to lose her.

God, my heart aches at the thought of that, at the idea of continuing my existence away from her.

Eliza's spirit has been calling out to me more frequently. I swear last night I closed my eyes in my room and I felt her. I saw her, she was trying to embrace me. I cannot lose that again, not when I'm so close to finally holding her again. I will not be able to survive this time. I need to call Markus or Victor after class and get them over here, stat! I know Markus is going to really give me hell when I reveal the truth. I'm not dealing with this shit for a second time!

I walk into the building and head straight for the classroom. I arrive early and set up the classroom. Shortly after I arrive, I hear a ruckus in the hallway. It is Camille again, struggling down the hallway with more paperwork, coffees, and a box of items.

Who is she working for that she constantly deals with this? She's not even an intern. I checked with the departments.

"Good morning, Mr. Fuser," I hear her say. I look down the hall as she goes inside several classrooms. And I hear greet everyone. She drops off their coffees, dropping off the paperwork items. Everyone says thank you to her.

I see her go to the end of the hall with the last cup of coffee. Suddenly, I feel her nervousness heighten; she feels terrified. I stand behind my door and listen to the interaction.

"Good morning, Mr. Wahlberg," she says timidly.

"Good, my dear," he says in an alluring voice. I immediately hold back a growl; I want to storm in there and rip him apart. I don't have to read his mind to know what he's trying to accomplish. Camille is very attractive. She looks like Eliza but with a heart-shaped face, plumper lips, pure blond hair. She's shorter than Eliza, with a naturally curvier body. Her breasts are rounder but slightly smaller. She's thinner than Eliza but with a natural hourglass figure like a professional dancer. Any man would love her. And I have learned several have had her. But she's not the type to sleep with teachers. She works her ass off.

I hear her start to leave, then I hear him. "Where are you going, angel?"

"Sir, I have to get to my first class." I hear the door close. "Cami, when are you going to stop denying me? I know your reputation. I could give you straight As. Just show me that you want me as I want you!"

I hear her gasp. I feel her terror. I decide to start quietly walking down the hall. I'm right outside the door when I start to smell her scent stronger.

"S-stop! Why do you do this?" I hear her ask.

"'Cause you know why. You know we're meant to be."

She screams, "No!"

That's it. I go to the classroom. I open the door. I see her kick him in the balls. Her skirt is hunched up. She looks at me, then runs to me. "Mr. Eldridge!"

I hold her briefly, trying to tell her that she's safe now. "Go to class," I order her, and she takes off, sobbing. I grab him by the throat and haul him to his feet. I'm seething! I want to kill him! He had her pinned against the counter, attempting to impale her from behind!

"You are fucking disgusting!" I mildly contain my rage as I punch him in the face and throw him over a table. "You're done!"

He starts to laugh. "That is rich, Mr. Eldridge. Your anger tells me everything. Seems she's denying me because you're already satisfying her!"

I sneer at him. "Or maybe I'm a gentleman who would never take advantage of a lady." I will find him later after school hours if need be after I calm her down.

I walk out of the room. There are several teachers in the hallway. "You!" I point to one. "Find Dean Richards! I want this piece of shit fired for sexual assault on a student!" I bark at everyone. I know my brother is not going to take this laying down. I leave the scene and walk back into my classroom. I'm enraged. I snap out of it when I see Camille.

"You have a class, do you not?" I ask her. I come off a little rude, and I don't mean to. I'm just very upset at what could have happened.

She looks at me, startled. "My teacher gave me the morning off. If you don't want me here, I will go." She starts to collect her stuff and leave, with a hurt expression.

"Stop," I say to her. I reach over and grab her hand. "I'm sorry. Seeing what happened just angered me. I don't want you to go," I tell her.

She seems to relax a bit comes closer to me. She steps into my embrace, buries her head into my chest, and cries.

"Do you want to leave? I will cancel class this morning," I ask her in a lulling voice.

She nods.

"Wait here," I tell her, and I step into the hallway. I see my brother walking away from the classroom. Mr. Wahlberg was detained inside.

"Richard!" I call to his attention. He turns toward me as some of the teachers look between us. I realize I just made a mistake and identified that we were previously connected. I ignore their questioning eyes.

"I'm going to take Ms. Williams home. I'm canceling class for today."

He nods, and in a whisper too quiet for humans, asks, "Who is she to you?"

I respond, "Eliza reborn. I feel her spirit inside of her calling out to me."

My brother's eyes flip wide open. A smile plays on his face. "Be careful, brother. She's human. Tread lightly."

I nod, collect Camille, and walk out of the school.

I notice her car is not in the parking lot, so I give her a ride in mine. She feels so right and perfect next to me. She shows me where she lives, and I drive her there. We pull up to the apartment building. The neighborhood looks a bit worn out. The duplexes look unkempt. Her apartment building looks like it could use some updating. The sign in front is weathered, and some of the steps are broken. I wouldn't trust my dog to stay safe here. She's in a cheap one-bedroom apartment. I continue look around. There is graffiti on the side of her building. The air conditioner on the main floor looks broken. A car drives by blaring rap music. There are several men in the car with gang attire on.

This place is probably the worst apartment building I have seen, surprisingly about ten blocks away from my penthouse. I park out front of her apartment.

"Do you want to come upstairs? After what happened. I don't want to be alone." I agree and follow her in. As I'm walking through the door, I notice the car slow up, and one of the men is eyeing Camille. I bite back a growl as we step inside.

I sit down on the sofa, and she goes into her room, supposedly to change. She comes back a while later in comfy clothes and a snuggly blanket. She sits down by me and lays her head on my shoulder to cry some more.

"I'm sorry you had to see that. I was not always such a slut."

I shake my head. "You're not a slut," I tell her.

She shakes her head in disagreement. "Yes. I am. I have had so many men, and I want to have you for the same selfish reasons."

I stroke her hair as she confesses.

"Now I'm not so sure."

Oh?

"I feel closer to you. I feel you're not Chase. You're not going to use me and dump me."

I turn toward her, and she lays her head on my lap. "Camille, you've been playing with boys. You have not had a man!" I tell her in a husky voice.

Her eyes widen, and she suddenly stares at my lips. She lifts herself up and brings her lips to mine. I deepen the kiss as she moans, and I lick her lips. They open wide for me. I plunge my tongue into her mouth. She adjusts herself to straddle my lap. I gently press her into me. I move my lips to her neck. She moans, and it sounds so sweet.

"Hunter," she says in a whisper I know so well. I cannot hold back anymore.

"Where?" I ask.

"My bedroom," she says.

I pick her up while she wraps her legs around me, and I carry her to her room. I lay her on the bed and work on claiming her body. We spend the rest of the afternoon in a heated, passionate embrace as we both scream and writhe in the pleasure only we can give each other.

Things escalated quicker than I expected. But I wouldn't change it for the world. I have not felt this happy in decades, even now as I lie here, wrapped up in her arms, caressing her naked back. She sighs as she snuggles further into my side. I cannot believe that after all this time, through all the emotional turmoil I have gone through, she's in my life!

I know this form is not the true Eliza. However, I'm overjoyed. I wouldn't change anything about Camille. She's everything that my wife was, plus more. I feel like she connects with me on deeper levels than my wife did.

I softly caress her bare back, and she wraps her arm across my chest. I kiss the side of her face, smiling, as she turns her head toward me.

"Hunter?"

I nip her nose. "Yes?"

She yawns. "I wasn't sure if you would still be here."

I stroke her hair.

"I'm glad. Honestly, it feels shitty and lonely waking up alone."

I slide myself down beside her and wrap my arms around her body. "You never have to feel that again. If you'll have me, I will be here."

She has a sleepy smile on her face as she kisses me lightly. I whisper to her, "Forever."

After she awakens, we spend the next several hours talking about everything. I share with her my business, and she's genuinely interested. She shares with me her annoyance with Allison. Apparently, in the family, Allison is considered the "perfect" sister, and both sisters seem to be trying to be Allison.

"Camille, don't try to be your sister. You are perfect just as you are."

She's shocked at first, then she smiles with a megawatt smile and hugs me fiercely.

I feel so connected with her each passing hour. I know completely that she was destined for me, and I'm so happy I found her. After some time lying in bed, we both get dressed. My brother texts me that we both have the week off class. Thank you, Richard! I inform her, and she starts to panic about being able to afford her bills.

The receptionist clearly was wrong. She informed me that the departments pay her for helping. "Camille, it is completely up to you, but I can help you."

She shakes her head. "Hunter, I don't know. I know you are well endowed clearly in more ways than wealth." She smirks, and I crack up laughing. "But I don't want to owe you money?"

I look her in the eye. "Camille, you don't owe me anything. I want to help you," I tell her, and she shakes her head, giving me another hug as she thanks me. This feels like the start of something beautiful.

Over the next week, we spend every moment together, and she spends every night in my arms as I bury myself deep inside of her. We wake up every morning in bliss. I never want this to end.

We arrive at class the following Monday. She now is positioned in the front row closest to me as I lecture. She's a very bright student and does everything she can to succeed. She's more like me than I realized when I first met her. She gathers up her books at the end of class, and I see out of the corner of my eye some schmuck approaching her.

"Hey, Cami."

She looks over her shoulder. "Jordan," she addresses him. I have my eye on this. I want to see what she'll do.

"So, I was wondering if you're free tonight?" I don't miss the salacious tone in his voice.

"Sorry. I'm busy from now on," she says in a cold voice as she walks away from him. The kid is flabbergasted, and I'm feeling proud. Yeah, punk, she's mine! I finish the class, discussing creative illustrations, and pack up to leave.

I notice Camille has already left this time. Later in the day, I'm driving, and I see her at the café. I realize that she left to go to work. I sit down and smile when she notices me. She smiles and winks at me. I'm in seventh heaven with this girl. After some time has gone by, she sits down next to me.

"Hey, babe!" She kisses me in front of everyone, to my happy surprise. I wrap my hand around the nape of her neck and crash my lips to hers letting everyone in sight know she's mine! When she starts to moan, I pull away, and she pouts.

"Sweetheart, you're working," I remind her as all her friends stare with their mouths gaping.

She notices and laughs a bit, then stands up to leave. As she walks by, I subtly slide my hand across her ass. That sexy ass. I will be claiming that again tonight. If she gets sassy with me, I'll do what I did last night. I bound her to the bed and claimed her. Man, did she come hard. Turns out this little minx has a kinky side.

I decide to head back to her apartment and wait for her. When I arrive, I instantly sense something is wrong. The door is slightly ajar.

I notice a scent that doesn't belong to Camille. I take a deep inhale lavender and peppermint. I push my way inside her apartment. What I see makes me hiss. Someone has been in here. Her apartment is trashed. Everything is thrown around. There is a rock sticking out of her TV. Her sofa is ripped up as if claws slashed it. Her windows are all shattered,

There is the word *Slut* written in red all over her kitchen counter and cabinets. I walk to the back hallway where her bedroom is. The bed is torn apart, again looking like a tiger mauled it. Her dresser is smashed. Her clothes are ripped apart. To my horror, there is a small doll hung in the bedroom closet. I immediately cut it down in disgust. I decide to check the rest of the apartment. Nothing has been stolen. I walk past the bathroom, and I notice the mirror. The message sends fury through my body. It is indeed a scare tactic to drive her away.

Die, human bitch! Go back to the gutter, whore!

I snarl in fury. The words are written in red, and I can tell it is blood. Camille doesn't own any pets, so I fear where it came from. I hope none of her neighbors are hurt. She'll never want to live here again after this. I find a cleaning solution to erase this message and clean her kitchen before she gets home. Once it is erased, I quietly exit her apartment and head back to mine. I make sure that I move with speed, so no one sees me leave.

I arrive back at the penthouse, and I head straight to my home gym. I punch the boxing bag directly into the wall. I'm so enraged and scared! This is happening sooner than I want it to. Fuck! Just when I finally start to feel happy, someone must start fucking it up.

I finish my workout, and I receive a phone call. I look at the caller and recognize Camille. I answer the phone—she's beyond hysteric. I don't blame her.

"Sweetheart, I don't want you staying there any longer. I cannot bear the thought of whoever it was coming back."

She tells me she thinks it might be Mr. Wahlberg or maybe someone else, and she doesn't feel safe there anymore. She doesn't need to worry about him ever again. I will never tell her. But I ended him.

I was running through the city and found him assaulting a different girl on the other side of town. He had just finished copulating with her, and in the process of fixing the situation, I snarled and tore him apart before he could kill the poor girl. I felt sick to my stomach and guilty I didn't end him sooner. If I had, this innocent girl wouldn't have been hurt. Now, he can never harm anyone again. I informed my brother of the incident, and he arrived with his own coven to erase the scenario.

Her question pulls me out of my thoughts. "Where would I go, Hunter?" she asks me.

"Come to my place, Camille. At least until you find somewhere new," I suggest.

She happily accepts. We have already been sleeping in the same bed for the past few weeks, and we are nearly inseparable. It makes the most sense. I will do anything to protect my soulmate. She belongs by my side.

"I will be over in a few hours. I have to go file a police report, and I need to let my landlord know."

I tell her I will go with her. I don't leave it up for discussion after what has happened. It occurs to me that I will need to stock my fridge with human food. I quickly run to the store and bring back enough food to stock my fridge for the next week. I know I will have to better stock it in a few days. Right now, this is good enough.

I meet her at her apartment, and I stay with her through the whole scenario. I hold her hand and wrap my arms around her as she recounts everything she witnessed to the police and her landlord. After a few hours of answering questions and regaling her traumatic episode, the police leave. I decide to return to my place and prepare for her arrival. As I'm walking out the door, I hear her blood-curdling scream.

I run into the bathroom. She hides her face in my arms as I see it, the reason for the blood I found earlier—there is a mutilated cat in the tub. How in the fuck did I miss it? I rush her out of the apartment, and I drive like a demon back to my penthouse. She's shaking and sobbing the entire time.

Fuck, I think she's going into shock. It is a short drive, thank heavens. I nearly jump from the car with her in my arms getting her inside as I constantly watch over my shoulder. I have a strong feeling that Bathilda has returned. If it is true that she's back, things are about to get dangerous.

This realization chills me to the bone. And memories of my last human night plays in my mind. None of us are safe.

CHAPTER 22

I held her throughout the night as her body shakes and she sobs at not only the horrific sight she witnessed but also the slaughter of her apartment. I rock her all night long until she falls asleep in my arms. I lay her on my bed, and she snuggles into my chest. I watch her sleep for a few hours, swearing an oath to protect her. Suddenly, I start to feel a crawling sensation go through me. My gums start to tingle. With horror, I realize then that the beast at bay has only been lying dormant purposefully. It's waiting to have her here, so it could strike.

I wrench myself away from her, detesting myself, my heart heavy. How could I have made her feel so safe when I am just as dangerous? I close my bedroom door and force myself to leave. The beast inside is fighting me, snarling, giving me vivid scenarios of how sweet and good her blood would taste.

"No!" I growl. I'm better than this. I convince myself to look at her as if she were Eliza. I would never hurt her.

The beast roars in fury, yet I fight him with everything in me. *I don't give a shit. I will not succumb. I will not let this vile monstrous side of me be stronger than me. I will not harm her,* I tell the beast, and he retreats into my mind, snarling.

I leap from my balcony. It's past midnight, so most of the humans will be either asleep or out partying. I need to hunt immediately to satiate the beast. I think, honestly, it might be a good idea to pick up some blood bags. I don't know why I never thought of it. I could adjust to blood bags. That way, Camille doesn't catch on to what I am. It would be devastating if she woke up during the night and found me coming home from hunting disheveled.

That happened once with Lucinda, and she nearly went into shock for a whole day before accepting it. Learning that Lucinda's family are witches, though, it was understandable why she was able to accept it. Camille, though, I don't know her family well enough. I know that she's human. But she never mentions her parents, just her sisters. I have a feeling something happened to them that she doesn't discuss. I push the thoughts out of my mind as I run. I start to concentrate on my hunting.

I slow near the hills of San Francisco. I have never been here before. I'm interested in the hunting possibilities. Suddenly, as I'm descending, I hear a growl behind me. I turn around to see a mountain lion perched nearby on a ledge, crouching to attack, as it senses the predator that I am.

What the fuck, it's still blood, I think as I let a snarl rip through me. It soars from the ledge toward me. I give it a swift kick, knocking it into a tree.

The mountain lion roars and charges at me. I charge as well. With speed, I dodge its attacks, jump onto its back, wrap my arms around its torso in a vicelike grip, and bite into its neck. Its warm blood fills my mouth. It is not as sweet as human blood. There's a tangy taste to it. It is then that I realize that it will suffice. Could it be possible? Could I survive like this? If I'm being honest with myself, I have always hated traditional hunting. I feel as though, with each life I have taken, my soul has fallen deeper and deeper into the blackness of hell.

Can I redeem myself through this alternative? Can I stop? It was Garrett who drilled into me the importance of human blood, yet I remember there were times where he would tolerate animal blood. Quite hypocritically, he would force me to hunt humans until I didn't want anything else. But he occasionally would indulge in it. Honestly, as I think back on the amount of hypocrisy Garrett practiced, I realize it was such bullshit! He knew I hated it. He knew in the beginning. I didn't want to. I hated the idea of hurting someone. I still do.

With this revelation, I feel as if I have awoken from a daze like I had been asleep for centuries. I stroll down to San Francisco and head into a clothing store. I'm a bit disheveled. I cannot return home like this. I locate one which I can tell is under vampiric management. A fellow vampire will not ask questions since they will understand.

"Hello, Your Majesty," she greets me in a low voice.

I nod. Yes, technically I'm the newly chosen vampire king. However, it has not been made public yet, so someone must be spreading the news! I groan.

I greet her and ask her where I can find a different outfit. After a few minutes, I'm dressed, and due to my status, she gives it to me freely. I walk out the doors and make the run back to the penthouse in minutes. I arrive to find Camille still sleeping in bed. I check the time on the digital clock and realize I have only been gone for three hours. I head toward the front room, sit down, open my laptop, and check my emails. I spend the next several hours focusing on some of my business.

Once that is completed, I still feel restless. I know Bathilda is lurking once again. I can feel it in my bones, like my body in being infected with acid spreading through it. Over the years of hunting her, I have developed a sickening sense. I can feel when she's near. It makes my body feel poisoned.

Eliza also has been with me in spirit, whispering to me that she's close. Eliza is greatly affected by Bathilda since the night of her death. She told me once that it is as if when Bathilda killed her, she took a bit of her soul. And Eliza can sense when she's near as well.

I can only hope she doesn't know where I'm living. I need to protect Camille. She's my life, my true second chance. This is my mission now. I stand to my feet and walk over to my harp. It used to belong to Eliza, and it took me many years to track it down. After Garrett sold the house, he also sold away all my human attachments, memories that I had with her, and never told me. I learned all this later when I wanted to bring some of them with me to America.

I was enraged at him and didn't speak to him for a week. It was then that I didn't trust him anymore. I have spent years hunting down some of the items we shared. I loved this harp.

As I start to play, I see Camille exit the hallway and walk toward me. She sits on the sofa in front of me.

"I didn't know that you could play the harp?"

I smile. "Yes. Do you like it?" I ask her.

She smiles sweetly. "I actually used to play when I was a kid"

Oh? "You did?" I ask her, surprised.

"Yeah. I have always found it soothing."

I smile again. "I do as well."

She cocks her head. "Who taught you?"

My smile fades at her question. "My wife did."

She looks at me with alarm. "Where is she now?" she asks me. I can hear her thoughts, hoping that she's not being a homewrecker. I let her fear wash away with my next words.

"She was taken away from me. We were attacked one night, and she was killed," I tell her in a bleak voice. Her face fills with remorse. I will not be open to the fact that she's my wife reborn, which would flip her out.

"I'm so sorry." She comes to me and hugs me.

"It was long ago. You are my life now."

She smiles at me sweetly. "I don't know, honestly, if I should be here. You have an intimidating aura, yet I don't feel scared of you," she tells me.

"That is because, my sweet," I say to her as I surprise her by lifting her up to fit into my lap, "you were made to be mine!" I set her down and crush my lips to hers.

I remind myself to sheath my fangs. She moans into my mouth while her arms go around my neck. I lift her in my arms, carrying her to our bedroom. I spend the next several hours that are left of the night burying myself inside of her. The house fills with her cries of ecstasy as she moans and screams my name repeatedly. I take her in every way I can possibly think of, so she will never forget that we belong together. I know that soon I will have to be honest with her. The beast inside is starting to grow hungry for her, and I'm fighting him with everything that I have.

As I swallow her salacious moans with a searing kiss, I hear a distant sinister chuckle from somewhere outside in the darkness. Someone is watching and waiting. The next morning, I lie in bed. I wrap myself in her arms again. I feel so blissfully happy. However, the horrors of yesterday's events are fresh in my mind. I'm ecstatic that she agreed to move in with me so suddenly. But this still spells danger. She's being hunted by that psychotic bitch. Because of me.

I don't know how she found out about her. But I know secrets never stay hidden in the vampire world. I need to be honest with her and tell her the truth before Bathilda comes for her. I turn to my side in the bed and watch her dream. I could stare at her sleep forever. She's so beautiful, and I love that she's mine. I start to fear.

For how long? What happens when she learns the truth? A side of me already knows the worst. She will run away screaming. As she should. I love her so much. But perhaps, it is best. I could watch her from afar. No! No, I squash that. I'm not a vampire stalker.

I need to be honest with her. If she hates me, I will learn to accept it. It will protect her and keep her safe. I lie here next to her, waiting for her to wake up. We have been together for almost a month now, and we have been deeply connected. It feels as if she has always been with me. That's because a small part of her has never left me. Camille doesn't realize it yet. I'm stroking her hair as I see her start to stir.

She opens her eyes with a smile at first, then sensing my emotions, she sits up with a frown. "Hunter? What is the matter?"

I smile and brush my thumb across her lip. *Will this be our last day together?* The thought stabs my chest with grief. But I must do this.

"Get dressed and meet me in the living room. I need to speak with you. It is serious, and it is something I need to tell you before we live together officially."

She stares at me while getting dressed, a deep frown on her face. I can feel her anxiety, her fear. She thinks I'm going to leave her. I would never do that. However, I know after this she will leave me.

I meet her in the living room, and she sits down on the sofa. Her anxiety is at a high-power level. "Camille, I need to be honest with you, and what I'm about to tell you may have you running and screaming away from me."

Her eyes widen, and she cracks a joke. "Let me guess: you're not human." She's trying to be sarcastic while downplaying her fear.

I look at her straight in the face. "No. I'm not."

She laughs slightly until she sees that I'm serious. She starts to cower into the couch.

"I'm not human, Camille, and I need you to understand this. I need you to think through us being together. You must also understand. I will never hurt you. If I go away for a trip, part of it is business, and part of it is to control myself."

She's wide-eyed like she's caught in a trance, frozen.

She asks timidly, "What are you?"

I was hoping she would never ask this. But she's always surprising me. I square my shoulders. "I'm a vampire." I tell her this and watch her go pale in fear. "Just know I would never harm you!"

She speaks in a fragile voice. "How would I know that?" Then she surprises me with the fury in her eyes. "I always knew your kind existed! I knew it! Did you murder them! Have you been stalking me my whole life! I have always felt watched! 'Cause I figured it out!" she screams at me.

I have no idea what this is about. "What are you talking about?"

She glares at me, "Do not play dumb! My parents!"

Her statement is like an electric shock to me.

"They were found near Navy Pier. I was eleven. Chests clawed up. Throats ripped open," she says as she cries. "Everyone said it was an animal attack. Animals don't rip people's throats out or drain their blood!" She screams as she cries.

I never knew this about her. It makes sense why she never talks about it. I don't know if I should comfort her. "Camille, do you really believe I would be that cruel? That I would do that? Have I not protected you?" I ask her as she continues to glare at me.

"It's what you do, isn't it? Destroy and murder innocent people? Is this your plan? Are you trying to lure me into this apartment so you can claim my life!" she screeches.

I'm hurt she would believe that. But I cannot blame her after hearing the truth of her parent's death. She believes in vampires, and she believes we're vicious killers. She's not entirely wrong. But that is not me anymore.

She needs to understand this, she needs to know that I have never been such a monster.

"No. I don't do that, not anymore. I did in my early years because my mentor was forcing me. But not anymore."

She stops crying, and her mouth falls open.

"I can read people. I know if someone is like, let me say, for example, a serial killer that has not found justice. I become justice," I tell her with a snarl.

Her eyes shoot up to mine in surprise. "Camille, I hate the thought of hurting people. I have never been that person. In my human life, I loved taking care of people just like I loved caring for my wife."

She's shaking her head. I can hear her thoughts: *That is too impossible to believe.* She needs to understand me.

"Do you remember what I told you about, that night when I said my wife died?"

She nods. "She died while I was protecting her. We were attacked by vampires. I was changed that night while trying to protect her."

Camille looks at me as if she's seeing me in a new light. She's finally starting to see me, so I continue the confession. "You aren't the first human I have been with. I dated one for several years. I would have loved to marry her."

She asks me in a broken voice. "What happened to her?"

"She unexpectedly died while we were on a camping trip. I thought it was werewolves. But the incident of her death, it was described exactly as you said." I stand up and pace the room. "She left behind her daughter who I raised. If you don't believe me, I will arrange for you to meet her."

I see her eyes widen in surprise at the truth of my words. "I will leave you right now, so you can consider what I'm saying. You need to decide the best choice for you." I say to her, "I understand your pain. But I will never hurt you."

She turns her head away. I walk away. Before I fully step out the door, I leave her with something else to think about.

"I'm truly sorry for what happened to them. I had parents too. I loved my parents. My brother is actually your dean." Her eyes fly open in shock. "He can tell you of my character. Know this as well: I will help you seek vengeance. And know this: I'm not a just vampire. But I'm under consideration to be the vampire king! So I mean what I say. I will bring you justice," I tell her with my powerful aura.

I turn away and walk away from the penthouse with my heart in a vice. I hear her gasp then. I hear her start to sob again. I hear her screaming my name, that she's sorry for everything. She must think I'm angry at her. I'm not angry at her. I'm hurt by how much pain she has gone through. I also know that being with me will be hazardous for her. I want her to have time to herself to make the right decision.

I walk away feeling like I'm leaving a piece of my soul with her. No matter what she chooses, I will try to honor it. I just hope that

I'm not forced to see her walk away. I take the elevator to the parking garage of my building and slide into the front seat of my BMW.

As I start to drive, I suddenly receive a call. I look to see who it is.

"Markus," I answer. He greets me and asks what the urgency is. I tell him about recent events. I tell him that I met Eliza's doppelganger. I tell him about what happened at the apartment and Bathilda's return.

I mention how I confessed everything about us to Camille and the truth she told me about her parents.

"There is apparently a lot been happening with you," he says sarcastically. "There seems to have been a number of slip-ups that were happening when those elder wretches were in charge! How could they turn a blind eye to the cruelty that she described?"

We talk more about it. And I leave him in charge of what is to be done. As far as Bathilda, he suggests that we get back to Chicago, ASAP! I doubt she's going to agree to that. I don't want this to be goodbye. I feel my heart dying inside at the thought.

CHAPTER 23

I continue to drive around Portland, feeling like I'm going nowhere or have nowhere to go. I'm terrified to come home and find her gone. I know that she would need her space, she should be a thousand miles away from me. It would be for her safety. However, I also wonder what she meant by "being watched all her life."

Did someone already know about her before I did? Was it because she discovered the truth? Either way, that means she has been in danger for years. That's a scary thought. I'm thankful that no one has attempted to harm her.

I drive back to the penthouse, heart feeling like ice. As I walk inside and find her gone, I crumple to the ground, fearing the worst has happened. I lie there for a while until I look up and find a note on the dining table:

Dear Hunter,

I don't even know how to write this! It took everything in me to leave, something in me was strongly urging me to stay. I just need space. I understand everything that you said. I know in my heart that you would never hurt me. I'm sorry for the harsh words I said. It was foolish of me to blame you for my parents.

Just because some people might be evil does not mean everyone is. I need time to think and make the right choice for me.

Love, Camille

I crumble the note and let the sobs rip through me. I fucking loathe what I am more than anything this moment. I feel like I have lost my life again, and I could not stop it.

I want the rip something to shreds. However, there is nothing I can think of that could help with this pain in my heart. I fall to the floor frozen. I know this is the best decision for her. She will be alive, happy and safe. She will not be tied to a soulless monster. I know that if she lives. I can move forward and live beyond this current pain. My rational side is telling me this. However, I don't know how I'm going to live without her.

Several days go by, and I hear nothing from her. I do my best to contain the pain in my heart. I'm constantly waiting for her to contact me. Once it has been weeks, I decide enough is enough. I decide to search for her. To make matters worse, she's not even in my class anymore.

I drive by the café where she works, and they inform me that she has resigned. Her friend tells me she found a different apartment, a position for her degree, and relocated to New York. I walk away from the diner, feeling like my heart is being ripped out.

My brother meets with me, and the pain worsens. "Camille, she, uh, graduated early."

I'm flabbergasted. "How?"

Richard informs me that she has had more than enough credits. She said she needed a change, so her teachers let her work virtual for the past couple of weeks, and she finished last weekend. He says how sorry he is, and I feel my heart trying to stop.

She completely left me. Wait, they said New York. It is crazy. But I have a condo in New York. I could wait a while, give her more space, and relocate there to be near her. I'm frantic right now, Bathilda is roaming around. And Camille just relocated across the country. I understand Camille doesn't know. However, it is too risky. Fuck! Camille! Why did you do this?

I walk out of the school, feeling an ever-deepening pit of despair. I run straight toward the Oregon Mountains. I need to be alone. I'm surrounded by forest when. I accidentally knock into someone, who I was anticipating seeing!

"Oh, hello, lovely," she purrs.

"Fuck you, bitch!" I snarl. I start to measure myself for strike. I sink into a crouching position to lunge at her.

She just laughs at me. "Oh, my Hunter! Are you sore because your little human bed toy dumped you?" Bathilda snickers.

How the fuck does she know? "What did you do? I should just kill you now!" I speak coldly.

"No, my love, you won't, and I know you won't because I have something of yours." Her words strike terror for Camille's safety.

I feel a chill go down my spine. I lunge at her, but she shoves me out of the way. It feels like we are playing a game of cat and mouse.

"Where the fuck is she!"

She laughs. "Who are we talking about? Oh, the human!" She paces around me. "I simply told her the truth, that you only want her because she looks exactly like your dear wife!"

My face pales. And I nearly fall over in shock. "How the fuck do you know?"

She doesn't answer me. "I don't care about your little human. Although, unless you want her to end up like the last little bitch, I would stop copulating with your food and make the right choice!"

I'm seething. "It was you! You killed Lucinda!"

She holds up her hands like she's being arrested. "Yeah, we did. That was fun!" She giggles as I hit her in the gut. She takes the hit, then bounces back. "Remember who you are, my love! Remember who they are to us!"

I'm snarling. Then. It dawns on me. "So, that means it was you behind the savage animalistic attacks!"

She goes white with fear as I say it. I grab her by her throat.

"Fuck, Hunter, get your hands off me!"

I snarl in fury, "That's Your Majesty to you, peasant!"

Her eyes grow wide, and her mouth hangs open. I'm just about the rip her when someone knocks into me at vampiric speed. The hit is hard enough that I'm thrown off the cliff. I reach out and dig my hands into the granite as I roll down the hill. By the time I reach the top, she's gone.

Fuck! I have no idea who fucking threw me down the cliff. But I don't trust Bathilda to stay away from Camille. It is evident that she killed Lucinda. She also is not working alone. I must get to New York. Fucking soon.

I leave the Oregon mountain range, with a sole purpose in my mind. I need to find Camille. I cannot believe that she abruptly left the way she did. No goodbye, nothing! The mere idea is painful.

Do I mean nothing to her? Was I originally a sex ride all along? No. I cannot think like that. What the fuck happened? I'm not going to get any answers here. I need to leave.

I arrive back in Portland. I inform my brother of my imminent departure. I inform him that I need to return home and apologize for any inconvenience it may cause. My brother, as always, is completely understanding and wishes me a safe trip.

I call Allison and ask her to arrange for me to travel to New York. I tell her that I have not visited the publishing office there in a long time, and I need to check on management and so on.

She says, "Right away, sir," professional as ever.

I head back to my penthouse and find a note there.

Hunter,

Stop avoiding the inevitable. Stop messing around with weak little humans. Join us, take your rightful

> *place as ruler of our world and rule this world as we*
> *know it. Stop attacking Bathilda as well. She's trying*
> *to prepare you, to become the king you are meant to be!*

The Master

I read the note, and I have no words. What the ever-living fuck! Who is this psychopath?

He doesn't understand the history I have with her. I decide to leave a note myself, with my little message, and I hope they are watching. It's not bad enough that these people have been stalking for God knows how long. I have known they were there for a while now. I have tried to ignore it 'cause all I want is to live my life and reclaim what I lost.

This group just will not let me. I can only imagine that they want me to become like my ancestor Abner, they were possibly in league with him so many centuries ago. They are probably just as wicked as he was. That is not who I am, and I have worked my ass off over the last several years to atone for my sins, to redeem myself before God in prayer, to become something of the man I was once before. I will be damned if I let some group of psychos turn me into a demonic, sadistic beast.

Dear Master,

> *You can take your thoughts me joining your twisted*
> *band of psychopaths. And kiss my ass. I will be king.*
> *However, I will do it the right way. I have no plan*
> *to turn into a sadistic demon like my ancestor Abner.*
> *He and his deranged wife deserved to be assassinated!*
> *I will never be like that. Bathilda is a twisted psycho,*
> *and I have no interest in being a part of any group that*
> *she relates to. Fuck off and leave me alone.*

Hunter Eldridge

I leave the note while looking around. If these people are in the area, I have no doubt they will find the message. I lock up the penthouse and start to make my way to the airport. I receive an email from Allison letting me know that everything is arranged and my Upper East Side Loft has been cleaned promptly. I message her back with a thank you. I'm so nervous. This is very impromptu, basically, chasing after Camille without telling anyone. I just need to know what is happening with her. I just cannot let her go, not like this. Not without any reasoning behind it.

While I sit through the flight, I remember Bathilda's words. She was the one who killed Lucinda. She and her psychotic coven were the ones for all the gruesome murders, she's responsible for Camille's parents. Everything hits me like lightning with clarity. They are also responsible for the attack that changed my life. I was blaming the wolves this entire time. I need to eventually call Molly. She needs to know the truth.

After a few hours, my jet touches down in New York City. I can feel my nerves sizzling. I have no idea where to look for her. New York City is incredibly huge. I have a feeling, though, that Eliza is going to sense me, and she will seek me out as she did before. The first order of the day is to get settled in my loft, then I may as well go to my company to check on progress before figuring out where to look.

I exit my jet and leave her in the hands of Connor. He has taken care of her for several years every time I arrive in New York. I hail a taxi and give them the directions to my Fifth Avenue loft. I was very fortunate to find this apartment so close to my publishing building. I can quickly walk to work when I'm here. Vampires in New York are more common than humans might think. The city that never sleeps creates the perfect hunting grounds for vampires. That is another reason for my being here. The last thing I need is for someone to take an interest in her as something other than a mate does. She could easily be hurt or killed here. Humans that walk around here are living in a vampire buffet zone.

I arrive at my building E. H. Publishing in a few minutes. No one here knows that I'm arriving, so this will be fun and keep them on their toes. The moment I walk into the lobby, Camille's scent hits me powerfully. She can't be here. Can she? My brother never said where she was hired at. What would the odds be that she was recruited here? I never mentioned this location in my lecture, she couldn't have known. I suddenly feel like jumping to the moon in happiness if I'm right.

I walk through the lobby and enter the VIP elevator. I exit the floor below mine where the secretaries work. The first step is to surprise Mr. Millard and his team. I notice they tend to slack. Every time I come in for a surprise visit he pushes them into gear. I walk into the room, and everyone stops what they are doing.

The building manager Gregory comes up to greet me. "Mr. Eldridge?"

I shake his hand, tell him it is a surprise visit to check on progress. He scurries away. In hurry. I hear him shouting at everyone that I have arrived unannounced, to pick up the pace—be perfect and be professional.

I chuckle to myself. He always did love to kiss ass. Suddenly, I hear a startled gasp, and I hear something drop. I peel my eyes away from Gregory. At a desk in the far corner, ocean blue eyes lock with mine, with a look of surprise.

Yeah, sweetheart. I found you, I think as her mouth gapes open while she freezes, and I think the biggest laugh of all: *She accepted an internship at E. H. Publishing? My little minx now works for me.*

I stare at her with a smirk that read, *If you were trying to get away, you failed.* Oh, this is going to be much more fun than Portland. She's officially mine in more ways than one, and I'm strongly thinking of some form of punishment for her behavior and little disappearing act.

The look on her face is confused but with the knowledge that she's in trouble. *Yeah, your sweet little ass is in trouble for the little stunt you pulled.*

Mr. Gregory turns to the sound and barks at her, "Ms. Williams. Clean that mess up."

She immediately lowers herself and does as she's asked. I want to scold him for his attitude. But he's not aware of our history.

Instead. I approach her and help her.

"Mr. Eldridge, you don't have to help me," she says.

"Mr. Eldridge? Have you forgotten me?" I ask her in a very low voice.

She looks at me. She's trying to hide her longing. Eliza is pushing through. I know it.

"My office in two hours. You have some explaining to do," I whisper to her. I stand up and walk away. I inform Mr. Gregory that I want to see her in my office in two hours sharp. As I walk away, I hear him scold her and tell her that she better pray she doesn't lose her job after this happens.

I hear her low chuckle. He has no idea that we are already acquainted.

Directly on time, she arrives in my office, looking like a little lamb about to be slaughtered. This room is soundproof, so we can talk without anyone hearing. I sit at my desk just staring at her. Her head hangs low, she knows I'm pissed, she knows she fucked up.

I keep my emotions in check. "So, you relocated?"

She just nods. "You just packed up everything and relocated very randomly to New York City from Portland? Finishing school early at the same time?"

She quietly says, "Yes."

I'm at a loss for words. But I find them. "Is this about us? You didn't need to go that far? Do I repulse you that much? You didn't seem like it when you were screaming my name?"

She gasps and stares at me.

"I said that I would give you time. I never expected you to completely leave me and relocate across the country?" I tell her in a broken tone.

Camille looks like she's going to cry. "Hunter, I never intended to," she says as she bows her head. "I was coming back to your penthouse. Then out of nowhere, my mind was filled with the desire to relocate. It was all I could think about. My mind told me to leave school and start my life over in New York City."

I pinch the bridge of my nose, understanding what happened. "Camille, do you remember what I am?"

She looks at me pale. "Yes" is all she says.

I need to be honest with her. "Camille, that was vampire mind compulsion that was inflicted on you from someone very dangerous, the same one I found out murdered your parents" As I tell her this, there is a fire in her eyes. A look of sheer hate.

"Where!" she growls out.

I tell her that I don't know. It is a group of sadistic vampires that I'm trying to track down. They are responsible for countless brutal deaths.

She starts to shake and cry. I pull her into my arms, and she gladly accepts. I bury my nose in her hair, inhaling the delicious scent of her.

"No more running!" I glare at her. "You and I are meant to be together. I need to protect you. But you running off to New York of all places." I shake my head. I tell her that these creatures are evil. "They knew, if you came here, you would be unprotected in a city which is like vampire restaurant."

She gulps as she starts to realize what I'm saying. They meant for her to come here, away from me, and possibly die.

I look at her again, and we both say the same thing. "No more running." I cup her hands with my face. "Whatever happens, we face together." Then I kiss her like a starving man in need of water.

She's all I see, all I want, and the one who I cannot live without. When I dismiss her to return to work, I also give her my compulsion, to come to my loft on Fifth Avenue after she gets off work. She's happy to accept this and informs me that she's staying at a family condo in Chelsea.

It seems that her grandmother was the niece of a British Lord Wellington, and he bequeathed her the condo. "No one lives there anymore, so my aunt, who is a lawyer, decided to remodel it for me."

"That is nice of her."

"She wanted me to have somewhere decent to live in the city." I didn't know her family was a bit connected to mine. I ask for the name of her grandmother, and I'm surprised to learn that I had met her. Her name was Althea Bentley. She was the niece of Eliza's sister's husband. I remember meeting her one time while attending the christening of their son, Conrad Wellington, She was just a kid at the time. She must have married into the Williams family after relocating to America.

Damn. It is a small world. I'm happily surprised to learn this news and thrilled that she's living in a decent house this time. That apartment in Portland was a piece of trash in a shady neighborhood. I hope that eventually she will live with me. I never want to be away from her again.

CHAPTER 24

Three hours later, the concierge in the lobby informs me that has a Miss Camille Williams has arrived. I immediately send her up. I cannot resist. After she enters the apartment. I take her into my arms and kiss her like she's the air that I need. She matches my kiss with equal passion, and I'm so thrilled she's here, which means she has accepted me.

I deepen the kiss and decide to let myself feel her. I use some of my powers to heighten the passion we're emanating. She gasps when she feels it. I back her into the wall with a growl.

"Oh God!" she screams. I wrap her legs around me and carry her to my bedroom. I throw her down on the bed, we shred each other of clothing.

I hover over her. "You're so beautiful, so soft, so warm, and mine." I growl as I start to devour her skin.

Her back is arching off the bed, and I have not even gone all the way with her yet. She sees my eyes start to shift. I'm fighting the beast.

"Go ahead," she whispers.

And I stare at her in shock. I shake my head. I know I can stop. But I cannot believe she's saying this. "Hunter. If I'm going be with you and accept you because I know you love me and never hurt me. I want to give all of myself to you" She tilts her head exposing her throat to me.

I struggle for a little while before sinking my fangs in. I hear her gasp and I hear her moan. I only take a small taste of her rich, warm, succulent blood. It is everything that I have ever dreamed she would taste like, the beast in me wants to devour more. Instead, I find the strength to force it down. I lick the wound instantly healing it and position myself at her entrance.

I whisper, "You are never leaving me again," as I sheath myself in her fully to the hilt.

She lets out a load moan and screams yes as I pump myself in and out of her. I hear her scream. "Never again, my love, my prince. My soul is yours." Her voice is blended with Eliza, and it makes me go wild with carnal lust as I reclaim her beautiful body for the rest of the night. I'm never letting her go again.

I'm still hyperaware of Bathilda's threat. I'm not going to take any chances with her safety. I have arranged security for Camille. She hates it. But she doesn't challenge me on the matter.

Time moves forward when a person least expects it. We have been together now for six months. Every day with her has been heaven. Three months after we officially settled in New York, Camille finishes her internship at my company. As a reward for her hard work, I promote her to executive assistant, and I have her relocated to my office. Mr. Millard is speechless and a bit irritated. I become hot tempered with him when he questions my decision. He bows his head, refusing to look at me, claiming that her performance is subpar.

I see through him. I know her work is excellent, and she's driven person. I read his mind and find that he fancied her. But she ignores his flirtatious attempts. I dismiss him, with a mind to possibly give Camille his job. He is honestly an annoying kiss-ass and lazy employee. He works hard but also slacks in other areas. Camille intimidates him, and I love it.

I love her fire, her drive to succeed. I offer her the position and she protests. But after I showed her the several perks, including a pay raise and a soundproof room, she relaxed and comes to love the idea. I wish I could convince her to return to Chicago, so I decide to promote Allison to district manager of that region, so Allison is thrilled, but when she asks me why, Camille comes slightly clean about our relationship, leaving out the vampire part.

Allison is angry at first, then realizes, Camille is finally committing and opening her heart again. She cries and is very happy for us. She hopes Camille continues to change for the better. Everything seems to be going well. Aside from the threats from Bathilda, I'm loving my life again. I just need to prepare for the worst-case scenario. Camille, who once objected to my security, is now grateful. I learned from her last week, while she was out finding food during lunch time, she felt watched. Her security guard located a new vampire who was stalking her while she was in the Indian restaurant.

The most disturbing part was the man who I could tell was a newborn was given her scent. I recognized her cardigan, which she said went missing a few days ago. So they stole my mate's scent. I tore the man apart in anger. No one touches my love. Never again.

Have you ever heard someone say, "Just when everything looks good, a storm happens?" Yeah, different from a century ago, this time. I expect that she-devil to show again. Why is it when I start to become happy, she tries to fuck everything up? The only difference is I don't realize my love is such a fighter. How funny it suddenly happens when we least expect it.

It is beautiful day in July. We are out on a date in Manhattan. I take her out for the entire day, while we have a free day, and I completely spoil her. Every day I make sure that she experiences the elegance of New York. I assign a hairstylist to assist in giving her a makeover that she chooses. She makes me nearly have a heart attack when she chose dark brunette, or specifically, "Deep Mahogany Brunette." She is beautiful beyond compare and is nearly the spitting image of Eliza. Good God, she's asking for trouble. I tell her that she looks like a goddess, and she melts into me. I keep quiet about the now-glaring similarities. She receives manicures, pedicures, facial treatments, waxing, and lastly, I send her with a personal shopper to designer quality stores on Fifth Avenue, letting her become the queen she was always meant to be.

After the entire day is done, she's spent close to one hundred thousand dollars. She feels very self-conscious about it, and she keeps on insisting that she'll repay the money. I won't hear anything of the sort. As far as I'm concerned what is mine is also hers. I assure her I don't care. I want to provide her with the world and give her everything her heart desires. After she's finished with her stunning transformation, I meet her at Rau Depierre Salon, and we depart to find a restaurant for dinner.

I arranged a reservation at a French restaurant in Manhattan, Cafe Carlyle. Very modern and sophisticated. We have plans afterward to tour the channel gardens. There is so much to do in New York City. Since it is her first year living here, I want to give her the adventure of a lifetime while she stays with me. I don't expect her to be here forever.

How long until she wants a family? How long will she stay with me and accept the idea of never having kids? It pains me. But it is true. We enter the restaurant, and I'm ecstatic that I am able to use my fluency. I watch Camille as she stares at me in wonder at how well I am about to speak the language. I tell her how my uncle lived in Paris. She becomes interested in my life experiences, where I have been. She asks me questions about Paris and many more things.

She tells me she has always wanted to travel. During college, before we met, she was also a language major and specialized in French, Mandarin, Spanish, German, and Russia. I find this fascinating since, over the years, I have become fluent in several myself. I'm excited. I finally have someone else around me to communicate within a different language. We immediately start to speak to each other in French, and it is so fun. I now have another thought in mind of eventually making her head over our international division. She's beautiful whether she has her natural blond hair. Her dyeing it, however, is a little unsettling. She looks identical to my late wife. Somehow I have a feeling it was an impromptu idea by that wife. It is a scary thought. I know my wife wants to come back but understands that is nearly impossible. Her body is no longer alive, so she's becoming content with Camille.

There are moments, when Camille is asleep, that Eliza freaks me out by taking over and waking up to be with me. This happened last night. I was resting with Camille. Suddenly, I heard Camille whispering my name at in the morning. I looked at her, and her eyes were a deeper blue. I felt as if I was seeing a hallucination in my mind. She was wearing a dress, and her hair was pinned back. I recognized it right away. This was an outfit that Eliza wore. I knew that Eliza was appearing before me in Camille's body. I threw myself from the bed, and she walked toward me. Her movements were seductive. She started to lower her dress for me. It was too much. Once upon a time, I had wanted this more than anything. Now I feel like, with Camille, I'm finally moving on, but my wife is possessing her body and becoming sexual. I try to walk away.

She started to accuse me of not wanting her, and she sealed her lips to mine. I fought my best until she stroked my ass like she used to. I lost it and claimed her for a while before I came to my senses. We talked, and I asked her to be at peace, to let me be with Camille. I was finally moving on like she wanted. She glared at me, and after a while, I could tell she left. My mind became clear, and Camille laid beside me asleep. I was freaked out for several hours. It was clear Eliza was trying to come back through Camille. I don't know if this is a good or bad thing. She's becoming like a dual personality.

I shake my head subtly, trying to erase that incident. I don't want to sour my dinner date.

We walk away from the restaurant. I was able to hire vampiric security in case anything was to happen. However, they have completely disappeared. I'm pissed. I mentally search for the guards that have now vanished.

I hear someone several blocks away. "Did you kill the guards, my pet?"

"Yes, Master. It was a bit difficult. But handled."

"Very good, my pet. You have been a faithful and useful aid for me. Daddy will reward you later, Bathilda."

"Thank you, Master. We will restore balance again. Hunter was a fool to claim a human. History will only repeat itself, sir."

"He will one day come to learn he was made for more wondrous things."

They both laugh.

I'm seething. I knew it was her. However, I couldn't recognize the man's voice. It sounds as if he were using a disguise. I don't like how frighteningly similar this is.

Out of nowhere, I hear a sinister laugh. Camille immediately takes out her phone and turns on the flashlight. I push her behind me.

"Show yourself, snake!" Camille yells into the darkness.

I look behind me and see her eyes filled with rage. I make her stay behind me.

"Hunter, I don't run from a piece of shit who cowers in the darkness. Coward!" Camille screams out.

I tell her to stop. They are vampires. "I don't give a shit. I won't go down without a fight."

Suddenly, I hear Bathilda. "Ooh my, finally, Hunter. A woman worthy of you. If only she wasn't a useless human. She'd make an excellent vampire."

I roar in fury.

Camille tries not to cringe, still glaring into the darkness.

Bathilda laughs like an evil witch. "You know you are not going to kill me. We have too much fun together."

I scoff at her. "You are chasing me all over the world for a century. Is just so comical. I did you a favor. I killed that little human, so we could be together. What did you do? You killed my sister."

I smirk, then she snarls at me and lunges. I pick up Camille and soar through the air. I take off running with her, jumping, and landing again in Rockefeller Center. She's shaken. She slaps herself on the face and gets into a fighting position. She's so strong.

"You're human, Camille." I glare at her.

"Do you really think I'm some dainty little princess? After the death of my parents, I spent years studying kickboxing."

I shake my head. "Admirable if the opponent was not immortal and thousand times more powerful." I shove her behind me again.

Bathilda comes from nowhere and snatches her away. Camille punches her in the face. Bathilda snarls. Without thinking, I grab the bitch's leg and I land a swift kick in Bathilda's gut. Camille is thrown through the air and lands twenty feet away with a scream as her body makes an impact with the fountain. I stare at Camille in horror, terrified of what I have just done. I feel sick to my stomach. My mind starts filling me with the worst-case scenarios. Dear God, please. Please. Do not let my second chance at love die because of me.

Bathilda charges at me again. I grab her by her throat as we both sail through the air and crash through more than two office buildings. I skid across a room into a desk. I roll over the top of it and feel my head hit a brick wall. I'm so thankful right now I'm vampire. Were I human, that hit would have killed me. I get back up. My head feels fuzzy. But I shake myself as she runs toward me. I counter her attack and knock her through a wall.

Finally, this bitch is going to die. She grabs me and throws me through two floors. I quickly turn around and shove her through every floor there is in the building. I watch as the metal and cement of each level cuts into both of us. I make sure she feels every break as we descend five floors.

She stands to her feet barely, body battered. If she were human, she'd be dead. She screeches at me. "You could have had the world with me, Hunter."

I snarl as I hit her again. "You ripped my world apart."

She swings at me, and I deliver a hard blow to her face.

"Just accept me, Hunter. Accept your fate. You could have your wife back."

I take off into a darkened area of the building luring her in.

I notice the E. H. House on the wall. I realize we are in my building after hours. Perfect. I know this building well. I hear her following me.

"Come on, Hunter. Enough. End this silly charade." She cackles. I hide behind an office door, waiting for her to pass as she steps into view.

"Gladly, you first." I snarl as I slam her into a wall and shove my hand into her chest. Her eyes go wide in shock as I rip through her chest and tear out her heart. Blood coats my hands as she falls to the floor dead. I crush her heart with my hand. I use all my strength to rip her head off. Her blood squirts from her body, filling the room and staining my shirt.

I sit down as I start to cry tears I can no longer produce. Everything she has put me through. All the despair and pain. Eliza, I have avenged you. At that moment, I feel someone kiss my check and whisper her name. It stirs my mind, and I immediately spring to my feet. Fuck. Camille.

I race back to the fountain where she lays completely still. Dear God, no. I cannot live through losing her again. I take her into my arms. I see a crack in her skull and blood covering her beautiful hair. I lick the wound. it immediately starts to heal. However, her heartbeat is faint.

Vampire blood has healing powers. I bite into my wrist, open her mouth, and force her to accept it. I need to save her life. I feel her slightly struggle. Then she starts to weakly drink, and I breathe a sigh of relief, she's going to be okay, she must be. I hold her and kiss her as I find her phone to dial 9-1-1 with only one thought in my mind as the rescue squad arrives to take her to the hospital.

Camille, my love. Please don't leave, I cry out in my mind.

I watch them as they load her on to the gurney, and demanded to ride with her to the hospital. She's so broken. I fight with the health-care professionals to stay with her. I fight against my vampire nature. My beast inside wants to drink from her. I know that will kill her. I run from the room, from the hospital, when they took her into surgery. I run as fast as I can into the mountains near Canada. I need to hunt so I can heal.

I find a bear and take it down with ease. I decide, after this ordeal, I'm going to try to commit to an animal-blood lifestyle. I want Camille to be happy, and I don't want her to ever fear me. I want to be able to live around her without the beast in me trying to attack. This is going to be a long shot. But I have to try.

I realize I'm in reach of my upstate mansion, so I decide to rest and change my clothes. I have not been here in years. It feels weird to be back. I go in the garden and visit Eliza. I talk with her there. I have avenged her after so many years of trying, and I pray that she finds peace.

I feel a touch on my hand and the whisper of a kiss. I feel someone embrace me and whisper, "Be at peace my love," then it is gone.

I sit in the garden and cry. I wish could produce tears. Crying for a vampire is weird. It feels like you are dry heaving. I brought justice after so long. It feels good, and I'm happy that I can finally move one. I have finally found love again. I look around the estate, and I start to consider making this my gathering place when I'm in the area to plan for my reign as king. I need a place separate from the council estate where I can meet with my comrades and no one else will hear what we discuss.

Once I return to the emergency room, I learn that Camille slipped into a coma. I sit down and bury my head in my hands. I cannot escape the guilt I feel. If she had not been with me, she wouldn't be fighting for her life right now. I walk out of the room. I need to inform Allison. I relay her the news that we were out to dinner, and we were mugged by a gang. I tell her there were six guys. I did my best to fight them off. But some took Camille and beat her up. We are fortunate that didn't get to do anything else. Allison is hysterical. I make arrangements to fly her out to New York.

After I hang up with her. I call Markus to see if he's in the area. I tell him what happened, and I need a cleanup for my E. H. Publishing House building. I tell him I finally killed Bathilda. I need her body removed, and also to stage a break-in and to make it look gang related. He agrees and sounds excited for some reason. Afterward, I email all my employees, letting them know they all will be switched to online work from home, claiming that I am remodeling to building, effective immediately.

It is been weeks of torture. I await the moment when my love will open her eyes. I miss her smile, her laugh, her sassy nature. Doctors are skeptical that she will never wake up. I know my Camille, though; she's a fighter. She will be all right. She must be. I have been hell on wheels with the doctors trying to pull her plug.

When they are not aware, I feed her some of my blood. Anything to help give her further healing. I stay by her side every single day, rarely leaving except to find blood and change my clothes. It was during some of these times that her family would come to visit. Some days I would be there; some days I would be absent to give them privacy. The minute they are gone, I come back immediately. I grow tired of the doctors and nurses trying to force me out, so I compelled them to let me stay by her side.

When they try to pull her plug for the final time, I compel them to never try it again. She is not leaving me. I will find a way to walk through hellfire to keep her by my side and make sure she's alive. This was too close of a call. If she decides to leave me after this, I will find a way to live without her. I will find a way to move. I only want her to be happy.

It is late one night, and I am relaxing by her side, praying to God for her to open her eyes. I only pray that God hears me. I have not prayed in a long time, since I was human. I used to attend mass with Eliza, and we would say prayers together during the evening before bedtime. She would pray for my soul to find peace, and we both prayed for God's blessings. After all these years, I feel like God has finally granted me the peace I have been searching for. The peace that makes me feel complete is Camille. I have always struggled in my faith. My time in war has led me to question God's purpose. But deep in my heart. I have never lost belief in God.

Now I understand God's purpose. I know that he has a will for everything. Everything happens for a reason, just as my new life has a purpose. I was destined to become a vampire. I was destined to claim the right of being king. I was meant to find Camille and protect her from the growing vampire threat that is purging society. I know the path I need to be on, and that path is with Camille forever and always by my side.

EPILOGUE

Life is ever evolving. Time changes everything as the years continue to move on. My life since that fateful night in 1860 has been nothing short of a roller-coaster. I have ridden many valleys, travelled through the darkest nights and have finally found my happy place. The light has returned to my life in the name of a woman named Camille Williams. I have had six months to reflect on it, and now I realize that all these years have been a waste. I understand Eliza wanted me to avenge her. However, that vengeance has also led my soul to dark places and my dead heart becoming tainted by hatred and bitterness. I became everything that Bathilda's coven wanted me to be until I met Molly. She pulled me away from the darkness and helped me find my way back to the light. Now, my shining light is Camille. She's my guiding star. Please, God, let her live.

Suddenly, I hear the monitor going berserk, and I feel a hand caressing my hair. I raise my eyes and look into the most beautiful ocean-colored eyes. I could drown in for eternity.

"Hunter?" she says in a groggy voice. I take her head in my hands, and with everything in me. I kiss her like I'm joining my soul to hers.

"My love," I say as I stroke the sides of her face.

Suddenly, she looks like she's panicking. I hold on to her hands, attempting to calm her down.

"Sweetheart, you're safe, your alive, your safe," I say as I start to hold her.

"What happened? Where am I? What day is it?" Her eyes roam wildly all over the room.

I tell her to focus on me, to take deep breaths. "I'm so sorry for everything that happened. I never meant for you to be hurt," I tell her in a broken tone. "Sweetheart, you have been in a coma for six months."

She stares at me in shock, and her face pales.

"They had to do a few surgeries on you. You had a cracked skull, a broken leg, two broken ribs, a broken hand, and you were covered in bruises."

She strokes my head, and I walk away from her. She looks at me confused.

"Hunter, what is wrong?"

I pace around the room. "This was too close. I cannot lose you, Camille. I cannot live without you" She stares at me as if she can read my thoughts. We are deeply connected.

She reads me like an open book. Camille has a way of seeing through all the bullshit and finding the heart of the truth. "But?" she says while looking at me. She knows I will not openly tell her what I'm thinking, so she constantly pushes me like this. Sometimes it is a fucking pain in the ass.

"I feel like I cannot continue to live with you. You can't survive my world, Camille," I tell her in broken tone. I know I need to let her go, to have a normal human life. If she agrees, I will do my best to carry on. I will hide my pain and hold her memory in my heart.

She looks at me. Her eyes become wide, and her face starts to become pale as she hyperventilates.

"I will understand if you want to walk away. I will even give you release papers at work if you want to go back to Portland," I tell her while trying not to cry.

Her face goes white, and she starts to thrash to get out of the bed. I go and grab her hands to restrain her.

"Don't!" she yells at me.

I stand back.

"Don't you dare leave me, Hunter Eldridge. After everything we have been through. Yes, that night was frightening as shit. I knew it might happen considering I knew the truth a long time ago. None of it is your fault. Blame that bitch."

Suddenly, I can feel fury radiate off her in waves.

I close my eyes. I cannot take her tears or her screaming at me anymore. I reach over and crawl onto her bed. I take her into my arms like I'm never going to let go. "Camille, my love, you don't have to worry about her anymore, she's finally dead. I don't want to be without your love. I just don't want to be the reason you get hurt."

She scoffs. "You are not the cause of this. Plus, you know me. I could literally break my neck by tripping on my own feet."

I try not to laugh. She's right. I have seen her trip on air.

"You have never done anything to hurt me. You saved me, Hunter. I don't know how. But I felt your power flowing through me numerous times, you pulled me out of the darkness my king," she says in a loving tone while caressing my face.

Hearing her say those words to me sends an abundance of happiness through me. She's not a vampire, and I doubt she would want to be one. But hearing her calling me king. That was amazing and somehow cements her place not only in my world. But further in my frozen heart, I remember the discussion we once had, where I revealed to her that I was in essence the vampire king. I just never thought I would say the day where she addresses me as such, and her statement is also cementing herself as queen. I'm beside myself with happiness as hear her next words.

"Hunter, I never want to be away from you again. I want to love you forever and never leave you" she says as she kisses me. I wish it was forever. I never want her to leave my side. But I doubt she would officially want that.

She kisses me as if she's searing her soul with mine, and I kiss her back with the same ferocity. Suddenly, I hear the medical equipment start to scream at us. I realize it is her heart monitor, and it sounds angry. I suddenly get a naughty idea.

I wonder? I think as I lean in further. I kiss her harder. She wraps her arms around me. I lie next to her, and I start to kiss my way down her neck. She starts to moan, and the alarm starts to grow into an annoying siren. I look up at it, look at her, and smirk. She finally notices what is happening, and she hits me on the shoulder. I fall off the bed laughing as she tries to cover herself in embarrassment.

I must let medical personnel know. I'm sure they saw the medical alarms going off. "Let's get you out of here. Let's get you home."

She giggles and shakes her head. I let go of her and run into the hallway, calling for the doctors to come immediately and attend to her. The nurses pour into the room to check on her and are shocked to find her awake. I'm so overjoyed I fall to my knees thanking God that he has not abandoned me.

I order food for her and insist that I take care of her. I have waited too long for her to wake while I sat helpless from the side. I'm never letting her be hurt again. I cannot live with myself if something were to ever happen to her. Several months of never knowing if she will wake up have been hell on earth. A week goes by, and I make sure that I'm full attentive to all her needs. I hire all the best doctors and the best physical therapy treatments. Anything my angel needs. She's smiling at me through her pain of physical therapy and recovery.

I'm amazed that she's not hating me for everything that she has gone through. She should be cursing at me, walking away from me. She has so much strength, and I'm amazed at how she rationalizes everything, placing full blame on the psychotic vampires as the ones responsible.

Within a few months of physical therapy, she's back to being her old self, and I love her resilience. I'm amazed that she still doesn't blame me or hate me. I'm also thrilled that with a little help from

Allison, she finally agrees to move back to Chicago with me. After everything that has happened, she wants to live closer to her family. No more living isolated away from loved ones.

It is officially the holiday season now. This is our second year as a couple. I have grown to love celebrating human holidays with her. I have missed these moments for a long time. Halloween is fun dressing up. Thanksgiving is fun. I host a dinner at my mansion. Christmas time is here, and I cannot wait to give her my present that I bought for her. I planned a party for our family and coworkers. Those who are vampires know they must be on their best behaviors.

I call attention to the crowd. "Everyone, can you gather around please?"

People are beginning to crowd me, curious and anticipation filling them as they await what I will say.

"I want to thank all of you for coming this evening. Camille and I are thrilled to have you here. We have had an incredible year. Business sales are up. Drama is way down."

Everyone laughs. I chuckle for a moment before becoming serious again.

"No, seriously, last year, I was terrified beyond belief. We had a close call, as many of you know. After her attack in Central Park, I stayed by her side through the entire six months. Everyday felt like I could just die inside as I waited for her to come back to me, because I cannot live without her."

She's slightly teary-eyed.

"I don't want to live without her ever, so if Camille will be the first to open her gift?"

She smiles and opens it to find a Tiffany's box.

I kneel next to her and let my emotions speak for me. She's crying because she already knows.

"Yes, a thousand times, yes." I pull her into my arms and kiss her with every emotion I feel. All our guests erupt in cheers for us.

She whispers into my ear, "Open your gift."

I see there is a card and a small box. The gift is an antique pocket watch. "I love it darling." She whispers for me to look at the card. I open it up, and it simply says:

Hunter,

> *My love, my life. Everything I want for eternity.*
> *Be my King. Claim me as your Queen, for eternity.*
> *I vow to never leave your side. Forever, My Love.*
> *Change me.*

Love, your precious Gem.

I stare at her with wide eyes. I never dreamed she would be asking this of me. Does she truly know what she's asking for? I would be in eternal bliss. However, how can she ask this of me? How can she ask me to take away her soul?

I will love her for eternity. But a part of me still wishes that I could grant her children, Molly is well over the age of fifty at this point. She's not a child anymore.

I take her in my arms and whisper, "Are you sure? This is what you want?"

She whispers back. "I want you forever. That is all I want," she says while we hug each other, and she nibbles on my ear. I stare at her face and kiss her passionately. My love, my life, my rare gem, she has returned to me, and I'm never letting her go. I cannot believe what she's asking of me. I take her into my arms once everyone has left and make passionate love to her whispering my love for her throughout the night.

Why do I feel, though, as if Bathilda's death was just the beginning? Why do I feel as if we are still being watched? Is it this insidious person entitled the "Master"? Whatever happens, we will face this world together. I'm hers, and she's mine. We will never be apart again, forever.

SPECIAL THANKS

Thank you to everyone who helped support this book. You have made my dreams come true.

Thank you to my loving husband, Samuel Marcelain. You are my rock. Through all the challenges we have faced over the years, you continue to be a beacon of light and emotional support for me. My love, you inspired me to push past my anxiety and make Hunter a reality. You helped with brainstorming ideas about the vampires and created my book cover. I cannot ask for a better man than you.

I hope everyone enjoys Hunter's journey through life until the end when he finds true love again. I hope everyone can see the how the goodness of his heart stands the test of time and how true love is rare to find, once it is found. If you love strong enough, it will always return to you. No matter how dark the road can be, love and light will always shine through.

Hunter will return. Look for Book 2: "Beloved Darkness" coming soon. Also, look for the spin-off novel *The Hybrid Daughter*, which is the behind-the-scenes story of Molly's life.

CPSIA information can be obtained
at www.ICGtesting.com
Printed in the USA
JSHW032147201222
35243JS00003B/38

9 781665 735308